Praise for *Enlightenment*

'A dark Conradian drama, set i   the past is always with us.'

                                                              ..... Pamuk

'A complex, often riveting novel . . . quietly stunning.'

Publishers Weekly (starred review)

'Freely is an almost perversely original writer . . . A brave, unflinching work of art.'

The Washington Post Book World

'[Freely] possesses an exceptional command of language . . . An ingenious novel about appearance and reality . . . You will not put it down.'

Library Journal (starred review)

'Byzantine in structure, mischievous in intent, it is as concerned with the garbled and provisional nature of truth as with the minutiae of repression.'

TLS

'Maureen Freely's engaging, beautiful novel reminds us not only of the importance of history, but of its inextricability from our present-day narrative: a past never really buried but instead looming and palpable, a taste on your tongue, the acrid taste of ash.'

Natalie Bakopoulos, fictionwritersreview.com

'Raises pressing questions about Turkey's willingness to confront its inner divisions.'

The Guardian

'*Enlightenment* is both a gripping novel and a powerful fictional version of the argument that Turkey does not yet subscribe to the levels of democracy and human rights required if EU membership is to mean more than a passport to economic improvement.'

The Independent

'Playing out against a meticulously realised backdrop of Turkey in the years following the Cold War that feels thoroughly authentic, this sinister, complex political thriller snakes to a remarkably subtle conclusion.'

Independent on Sunday

To my mother:

keeper of the mysteries

SAILING THROUGH BYZANTIUM

A novel

Maureen Freely

To Abby
Hope that te
nxt time we
meet we'll
be there...
at a happier moment.

Maureen Freely
Breadloaf
6. 6. 17

LINENPRESS

Published by Linen Press, Edinburgh 2013

1 Newton Farm Cottages
Miller Hill
Dalkeith
Midlothian
EH22 1SA

www.linenpressbooks.co.uk

A CIP catalogue record for this book is available from the British Library.

Cover photograph: © arcangel-images.com
Cover design: Zebedee Design, Edinburgh
Typeset in Sabon by Zebedee Design, Edinburgh

Printed and bound in Great Britain by CPI Antony Rowe

ISBN 978-0-9575968-1-8

In the old bohemian quarter, once hidden, now restored . . .

I stand in this great room, with its golden floors and dusted, polished artefacts, and I grieve for the old clutter: the rolled-up carpets, discarded high heels and curling clouds of smoke, the laughter swirling around the punchbowl and the strawberries floating inside it.

Once again I wonder why my dear friend Dora has gone to all this trouble. If it was her idea to drape those shawls so prettily across the back of the ancient chaise longue. If the peacock feathers in the copper vase next to it are dry at last, after decades of sitting in the dregs of drinks. If it's still a bust of Beethoven beneath that black velvet hood, there on the baby grand.

On the wall before me, and taking up most of it, is a photograph of my mother in this same room, beside this same piano, on the night fifty years ago when the world almost ended. And I know I should be studying its every line and shadow, because there is a gap I need to fill, a black and bottomless pit. For while I can remember every ship and shop we passed on our drive into the city that evening, and every minute I wasted sulking in the musty stairwell, I can remember nothing from the moment Dora took me across this room, shielding me from the embers of swirling cigarettes, bending and swinging to the rhythm of the grown-ups' laughter.

'So,' she says now. 'Have you found yourself?'

She nods in the direction of the photograph. She smiles, to give me courage. We are standing in the middle of the room, and from this distance, the lettering along the bottom is no longer legible, so I can stop wondering how Dora could know the names of everyone in the photograph or be so sure it was taken at one minute to midnight on Saturday, the 27th of October, 1962. Instead, I can appreciate the composition: the extravagant creatures draped over the baby grand, the man bent over the keys, his hands dark and spidery. The tangle of legs, shawls and startled profiles on the ancient chaise longue. The hooded Beethoven, staring into the middle distance. My father, in his goatskin, on the floor. Clinging to the handlebars of her overturned tricycle, our hostess, the celebrated artist who is also Dora's great aunt. She is clutching her heart, and gazing up at my mother, who is singing with her arms outstretched, her head thrown back, her foot tapping and her dark curls dancing.

'You still can't see it, can you?' Dora says. She takes me closer to the picture, and with her free hand she traces a path amongst the legs and the high heels. And there I am, a blur beneath the baby grand. My hands are flailing, as if I've just tried to lean on someone who is no longer there.

I ask Dora whose idea it was, to throw an End of the World Party. She waves a dismissive hand. 'Who knows? It could have been anyone. You know what they were like.'

I tell her I still find it galling.

'Of course you do,' Dora says. 'You were never a bohemian. But even so. You survived, didn't you?'

I'm not sure I did.

By now we are at the window, which is not as dark yet as the one in the photograph. And there we stand, watching the ships, which are low in the water, just like the *Felix Dzerzhinsky* and all the other ships the Soviets sent through this same waterway fifty years ago, when it was secretly arming Cuba with nuclear weapons.

I ask her if she remembers them. She nods, but says nothing.

When she at last breaks the silence, it is to say she knows how hard it must be to be back in this room again. But there's no longer any point, she says, in bearing grudges. Because it's not a joke this time. The perverse but beautiful little enclave we inhabited as children is no longer. This room is all we have left.

The time has come to say our goodbyes, she says, and although I fail to grasp her logic, I find solace in her voice, which is hushed and rushed and wants to take me home. So I let her words roll over me, as Istanbul fades into an azure dusk, with only the street lamps to trace its shores. One by one, the palaces and mosques of the old city are illuminated, as I think back to when my mother could light up the whole world like this, just by telling me a lie.

1

Her lies

They changed with every telling, as perhaps they had to do if they were to convince a child like me who asked too many questions. But her first and most inspired lie, about the butterfly, was the one that changed least. It began without fail in a Brooklyn brownstone in the winter of 1938, with a girl idling a Sunday afternoon away in her father's favourite armchair, fiddling now and again with the dials on the radio at the tail end of a roast beef dinner she had politely but resolutely refused to touch, until happening upon a voice singing its soul away in a language she thought must be Italian, though she had no proof.

The girl, whose name was Grace, was only nine years old in the winter of 1938, but she had listened to enough radio dramas by then to know that this man was in desperate straits, teetering, perhaps, on the edge of perdition, and though she could not understand a word he sang, she could follow the tenor's meaning. Look out the window, he pleaded. There is more to the world than meets the eye. The lights in the brownstone across the street are but illusions. So please, look right through them. Seek the horizon, for beyond it is your fate.

The singer's name would remain a mystery, because when the announcer came on at the end of what Grace did not yet know to be an aria, the family chorus drowned him out. Turn off that racket! cried her aunt, who lived downstairs. She clapped her hands over her ears, while the others applauded her with laughter, failing to notice that Grace had turned the volume down only to turn it up again, notch by notch, once their backs were turned. And so it was that Grace was able to hear the life story of the next singer, and embrace it as the blueprint for her own future.

Because this second soprano had begun her life in Brooklyn, only streets away from where Grace herself was now sitting. But then she had done what no one in Grace's cosseted circle had ever even considered: at the same age as Grace was at that precise moment, she had persuaded her parents to abandon Brooklyn's safe brown streets for an adventure that would take her to all the great capitals of South America. And in each and every one of them, she had studied Voice. After travelling across the Atlantic 'in lieu of college' to study with the even greater Voices of Rome and Paris, she had returned to the city of her birth to attend the Julliard School of Music. And now here she was, on The Metropolitan Opera Auditions of the Air.

Though the announcer had said that 'this fine new talent' would be sure to convey the delights of being young in Paris, Grace knew at once that she had somehow left her soul there: to sing of those delights was now her only way to breathe. It was not until the third piece, a duet sung in what she thought might be French, that she grasped the key to the mystery. Whatever their language, this soprano and this tenor sang with one voice. They were urging her to embrace life without fear, for to keep one's heart open was worth any price.

The setting for this duet was an oasis in a desert, and now the tenor had become a young monk, the soprano an innocent maiden soon to join a nunnery. Rather than reveal their true feelings, they sang of bathing their hands and lips in water. Hands and lips, Grace thought. Had the nuns who taught her ever bathed their hands and lips? She took this question to school with her the next morning, and after gazing out the window at another row of brownstones, which would, if she could look through it, have revealed another row just like it,

11

she lifted her eyes to the weak lemon sun hanging above them, and under her scrutiny it seemed to slip from its place, like a cardboard disc inexpertly fastened to a stage set. When her eyes returned to the classroom, everything inside it – the rows of desks and straight-backed girls, their braids fastened with identical white ribbons, the dry husk of a nun tapping her stick against the blackboard – seemed paper thin.

Until that moment, her life had been ruled by ragtime, because her father, who owned a radio repair shop, could play it by ear. He had a few standard bass chords, and to these he could add any tune after hearing it just once. On Sundays when the weather was good, they would go out in the family car to Sheepshead Bay, where her mother's best friend's husband rented out fishing boats. Down the road from their house was a piano bar called Max's, and if her father could be persuaded to play, there would be another round of highballs as the two families crowded around the piano to sing along, and woe to the child who had the temerity to mention homework. Grace never lost her love of ragtime. But after her conversion to opera, ragtime came to remind her of a cradle, rocking in place.

From time to time her father would let a few blue notes waft in, but if he saw so much as a single spirit wilting, he'd switch to something with more bounce to it, like *Oh You Beautiful Doll*, or *I Can't Tell a Lie*. Perhaps that was why even he, with his musical ear, was not partial to opera. But he doted on Grace. And her rebellion against roast beef had shaken him, as had her refusal to explain her reasons. The truth is she'd turned against roast beef because she'd overhead her father telling a visitor that he, the cook of the family, served it every Sunday on account of his eldest and youngest children being just crazy about it. When the visitor asked about Grace, he'd said, 'Oh, *she'll* eat anything.'

She never told him how mad, how *hopping furious*, that had made her. But with opera as with roast beef, silence proved effective, because soon her parents had agreed to let her listen to opera once a week, even if it hurt people's ears a little.

Usually this would be on Saturday night, when *The Chicago Theater of the Air* offered one-hour adaptations of works deemed suitable for family listening. So most ended happily ever after; with exceptions edited to minimise their sting. Because no one wanted to listen to a ponderous historical lecture by Col Robert R. McCormick during the intermission, Grace had agreed to turn the dial way down until he was through droning on and on about some battle no one cared about. But one night she was listening to *Madame Butterfly*, and, fearful of missing the opening strains of the second half, she turned the dial up a minute too soon, whereupon they clapped their hands on their ears in unison, chanting *turn off that racket*! To drown them out, Grace pressed her ear against the radio. She closed her eyes until she had left her father's favourite armchair for the tragedy still unfolding in a Japanese garden, halfway around the world.

Was it true, Cio Cio San asked, that, in foreign lands, a man would catch a butterfly and pin its wings to a table? It was, said Colonel Pinkerton, but only to keep it from flying away. Embracing her, he added, 'I have caught you. You are mine.' And she replied, 'Yes, for life.' But by the intermission he had abandoned his butterfly, and though he returned, it was only to stain her honour and take away their son. There was just one thing he hadn't been able to take from her, and that was her voice.

So when the nine-year-old girl who would become my mother went to bed that night, a butterfly flew in after her. 'Beware!' it cried. 'Keep your wings well hidden. If you don't, some man might try to pin them to a table. Then he'll board a ship, promising to return for you, just as soon as the robins make their nests. But you trust him at your peril.'

'Why?' Grace asked. And then the butterfly told her: it is still a man's world – even in 1938, when ladies could at last wear trousers, and sing on the radio, and travel across the ocean in lieu of college, there to bathe their lips and hands. If Grace wanted to spread her wings one day, she had to do more

13

than to dream of the horizon. She had to make a plan, and then she had to stick to it. 'Last but not least,' said the butterfly, 'You must never, ever trust a man boarding a ship. Even if he's promised to take you around the world, don't take his word for it. Make sure you're right there next to him, holding the tickets.'

Young Grace thanked the butterfly and took her words to heart. She made a plan, and for the next twenty two years, she stuck to it, with such discretion that it wasn't until the summer of 1960, when we were packing to leave for Turkey, that my grandparents had the first inkling. They'd forgotten the operas by then, and the roast beef, and the string of eligible but deadly dull suitors Grace had refused just as firmly as roast beef. She'd been such a good girl, after all – going off to secretarial college with a skip and a smile, and then finding herself a nice job in that shipping company, and never once complaining (as did so many other girls her age) that she couldn't buy her own clothes. At the end of the month, she'd just hand her pay cheque over. She even thanked them for the lunch money they left for her on the sideboard each morning. They had no idea that she was saving it up to enrol in the St John's Great Books Program, or that from the day she did, she was reading Greek philosophers to and from Manhattan on the subway, or that, if ever she took a shortcut through the lobby of the Waldorf, she'd pretend to be looking for the porter with her trunks.

When Grace came home late on Tuesdays, they thought she'd been out at the movies with Estelle, her chum from stage school, with whom she'd once starred in a tap extravaganza called *American Patrol*, dressed as George Washington. What she really did was to go to a musical academy in the Lower East Side where she was the only white pupil. Even on that Sunday afternoon in 1947, when she went with her family to a piano bar in Flatbush named the Welcome Inn, to stun all in attendance with her new repertoire, it never occurred to my grandparents to ask how she had woken up that morning, suddenly able to sing the blues.

Propping up the bar that day was a wild boy just out of the navy. After listening, awestruck, to Grace's rendition of *Stormy Weather*, he had come over to introduce himself. And soon it was Grace doing the listening, as she sipped her ginger ale and the wild boy knocked back one beer after another, talking of his wartime adventures as a frogman in the Pacific, and his journey overland to China through the Burmese jungle just before they dropped The Bomb. Before long he was asking for advice. The more Grace's eyes widened, the more he talked about ships. And books. And philosophers with strange names. This set the tone for the courtship – day and night, he would talk about ships, and books, and philosophers with strange names. He would drone on and on and on until my grandparents' eyes were rolling in their sockets and there couldn't be a thing they hadn't heard a hundred times before (about ships, and the ports they visited, and the cockamamie ideas those philosophers had cooked up in those ports, but then, if Grace so much as smiled, he'd start up on a new story.

How relieved my grandparents were to see marriage bring him down to earth. This was not to say he hadn't worried them sick on occasion. First there was that bad business at Fort Monmouth. If it hadn't been for wise, old Mr Guttman, keeping him on the straight and narrow, God only knows how it might have ended. But by 1960, the tearaway had become a father of three, with a brand new PhD in physics that was getting him enticing job offers from some of the biggest colleges in the Tristate Area, not to mention Washington DC and NASA. My grandparents were innocently hoping that he wouldn't want to take us too far away, and so they were rooting for the nice community college in their own township.

This was because they knew nothing of the promise my father had made Grace when he had proposed to her twelve years earlier. They would have been shocked to hear that (as she sat there perched on a tombstone in the cemetery where her future father-in-law worked as a gravedigger) it had been Grace who had set the terms.

2

The secret pact

Every night from as far back as I could remember, my sister and I would pad downstairs after bath time to sit on the sofa while my father spun the globe, telling us about the countries we would visit one day, just as soon as he got his doctorate. He would point out the capitals and then he'd test us. So a week before his graduation, when he told us he'd been offered a job at an American college in Istanbul, and asked me if I knew where that was, I could tell him that it was the purple country that was shaped like a crumpled box.

I did not know how unnatural it was for a child like me to know such a thing. Since my parents' families had arrived on these shores, no one had ever travelled for pleasure, for the simple reason that they believed that all the pleasures in the world were right here. This is just one of the startling facts my grandmother presented to me when I went to stay with her at the end of August 1960, ten days before we were due to leave for Turkey. She'd spent the whole week spoiling me with Tang, and ginger ale, and maraschino cherries, and lots of other things I'd have to do without in Istanbul. On the last night they had planned to take me to see Jack Lemmon and Shirley MacLaine in *The Apartment*, and even now, when I see some mention of that film, I am returned to the despair of that afternoon when I went down with a fever so slight that my parents would have just given me a pink aspirin and sent me back outside to play. But my grandparents were not the kind to take chances. They

16

parked me with my aunt, who lived next door. 'You poor little chickadee,' she said. 'You're upset and I don't blame you. It's not fair to drag children halfway across the world like that. Not if they don't want to go . . .'

When my grandparents got back, they sat me down next to the darkened plate glass window in their kitchen and treated me to another ginger ale with a maraschino cherry. 'You know,' said my grandmother, 'that movie was pretty racy. It's just as well you didn't come.'

I asked her why, and it was my grandfather who answered. 'They should have called it *The Bedroom*!' My grandmother shushed him. I didn't like it when she did that. So I said that a film called *The Bedroom* sounded pretty tame to me. After all, I'd seen three films by Satyajit Ray that summer. Not to mention *Ivan the Terrible*, and *On the Beach*.

'You saw *On the Beach*?' said my grandfather.

'Who took you?' my grandmother asked. Then she answered her own question. 'I bet it was your father.'

I didn't like it when she spoke like that. So I told her the truth. I began with the recurring nightmare I'd been having for months now: there'd be an air raid drill at school, and after the all clear, my teacher would send us all home, but just before I got there, I'd see a mushroom cloud rising into the sky. I'd reach the house to find my mother at the wheel of our car, and my father sitting next to her with his arms folded. 'Hurry up and get in,' he'd say. 'We're off to the doctors to pick up our suicide pills.' Just like *On The Beach*! I wanted my grandparents to know that every time I had this nightmare and woke up screaming, my father would always be right there with me until I stopped trembling, never leaving until he was sure he had taught me what *On the Beach* really meant. 'Jeez Louise,' said my grandfather. My grandmother shook her head. 'What could a movie like that teach a sweet little girl like you?' So I told her. It had taught me what a dangerous game our President was playing, stockpiling nuclear weapons just to scare those madmen in the Kremlin. I don't think I knew what stockpiling meant then, and neither could I have named the madmen in the Kremlin, but I liked saying the words. And in spite of myself, I thrilled to the silence that fell after I said them.

'Your father told you that?' my grandmother asked.

I nodded. 'He thinks every last politician in this country is insane. Except for Adlai Stevenson, that is. But look at what the Republicans did to *him*.'

There was another long silence, and then my grandmother rose wearily from her chair, saying, 'Let's go down to the den to see if we can find you a nice movie on TV.' We were in luck. James Cagney was strutting across a stage. When I was back at the table next to the plate glass window, eating what was known in the family as an 'ice cap', my grandmother said, 'I love that song he sang at the end there. Do you know which one I mean?'

'*It's a Grand Old Flag*?'

'It's not a question,' she said. 'It's the truth. Are you going to take one out there with you?'

I didn't think so. 'It would fill up the whole suitcase.'

'Well, just make sure you think of our grand old flag, every night before you go to bed. It never hurts to remember who you are. Especially out there in Turkey. From what I hear, that place is just crawling with Communists.'

'It is?' I said.

'Oh yes,' she said. 'The Soviet Union is just next door. Didn't your father tell you that?'

After all those nights spinning the globe, he hadn't needed to. But I hadn't expected that my grandmother would know, too. When I told her so, she asked me why not. I explained that my father had asked me not to tell her. 'He said that?' She then asked what else he'd asked me not to mention. I listed the most important ones: Republicans, Bing Crosby, the Pope, and Lawrence Welk. When she asked why, I went into some detail.

'He told you all this?'

I nodded proudly. 'I might be only eight years old, but he says I can understand things better than most grown-ups.'

'He's right about that all right! But I bet there are some things he hasn't told you.'

'What kind of things?' I asked.

'First let's get you another ice cap.'

I could still feel my grandmother's words scraping against the sides of my stomach when I walked into the kitchen the next morning and found my father standing at the counter with my grandfather. They were examining the transistor radio that Mr Guttman had given us as a going-away present. My grandfather – the proud owner of a radio repair shop until moving to the suburbs – pronounced it a fine specimen.

Mr Guttman was at the table, finishing up a piece of cake. As he put down his fork he told my grandmother it was the best he'd had in donkey's years. My grandmother smiled, because she liked him. And when she turned to Mr Guttman and said, 'So you haven't talked our son-in-law out of this cockamamie job?' there was some softness in her voice. When Mr Guttman said, 'No, I'm afraid I didn't even try!' she did not lift her hankie to sob into it. Not even when he tried, one last time, to assure her that my father and mother and sister and brother and I would be blissfully happy and even safe in the place she still called Over There. 'I know it's hard to imagine,' he said. 'But there is no city on earth quite as beautiful. I saw it as a boy, you know. I can still see it in my mind's eye.'

My grandmother sighed. 'I bet you don't see any churches, though.'

'Oh, I see every kind of church. It's like Jerusalem. Like New York! Like all great cities, it embraces all the great religions!'

'Well, that's a relief,' said my grandmother, her smile almost surfacing.

'Now that's more like it,' Mr Guttman said.

All the way back to the house we'd soon be leaving, Mr Guttman talked about the grand tour he had taken, and the magnificent cities he had seen from the windows of trains and hotels and the portholes of ships when he was still a boy and his family still owned half of Philadelphia. I was sitting right behind the driver's seat. I could see him smiling in the rear view mirror speckled by sky and trees. Wasn't it a beautiful day? Wasn't it better than a postcard?

When we walked into our living room, to find its walls stripped bare and lined with trunks and suitcases, my legs sagged. 'There, there now,' said Mr Guttman, lifting me onto the sofa we weren't taking with us. 'It's not the end of the world. It's just a house! There's another beauty waiting for you over there, you know. You just wait and see.'

That was when he gave me the little leather satchel with the sketchbook in it. That took my mind off things, for a while.

But later, after Mr Guttman had left, and I was back on the sofa, sitting next to my father, watching him spin the globe we were not taking with us either, at last I had the chance to ask him the question that had been weighing on me, ever since my conversation with my grandmother the previous night:

'Why don't you love your country, by the way?'

'Who said I didn't love my country?' my father asked. Then he answered his own question. 'What else did she say?' Not wanting to lie, I told him what my grandmother had said – that he'd been born with the face of angel. That there'd even been a time when he seemed destined for priesthood. But then, she said, my father had read some book or other that had planted the seeds of doubt in him. Or maybe it was the war. Sometimes people came back from the war a little strange. Whatever his reasons, my father had come back from the war an atheist He'd spent the next four years trying to turn my mother into one, too. My grandmother wasn't sure if my mother had really lost her faith, but even if she hadn't, the sad fact was that she never responded when my father bragged that my first words had been, 'God does not exist'. My grandmother thought my father had perhaps taught me those hateful words to spite her. She said that if it hadn't been for her, I would never even have been baptised.

20

My grandmother said it was my father's teachers who had taken him so far from God. Even at Iona College, where the teachers were mostly priests, there had always been someone sowing those seeds of doubt. And when my father had moved on to do his doctorate at NYU, he had fallen in with 'all those refugees'. Though they'd pretended to be physicists, really they were spies in the pay of the Soviets. They'd been sent to America to find out how to make a nuclear bomb. Fortunately, the FBI had caught the worst two. Mr and Mrs Rosenberg had been condemned to the electric chair, so no one had to worry about *them* anymore. But other dangerous refugees had slipped through the net, and my grandmother was pretty sure that one of them had found his wily way to Fort Monmouth, which was, after all, the same research lab where Mr Rosenberg had worked during the War, and where my father was working when Senator McCarthy exposed it as a hotbed of Communism.

The Senator had gone on to identify more than a hundred subversives there. Naturally, my grandmother had assumed my father would have been happy to get them out of his hair. But no, instead he'd gone into a fury, insisting they were innocent. In the end, and for this she thanked God and Mr Guttman, he'd kept his head.

But when my grandmother heard what my father had taught me about the Pope, the Grand Old Party, and two of the best entertainers of our time, she had to wonder what other ideas 'those refugees' had planted in his head. So I should be on my guard, just in case something went wrong 'Out There', and we met more of 'those refugees', and they tried to feed me propaganda.

After I had told my father an eight-year old's version of all this, he spent some time spinning the globe. Then he stood up and said, 'It's a beautiful evening. Let's walk out to the arboretum and find a few more trees.'

We walked to the lake in silence. When we reached the bench next to the redwood, I brought out my sketchbook – not the new one Mr Guttman had given me for our travels, but the old one, with all the trees. Normally my father would have asked to see the sketches I had done of the trees we were leaving behind – I'd been working on trees all summer and this evening's redwood would be my thirty-eighth. But that night he told me a thing or two about 'those refugees' my grandmother claimed to know so much about. 'Do you know where they're from?' my father bellowed. 'Do you know why they had to come here?' He told me about his former boss, one of the finest minds in physics: he had lost every last member of his family to the gas chambers. He'd fled to America from Germany with nothing. He'd given his new country everything he had. 'It would not be far-fetched to say he helped us win the War. And this is how we thank him? By dragging him into a kangaroo court on these insane trumped-up charges? You know why that crackpot McCarthy turned on this wonderful man? Because he was Jewish – like 98 of the 100 men McCarthy hounded out of their jobs over there.'

'But I thought . . . you said . . . I thought Mr Guttman never gave up on them.'

'Of course he didn't! It's thanks to him, and only him, that at least some of them have their jobs back. But it made them all fearful. And that was the point of it – don't you see? This witch hunt never had anything to do with Communism. What we are looking at here is anti-Semitism, pure and simple. I've told you what that is, haven't I? Good. I'm glad. We had to fight a war to stamp that out, and if people ever forget it, we'll have to fight another one.'

'Maybe that's what Grandma is afraid about,' I suggested. 'Maybe she's afraid of the next war. She's seen *On The Beach*, too, you know. She thinks that we should stay together, just in case the Russkies drop the Bomb on us. If we have to take suicide pills, she wants us to take them all together.'

My father didn't say anything for some time after that, and when he spoke again, it was like he was trying to keep calm while someone strangled him. 'Listen,' he said. 'Your grandmother is a good person, and you must always remember

22

that. But she's never really approved of me, and right now she's furious, because if she had her way, we'd be moving into a house right next door, like your aunt. And who knows, we'd be building some goddamn shelter at the halfway point, even though it would do us no good if they dropped it. We'd all die anyway. I hope you know that. You know why they keep talking about bomb shelters? For the same reason they terrify you schoolchildren with those air raid drills, and make you lean against the wall with your heads between your knees while that deafening siren blasts your little ears.'

Staring at the lake in front of us, he clenched his fists. 'None of these idiot measures will save anyone! I'm a physicist, for Christ's sake. I should know. No – the point of all this is to scare everyone stiff, so when an insane dipsomaniac senator comes along and yells Communist . . .'

I asked him what a dipsomaniac was. 'Oh, come on now, you know that,' he said. 'But it's not his drinking I care about. It's not even the man himself. It's the rest of this goddamn country. We just sit here and let him go after anyone who doesn't look American enough, or patriotic enough, and then, when they've locked up thousands of innocents and destroyed careers . . .'

They? I asked. Was there was more than one dipsomaniac at large? Oh yes, there certainly was, my father assured me. They were all in cahoots, and together they had created such terror that no one dared make a peep. 'And then these cynical bastards go on television to claim that they are making the world safe for democracy. And a lot of people are fool enough to trust him. Including your grandmother. She thinks I don't love my country? The truth is I'm ashamed of it!'

Did that make him an un-American? I asked anxiously. It certainly did not. On the way back from the park, he tried to explain why I should never, ever call someone un-American, just because they criticised their country. But so many of the big words were new to me. And each time I asked him a new question I provoked another burst of anger. By the time we

23

got back to our street, his voice was so loud that my mother could hear us from the other end of it. She ran to the window to see him striding down the sidewalk, his arms flying all over the place like Buster Keaton, while I practically had to canter to keep up.

Over supper – never before had I been invited to join them for one of their candlelit meals – my father asked me if I understood why he was so upset. I didn't like admitting that I didn't understand everything he told me. It made him look so disappointed. So I asked a question instead.

'What's a Communist sympathiser, by the way?'

'Did she call me that, too? Jesus Christ,' he said, and he stood up so fast his chair fell over.

'Darling,' said my mother. 'Darling!'

'I'm sorry,' he said. He picked up his chair. 'Maybe the best thing is to begin at the beginning.'

For the next two hours, as the candlelight cast his face into one strange shape after another, he told me about the broken promise that was Communism. It had risen out of a noble dream – to free a working man who'd been put in chains – but over time it had replaced the old tyranny with a new one. After describing a bewildering array of world wars, revolutions, and uprisings, my father said, 'So if there is one thing I want you to understand from all this, it's how many ways there are to kill democracy. That's why I want to get us out of here, before it's too late.'

After supper, when my mother was doing the dishes, and I was sitting at the kitchen table, cradling my head to keep it from exploding, my mother asked me if I was feeling feverish.

'No,' I said, but tears were rolling down my cheeks, so she brought me a hankie. 'Why he is in such a rush to get us out of here?' I asked. 'Before it's too late for what?'

My mother sighed and sat down. 'Listen, he's just upset tonight,' she said. 'And when he's upset, he exaggerates. That's just the way men are, you know. Which is not to say I don't agree with every word he said. But it's not the whole story.'

She took my hand. 'Do you want to know the *real* reason why we're going to Turkey on Monday?'

That was when my mother told me the story about the opera singers, and the butterfly, and the promise my father had made to her the day they got engaged.

Afterwards she said, 'Do you feel a bit better now? We're going to have a wonderful time out there. The time of our lives. Look, doesn't even Mr Guttman say so? A whole new world awaits us. We'll see things I could only dream of when I was your age. You'll touch the Parthenon with your bare hands. And the Pyramids, and the Prado, and the Blue Mosque, and Pompeii, and the wine-dark sea. It doesn't matter what other people think. In my book, you're the luckiest children in the world.'

'What will we do if we run into Communists out there?'

'Oh, that's easy,' she said. 'We'll look straight through them.'

3

The new world

Sixteen months later, when we travelled to Egypt on a Soviet liner called the *Felix Dzerzhinsky*, surrounded by anxious spies of all allegiances, we would discover that you couldn't traipse through the heart of the Cold War and go unnoticed.

But first there was Istanbul, endlessly unfolding. There was the Bosphorus, carrying the waters of the Black Sea into the Marmara, the Mediterranean, and beyond. Its villages were connected by the ferries that darted back and forth between Europe and Asia. There were no bridges. Along each shore ran a single road, which dipped inland at intervals to make way for rows of restaurants on stilts and waterside mansions. Here and there were clusters of new apartment buildings, but most village houses were wooden, and slowly disintegrating. Rising above the villages were private woodlands. In late spring, when the Judas trees bloomed, the hillsides were splashed with magenta.

Our new apartment, from whose enormous balcony we could see all this, was perched on a hill between the little coastal town of Bebek and the great castle of Rumeli Hisar, built by Mehmet the Conqueror in 1453, the year he took the city from the Greeks. On the Asian shore, just opposite us, was a much smaller castle, built by his grandfather, next to once-grand *yalıs* with their overgrown waterside gardens. There was a little river that sent a ribbon of muddy water into the Bosphorus every time it rained, and next to it, a wedding cake palace in which I never saw a single light burning. Because we were on the slope of a promontory, the European and Asian shores to the south of us seemed to blend into a single mass – until a Soviet tanker sliced through the illusion, coming right at us. When it veered away to take the next bend, every windowpane in the house really would clatter. But once it was gone I could, if I narrowed my eyes, imagine the Bosphorus as an almost-lake again, criss-crossed by ferries that always came full circle.

During that first year, on Saturday mornings, we would take the ten o'clock ferry to dart back and forth between Europe and Asia, trembling to a stop at each landing stage while one man fastened the thick and rotting ropes, and another threw down the wet and rotting serrated planks that served as gangways, even as the passengers surged forward, jumping across the gap that – had they misjudged the distance – might have pulled them into watery graves. But they didn't seem worried. They never lost their serenity. Their fates were written – that must be why. Soon they would vanish into the leafy lanes that curled up the hill, while we pulled apart to slip along the shore, past mosques, restaurants, and the burnt-out shells of palaces, and men in undershirts who were eating breakfast in the gardens of their seaside villas. The domes and minarets of the Old City would emerge from the mist, and before I had a chance to steel myself, we were walking through the great untamed expanse that was Eminönü and winding our way through the honking armies of Plymouths and Chevrolets fighting their way on and off the Galata Bridge which was then the only conduit across the Golden Horn. Though my parents could see where we were going, my sister and I were caught between angry and glistening chrome fenders. I clung to my mother's hand, the little leather satchel containing Mr Guttman's sketchbook clamped beneath my free arm. When the thousand pigeons in the courtyard of the New Mosque took flight at the sight of us, my sister and I would shield our eyes while our parents smiled fondly in the never-dented certainty that these pigeons, like all other creatures on earth, meant us no harm.

But already they'd be moving on, drawn towards the Old City's shadowy streets. It was the Byzantine column propping up the Ottoman house that held their attention now. It was the trace of a submerged palace in the cemetery next to the mosque. Unless you counted the 1898 Baedeker, there were no guides to the city in those days. We could find our way to the Blue Mosque and Haghia Sophia and Topkapı Palace by following the skyline, but before long many of the places we wanted to visit were blocked to us, sealed behind rusty padlocked gates and we had to wait until a suspicious caretaker arrived to unlock them for us. The neighbourhood boys pelted us with Turkish questions until at last the one who was studying English stepped in to translate. The questions were always the same. Where are you from? What are you doing in Turkey? Why are you we interested in this dirty old building when there are so many modern ones to admire on the other side of the Golden Horn? Are you perhaps spies?

Even my father's students at Robert College were perplexed by our behaviour. Most were Turkish, heading for careers in business and engineering and couldn't understand why a nuclear physicist would want to take his wife and three small children to the cobblestone labyrinths, collapsing wooden houses, gypsy encampments and crumbling Byzantine walls of the old city. But now and again, a student would come with us, and by the time we had located the crumbling church behind the rusty padlocked gate, it would emerge that he knew more about these streets than he had let on. In fact, he had grown up just down the road – in Fatih, with his Albanian grandmother. In Beyazıt, with his father, who was really Bulgarian. In Galata, next to the synagogue. In Balat, until his family had left for Greece in 1955. In Kumkapı, which was still largely Armenian, despite the events of 1955.

The events themselves would remain unexplained. I remember how they would react to my father's pressing questions and how the snippets they offered never quite added up. Shadows would pass across their startled eyes. Could we be serious? Did we not understand? Then it would hit them. We must be innocents. We must honestly not know. They opened their arms to us, invited us to gardens and islands and coastal villages and taverns that would have remained closed to us forever had they not been at our side.

In those days, Robert College was run by a staid and worthy board in New York, but most of my father's colleagues turned out to be adventurers like us. So every Saturday, our group grew larger. And in the evening, when the six-o'clock ferry had brought us all back to Bebek, we would stop off at a garden café called Nazmi's. 'Just for one beer,' my father would say, but we rarely got home before eleven.

And when we did, we had an army of new friends with us. I would fall asleep to the sparkle of their laughter. There was always a note of surprise to it, as if none of them could quite believe their luck. Like my father, they had taken jobs at Robert College without knowing much about the place. They had just wanted to get out of America for a while: see a bit of the world and take a good, long breath before Life took over. Who could have known that this random leap would land them in this great and ruined beauty of a city?

For two thousand years, Istanbul had been one of the world's great capitals. Now it was just another disintegrating city, important only for the great waterway that passed through it. The Istanbul I knew as a child was a theatre: we sat on our balconies, watching the ships. Though we could read their names and identify their flags, we never knew where they were headed, or what they were carrying, or why. Some people solved the mystery by imposing on them their worst fears. They would hear the ships passing through the night and slide under their blankets. But not my parents, who would rise from their beds the moment their apartments began to tremble and walk out on to the balcony to see the great black hull cutting through the night. But not my parents, who would rise from their beds the moment their apartments began to tremble and walk out on to the balcony to watch the great black hull cutting through the night. And there they would sit, staring right through it.

4

Intimations

But even in those early months, I had intimations of what was to come. While foghorns blared and searchlights pierced through the night, and our curtains, and the electricity went on and off, while my parents and their new friends sat out on the balcony, laughing the night away, I tossed and turned in my bed. I could see only its faintest silhouette and as yet had no idea what it was.

Already I was sorry I had not found room in my suitcase for a flag. I was unsure about the one I conjured up each night after my mother turned my lights out. Had I given it the right number of stripes and the right arrangement of stars, the correct shades of blue and red? With my eyes closed, I could see it rippling in a breeze. I could see my lost classmates with their hands on their hearts, reciting the Pledge of Allegiance. I would recite it with them, but some nights I'd stumble over the words. Or I'd wonder about them. What did it mean for a nation to be indivisible? What was the difference between pledging allegiance to a flag and pledging it to the republic for which it stood? How could a republic stand for something anyway? I would ask my father about it, but not in the morning – he'd have a headache then. I would wait until supper. I would imagine the look he'd give my mother, as if to say, *What a brain this girl has. She asks better questions than the President of Robert College,* and for a moment I'd feel proud.

On other nights I'd take myself back to my old music class,

back in my old school. My best friend Shawna would be in the front row and next to her would be our almost-best friend Kathy, who would have taken my place by now. Did they ever think of me? If they did, were they sad? I would imagine them sitting there, waiting for our teacher – their teacher – to sit down at the piano.

And as she pounded out the first strains of the *Battle Hymn of the Republic*, I'd think again about the halls of Montezuma. Where were they? How far was it from this place to the shores of Tripoli? Why did the United States Marines have to go there? Didn't they ever get tired? I imagined the men setting out on yet another long journey, each one holding a flag. I saw them fanning out across the globe. I counted the countries currently in crisis – because I knew so much more now. Since arriving in Turkey, I'd been reading *Time* and *Newsweek* from cover to cover, and all the cartoons in the New Yorker. When the static on Mr Guttman's radio wasn't too bad, I even listened to the *Voice of America* in Special English. So I knew just how many battles our country was fighting on the land, on the sea, in space, and even in the hearts and minds of misguided youth. On each and every continent, there were dominoes falling, as marauding bands of Communists plotted together to rob whole nations of their freedom. The cost of defending them was astronomical, forcing President Kennedy to go to Congress *yet again* with his cap in his hand. He had been met with a cool reception, but this King of Statesmen had taken it in his stride.

These were extraordinary times. Civilisation itself was under threat. If freedom was to triumph, we were to stop asking what our country could do for us, and ask instead what we could do for our country.

But how could I know what to do for my country if I wasn't even there? I'd peered into the night and tried to see through it, all the way back to my old house where the lights didn't go on and off at whim like they did here, to my street, to my lost school and my lost best friend Shawna, who had the same birthday as I did. I conjured up our last party – the twin tube cakes, placed together to form an eight, and the matching pairs of high-heeled sandals that our almost-best friend Kathy had given us, and the twin presents all the other friends had brought, and the skirts we'd made from green crepe paper, so that we could dance like Hawaiians. I remembered my hula hoop, and the candy store on the corner, and the cranky old man across the street, who never threw back any ball so unlucky as to land in his garden and who shook his fist if we slid down the Mud Mound when it rained.

I returned to the Pine Pool and the Quarry. I felt the coolness of a supermarket on a summer afternoon. I ran across the sand at Island Beach, and walked all the way to the bend with my father, collecting driftwood. With my Brownie camera I photographed the sunset. In the back seat between my sister and our baby brother, I slipped down in my seat and watched the treetops flying past. In the back seat of Mr Guttman's car, I would name them. I didn't even know the names of the trees in Istanbul. In America I'd known them all. But if ever I reached out to touch an American tree which I knew by heart down to the last detail, it would float away from me. Already I was outside my own memories, looking in. Already other people's words were getting in the way.

There were more words now, floating in from the balcony, with no laughter to punctuate them. I could tell from the respectful hush that the newcomers who had joined my parents and their friends that night had at last been invited to tell the story of how they got here. I would leave my bed. Taking care not to step on the creaking floorboard, I would slip into my parents' bedroom. And if the night was warm enough to warrant an open window, I would sit in the windowsill and listen to their mysterious laments about an America where all minds had to march in step, where men who had fought a world war were forced back onto tracks so narrow that they had to keep their eyes on the ground for fear of falling off them, where girls with college degrees and myriad talents were dragooned into typing pools and stifling marriages and never ever allowed to sing the blues.

32

Whole families were condemned to suburbs where brainwashed neighbours ostracised you if you so much as suggested that Senator McCarthy was a scaremonger or expressed second thoughts about adding fluoridate to your water. I was not quite sure who exactly had done the brainwashing: my parents and their friends referred to them only as 'those people'. Neither could I understand why 'those people' ruled by fear, or why they were so hell-bent on suppressing the very things that had once made America so great. Hadn't they noticed what my parents and their friends saw so clearly: that whole flocks of the best and the brightest were taking flight?

'Taking flight'. I knew this was a metaphor, but I could also see it – a great swarm of free spirits rising into the sky, and heading off in all directions, in search of . . . what? 'A place where we can be ourselves,' I heard them say. 'A little corner of the world where we can slide beneath the radar, surround ourselves with kindred spirits, live by our own lights, without anyone being the wiser.' This, too, conjured up a picture: my parents and their friends bathed in light, sitting at a table on the edge of a great stage. But it worried me, because this stage did not belong to us, and we were only guests.

Supposing we had to leave here? Where would we go? Had I been a normal child – a child who was good at tether ball, and preferred hopscotch to reading – I would have welcomed the prospect of going 'home'. I might have known that – whatever the grownups might say on a balcony at midnight – the America I knew was still there. But I was not a normal child. I lived to read. I read to live. I would come home from school and curl up on the sofa with whatever book I could lay my hands on. I floated inside a swarm of words that bore no connection to the known world. And after mixing Philip Roth with Nancy Drew, and Ellery Queen with Robert Frost, there was little connection, either, between the America of my memories, and this other America where fashionable murderesses

33

wore turbans with their fox skin coats, and teenagers tore around in roadsters, and couples expressed their love for each other by taking diaphragms (lungs!) into bed with them. Though after reading of such horrors I could understand, perhaps, why good fences made good neighbours.

And why we had left.

5

Monday morning

But on Monday morning I woke to find my sister sitting on my feet, in conversation with Lightie and Keenie, who despite being imaginary were her closest friends simply because they hated me. They lived in the tree just outside my window, she claimed. They could read her lips through glass, which meant she didn't have to use her voice to converse with them, but she did use her voice, just to upset me. I felt that trembling, high-pitched hum grating on my ears, and all my wisdom washed away.

Then my sister was not just babbling but going through my chest of drawers, because she'd lost another sock on the way home from school, or ripped her blouse or poked another hole in her cardigan, so she was trying to make off with something of mine instead. It wasn't just that I didn't want her stealing my things; I didn't want her ruining them. I did not yet know that it was not my sister to blame for the destruction but a college workman who lay in wait for her every morning, in case she was walking to school alone.

I pulled one foot out from underneath her to give her the kick I still thought she deserved. She threw back her head and roared like a dying lion until my father came running. The disappointment in his eyes was genuine. He could never understand why I acted like a child. That was my sister's privilege, not mine.

I'd get the scolding from my father while my sister cried into my mother's skirt. She kept this up until she was granted the day off school – a day's reprieve, as we now know, from the paedophile workman. But this victory didn't stop her, and I would hear a note of triumph creeping into her sobs as my mother undid my braids and pulled a rough brush through my tangles. With each yank I yelled louder. With each yell, my sister, who was sucking her thumb by now, would wrinkle her nose in triumph. My mother didn't see this. She didn't know why I lunged forward. But because her hands were on my braids, she had no trouble yanking me back. Mute with disgust at my roar of pain – which was exaggerated, but still, there was the pain inside, the wound she couldn't see – my mother abandoned me for the kitchen. I stood at the door to watch her cut two thick slices of bread and coat them with Sana, the only margarine you could buy here. And how I hated it, *execrated* it, especially in the morning, when my head ached, and I couldn't leave yet, because there was still one braid unbraided. But I knew better than to tell my mother that. I didn't want her calling me a child. I would stand there like a stone while she clapped a slice of bologna between the two slices of bread. 'You'd better get going,' she said. 'Or else you'll be late.'

And so I stepped outside to face the cruel world: the wooded slope and the steep cobblestone road and the apartment dwellers glaring down at me through their dark blank windows as I walked past the tennis court and on to the Twisty Turny. I sobbed my way up the steep stairways that cut through the switch backs, blind to the bushes that harboured the truth. As I walked up the path that skirted the college infirmary, my tears finally cooled. Outside Albert Long Hall I paused to blow my nose, choosing a bench at the terrace edge that my father could not see from his office window, not unless he craned his neck, but after failing to locate a handkerchief, I reminded myself he wouldn't be looking for me anyway. Because I had disappointed him. Because he had better things to do, now that he had banished me from his life and mind. As I waited for my tears to dry, I imagined my mother on our balcony, smiling at my toddler brother, who would be crouching on the tiles, pretending that the stick in his hand was an airplane. My sister would be nestled in my mother's arms with that stupid thumb of hers still in her lying mouth. And my mother would be saying, 'Don't worry, darling. Mimi won't be bothering us again today.' Soundlessly I would reply: 'I won't be bothering you again ever!' Steeled by righteousness, I would head down the White Walk, turning right into a cobblestone lane that was steaming with the fresh manure from horses and donkeys, and the packs of dogs to be avoided at all cost, because they hadn't had rabies shots.

With luck I would pass without incident into the little square with the marble bench under the hundred-year-old plane tree, and from there to the green shuttered white stucco building that was Istanbul's only international primary school. If I was lucky, I'd walk up the path to hear the bell go. I'd see the Principal standing at the top of the stairs, and the children lining up. We would file in grade by grade and get straight to work, and once I was sitting at my desk, I would know what was expected of me, and how I wanted to do it, and before long I would forget that I was alone, unloved, abandoned and replaced.

But if I arrived early, I had to walk through a game of Horses. I was the only child in the entire school who did not see the point of Horses. If you were a girl this was what you did. You whinnied and pranced around the playground in feeble circles, pretending not to notice as the boys – the Horse-Catchers – advanced in posses, swinging imaginary lassos. You squealed hopelessly as they carted you off to some makeshift corral, where you had to remain, whinnying and flaring your nostrils, until the bell rang. I had known from the first day that I didn't want to play that game and yet I regretted having said so, because I was never asked again.

I melted into the image they formed of me. A smallish girl with crooked bangs and a lopsided parting that made one of her braids a lot thicker than the other, who had so few clothes that they imagined she'd come to Turkey with only an overnight bag. A girl whose supply of books was limitless. Who seemed to be in a competition with herself about how many trees she could sketch, even though the drawings looked nothing like the trees there. Who was the teacher's pet, because of all those long words she knew. Who always brought the same boring bologna sandwich in her lunch box and who stared hungrily at the lunch boxes the consular children brought in, because their parents had PX privileges and therefore access to Tang, maraschino cherries, Hostess cupcakes, and other delights she'd once taken for granted. Who was just terrible at tether ball, volley ball, basket ball, medicine ball, or any other ball you cared to mention, and so the last person to be picked for any team. Who should have laughed it off when the boy at the next desk called her a Communist, but instead launched into a tirade about some fort in New Jersey, and what Senator McCarthy had done there to innocent physicists whose families had died in the gas chambers, until the boy, stunned and stupefied, fell back in his chair and asked the girl next to him to get him an oxygen tank before he died of boredom.

This boy's father worked for the US Consulate. The girl's father was supposed to work for an oil company, but following his arrest two years later at the Turkish-Bulgarian border, he turned out to be an arms dealer. Both the girl and the boy lived in the building next to ours. There must have been twenty American families living in our neighbourhood and to a passing stranger we might have given the impression of a community: we children all knew each other, and our mothers made a show of being civil. But the fathers did not mix. There were the ones who taught at Robert College, who wore corduroy jackets and Hush Puppies and had hair long enough for you to see what colour it was, and there were the Cold Warriors, who had crew cuts and worked for the consulate or were in Turkey because their companies had sent them here on a rotation.

These warriors were so scary that even their own children clutched their thighs at the sight of them. Which was a good thing, I thought. Because no matter how hard I tried to walk home ahead of them, those children would be waiting for me on the bench by the tennis court. From my hiding place on the edge of the Twisty Turny, I waited for the veneer of protection their fathers unwittingly provided. It would, as a rule, be half past four on my Mickey Mouse watch when they emerged from their chauffeur-driven cars, flashing sunglasses, sharp suits, and thin-lipped frowns. Minutes later, they'd be bounding across the empty lot in their sneakers, slapping their rackets against their white shorts.

As they arrived at the bench, each claimed his own child with a cursory tap of the racket, asking, 'So how did the test go?' or 'Go home and help your mother,' and, for a few illusory moments, I imagined that I too was under their protection. I'd make a run for it, scuttling past the danger-bench as their scary children muttered the epithets of the day: *Creep. Jerk. Knucklehead. Numbskull. Spaz.*

I pretended I hadn't heard them. But sometimes I couldn't stem the rage washing inside me. I'd turn back and say, 'Just tell me what I did to deserve this. Just tell me!' They'd pretend they didn't hear. And so it went until, one day, the Admiral's wife caught them in the act.

She was walking up the Twisty Turny, swinging her groceries in a string bag. She heard her husband's cauterised curses rising from the tennis court. *Dang! Shoot! Fiddle and drumsticks!* Did she hear me pleading? Did she hear the bench children sniggering when I tripped and fell?

'That's a nasty cut you have on your knee there,' she said. 'If I were you, I'd go home and get a band-aid.'

'We don't have any band-aids,' I replied.

Leaning over, she lifted my chin. Her eyes were brown, but flecked with yellow, and as she studied me, nothing moved in her long unlined face. With an almost silent sigh, she took my hand. 'Then how about some cookies?'

She lived in the penthouse of a building at the top of our road, and there was a moment just before she closed the door when I remembered I shouldn't trust her. She was a stranger, after all. But there, beyond her terrace, was the Bosphorus. And when I leaned over the railing, I could see our kitchen window.

I turned around to find the Admiral's wife gazing down at it too.

6

In the picture

In the picture, taken at one minute to midnight, on the 27th of October, 1962, the Admiral's wife is standing behind the baby grand, beside the dark window. There is just the hint of a smile, hastily suppressed, but her gaze is unabashedly watchful. She's keeping us safe from all those anxious spies who have also been watching us, ever since the *Felix Dzerzhinsky*. That bundle of shawls on the ancient chaise longue – that's Sergei, the ship librarian. And there, in the shadows, is the Turkish Ambassador to Egypt, with his assistant, the young İsmet, and his old friend, William Wakefield, who is checking his watch. The white-suited figure at the far edge of the picture I take to be the Admiral himself.

I still don't know his wife's maiden name. Only rarely did I hear anyone call her by her first name, which was Hope. People usually referred to her as 'the Admiral's wife', in the same breath confessing they had no idea how she had ended up marrying an Admiral because Mrs Horace Harrison was a Quaker. She told me herself that same afternoon she took me home to clean and dress my knee. When I asked her what a Quaker was, she explained that a Quaker believed that no man stood between her and God. She believed everyone had a light inside them. She valued silence, and she opposed all wars.

'Even the good ones?' I asked, when she sat me down in the kitchen with a plate of chocolate chip cookies and a glass of ginger ale. I hadn't the nerve to ask her to add a maraschino cherry. She explained that she had indeed served her country during the Second World War. 'But not in quite the way you'd think.'

She cast her eyes downwards, as if to oppose all wars once more. Looking up, she asked, 'And what of thee?'

Thee was a word I associated with the 23rd Psalm, and my stern but loving kindergarten teacher, now an ocean and a continent away. She had read it to us every morning after the national anthem. I could still hear her voice. Perhaps this is why I decided to tell the Admiral's wife the truth as it appeared to me at that abject moment: how lost I was. How much I missed America. How much my parents loved this strange new world. How much they loved my sister and brother, how much less they loved me.

'Oh I'm sure that's not so,' I remember the Admiral's wife saying. The silence that followed was inviting. So I kept talking – about Horses and Sana margarine, about the boy who'd asked for an oxygen tank simply because I'd tried to explain to him what Senator McCarthy had done to some of the world's greatest physicists, but mostly about the thing that had been worrying me since the party at our house the previous Saturday, which had ended with my father and others running down the hill at dawn and stripping off at the edge of the Bosphorus to dive into its treacherous currents, despite the entreaties of Amy Cabot, my father's best friend's wife. Was it true, I asked the Admiral's wife, that they had risked offending the locals, and perhaps getting arrested and even *deported*? My confessor's clipped and noncommittal answers invited more questions, which tumbled out one after the other. Why did grown-ups contradict themselves? Why did Philip Roth take lungs into bed with him? Had the Admiral's wife ever crossed paths with a marauding band of Communists?

A look at her watch confirmed that it was supper time. I was very welcome to visit again, though. Any afternoon.

7

A silent house

It would have been two or three days, or two or three visits later, that I arrived home to a grim silence. What was wrong this time? Why had my father come home from work so early? And why was my mother looking at me like that? 'Come into the living room,' she said. 'We need to ask you something.'

It emerged that the Admiral's wife had paid my mother a visit that afternoon, bringing with her a care package with four sticks of real American butter and three boxes of American band aids, as well as a batch of peanut butter cookies and a really good hairbrush that might help my mother clear a few of the tangles that the Admiral's wife had noticed in my hastily braided hair. My mortified mother had invited her in for a cup of coffee. After an awkward exchange about how wonderful it was to be living in Istanbul of all places, and on the Bosphorus to wit, and how enchanting it was to see a child as young as my brother amuse himself with nothing more than a cup and a rolling pin, the Admiral's wife had subjected my mother to a string of well-intended but humiliating questions, quickly establishing that my mother had not been to college, had no profession to call her away from her family responsibilities, and was hearing for the first time that I'd been suffering from nightmares about couples who did strange things with lungs in bed.

'What the hell did you *tell* this woman?' my father asked. I had hardly begun my list when he slammed his fist down on the lamp table, so hard it sloshed his beer. 'This is just preposterous. Did you hear that, Gracie? She told this woman about Hector and me swimming in the Bosphorus. Swimming *nude* in the Bosphorus. She asked this woman if she thought it might get us deported!' Turning back to me, he said, 'Don't you know to keep your mouth shut around people like that? Do you have any idea who this woman's husband is? Don't you realise that *she* is the one who could get us deported, with one quick call to the college president?'

'She'd never do that,' I said. 'She's a Quaker, and she values silence.'

'Jesus Christ. Gracie. Are you following this?' Turning back to me with a gruesome smile, my father said, 'So I take it that while this woman was busy valuing her silence, you gave her chapter and verse on your own religious leanings.'

Why was truth such a cruel master? 'Actually,' I said, trying for a voice that might bolster up my courage. 'Actually, I told her about *you*.'

'You told you about *me*. Now that's reassuring. What exactly did you say?'

'Just about how you almost became a priest. And what I thought about it. I mean, I was wondering what it would have been like, not to exist. I mean, if you'd become a priest, because then you wouldn't have had any children. Why was it wrong to say that? It's the truth, isn't it?'

Emitting a hollow laugh as he hit the side of his head, my father turned again to my mother. She had her head bowed slightly, so I couldn't see her eyes. 'Gracie,' my father said. 'Gracie. Look up, for Christ's sake. For God's sake look at me. Why do I have to do this all alone? Why aren't you helping me?'

'Why do you talk about Christ and God so much,' I asked, 'if you don't even believe in them?'

Later, much later, my mother came to sit on my bedside, to smooth my matted hair and tear-streaked cheeks, and to tell me that she was sure that everything would be fine, just fine, because my father understood now that I was a child who had deep thoughts and was genuinely puzzled by his many and urgent appeals to Jesus Christ. She also told me that when I had been invited into the Admiral's wife's lair, I had been plied with peanut butter cookies and actively encouraged to pour my little heart out but had meant no harm in saying so much. My mother then told me about the silver lining in this cloud I'd brought over our lives: I was going to learn from my mistakes. I was going to understand from now on that I couldn't just go around telling everyone and his uncle how many beers my father drank on a normal night or what he thought about Senator McCarthy or why he had reason to believe that the Admiral – whom he had only ever seen playing tennis – might be a spook. She kept using the word discretion, and when I asked her what it meant, she said, 'It means not talking. It means keeping the really private things in your life just a little hidden, just a little secret.'

That didn't make sense to me, especially when I thought about it later on, after all the rituals of apology were over, and my father and I were friends again, and I had eaten everything on my plate, and everyone returned to a strained version of normal. I went to bed to toss and turn with the questions I had accumulated over the evening but not dared ask. Why had I been punished for telling the truth, when the truth was so very important? If discretion meant keeping your really private things a little hidden, a little secret, and if it was something adults learned never to forget, then why had my father and his new best friend Hector Cabot run down the hill at dawn to jump into the Bosphorus in their birthday suits for all to see?

In the living room, my parents were talking in low voices. I crept to the door, which was ajar. 'The lip on that girl!' I heard my father say. 'The disrespect!'

'Oh, I know,' said my mother. 'I know. It's terrible.'

Her betrayal went through me like an electric current. How dare she, after all she'd said and promised? As if in response to my silent rebuke, she added, 'I do think she was being sincere, though. It's just that she's confused. The Admiral's wife also called her precious,' my mother now recalled. 'Or to quote her exactly . . . she described our Mimi as *terribly* precious.'

My father let out a deep sigh, which my mother echoed. When I floated back to bed, the words played in my head like a heavenly harp. Precious. I was precious. And it was terrible to be precious. Just terrible. But as my mother had then reminded my father, it was not necessarily a bad thing.

My father went out that night. My mother insisted. 'You need to relax. You need to spend a few hours with Hector and the boys. No, honestly,' she'd said, although I could tell that she secretly longed for him to stay at home. Was this discretion, too? If so, why would it be dangerous to tell him the truth? Why was my father not to know what it was like in this house when he went out with his new friend Hector Cabot, and why was that beer hall they went to called the Passage of Flowers even though the only woman allowed into it was a large-busted bleached blonde accordionist named Madame Xenia? I would wake up to a night punctuated by searchlights and foghorns and the click of the electricity going off, and then on again. I would hear my mother pacing. Stepping out onto the balcony. Fixing a cup of linden tea and going back to bed to read.

That night I crept into bed beside her. The Herodotus she'd been carrying from room to room was sitting on the bedside table, replaced by a green and white striped Penguin mystery by Marjorie Allingham. I was reading the book I'd found on my father's bedside table, by an Englishman who'd disguised himself as a native and gone to Mecca masquerading as a believer, knowing all along that recognition could lead to an instant and gruesome death.

The ships came and went, the frames on the wall clattered, a searchlight passed across the curtains, followed by the beams of a car rounding Akıntı Burnu, the Point of the Wild Currents. The lights flickered, but came right on again. Then the book pulled me away from all of this and into its forbidden world.

45

I was straightening my pillows – because my eyelids were drooping, and I wanted to stay awake, because my intrepid hero had again evaded detection and was fast approaching the Kabaa Stone – when I felt my mother's hand on my arm.

'Precious,' she said.

Precious.

'That happened to me too, you know?'

'What happened?'

'I was carried away.'

She'd been carried away at about my age, in Brooklyn, with a lady she'd helped home from church one Sunday. The lady had invited her in for milk and cake and politely asked about her life. At first my mother had been at a loss: no one had ever asked her such a question. Then, without thinking about it, she had blurted out that she was an orphan. An orphan? Oh dear me, came the shocked reply. How had this terrible thing happened? My mother had supplied the first details that came into her head: it was a complicated story involving ship captains and consuls and betrayed butterflies in Japan. It had not occurred to my mother that the lady would want to take this tragic tale back to church with her the following Sunday, to gather alms for this waif who so longed to be an opera singer. By then it was too late.

'They were so disappointed in me.'

'Who?'

'My parents. They just couldn't understand why I would make up such a story.'

'I never make things up,' I said.

My mother laughed and swept back my hair.

'Oh you will,' she said. 'You will.'

8

Lessons

By now, my lessons were well under way. They were woven
into the household routine.

Each day, when I returned from school, it would be with a
question that had been plaguing me. I would think of another
as I followed my mother from the kitchen to the balcony.
Lingering at the supper table, I would argue with my sister
about which question was most urgent. And then, hands
tapping, feet swinging, we'd count the passing minutes, waiting
for our mother to give our brother his bath and his bedtime
story and at long last put him to bed.

From there it was back to the kitchen to make us linden
teas, or hot toddies without the whisky. We'd wait, as instructed,
until she'd settled into her chair, tasted her drink, and looked
up, with a smile.

'So then. What would you like to hear?'

Tell us about the shipping company, we'd say. Tell us about
the blues school. Tell us how the nun knocked your head against
the blackboard, when you came back late from lunch – even
though it was not your fault because your mother had taken
too long putting your food on the table. Read us that poem
again, and tell us why, when you first read it, you tried to
shout it from the rooftop. Tell us what your mother did
afterwards, and what she said about that poet. Tell us how
you felt when they told you only boys went to college. And
what it was like to share that small room with your sister when

47

your brother had a room twice the size. Tell us why, when you were our age, you thought life would be so much better, if you were a boy. Tell us why you're glad we're girls.

Each time my mother told a story, she embroidered it more boldly. With time, all the stories blended into a single drama – the long road to the grand but never-to-be tragic opera in which we now lived. What trials she had endured along the way! There were the kindly but blinkered souls who had told our mother that with her looks, she could make a perfect match. There were the suitors, each with his own tiny dream – a fine new furniture store in Westchester, an accountancy firm in Flushing, a ranch house in Lodi that could house a family of six. She looked at these nice men across the nice tables at the nice diners after the nice Broadway shows and she smiled politely, but her mind was still alight with visions of that other world glimpsed at the blues school.

On two occasions, she'd been taken to Carnegie Hall and on to a famous Broadway restaurant, where the star of a show they'd just seen was entertaining her closest friends, and still she clung to her dream. By imitating their every gesture, she made them all real for us: this was the way they threw their Spanish shawls over their shoulders, this was how they held a Gauloise. This was how they spent their lives: wafting stylishly from song to song, and from wild adventure to dangerous romance, somehow preserving their fine complexions.

But between their world and hers was a giant chasm. It was for them to play out the great dramas of life, and for her to look on. Until one day she happened to catch sight of my father, entering stage left . . .

Whenever my father overheard her telling us this part of the story he would leave his desk and stand in the doorway, arms akimbo, and would say, 'You know why it was stage left, not stage right, don't you?'

'Oh darling. There's no need to . . . ?'

'Do you know what my nickname was when your mother and I first met?'

48

We did. It was CS, short for Class Struggle. My mother's family hadn't thought that too funny. They hadn't laughed either when my father was working at the post office and redirected eleven hundred soda siphon advertisements to my mother's home address. Or when he and his best friend found a gravestone with my grandmother's name on it, and left it on the doorstep.

'But the topper' my father said, 'was that time in the cemetery itself.'

'Actually,' my mother added, 'I don't think my parents ever heard about that one.'

'I bet they didn't,' my father said. Turning to us, he added: 'You know which story I mean, don't you?'

'Was it when you were courting?'

'Darling, do you really think . . . ?'

Overriding her modest plea, my father continued, 'Yes, I do. In fact, my blood chills just at the thought of it. Imagine, girls, we were sitting on that gravestone . . . '

'Just sitting,' my mother would murmur.

'We were sitting on that gravestone . . .'

'Laughing at a joke . . .'

'Yes, that part is true. We were sitting on the gravestone, laughing our heads off, when I just happened to put my hand down on the stone. But it was not the stone I touched. It was *another man's hand* . . .'

After the story, when my father had gone back to his desk, my mother always said: Never learn to type. If you never learn to type, you'll never get stuck in jobs that go nowhere.

'But if you'd become a blues singer, we wouldn't be here.'

'But I didn't become a blues singer. I chose to have you, and here you are. Did you know that from the moment I set eyes on you, I saw straight into your souls?'

My sister was the one who was most like my mother – the classic second child, so often overlooked, so cruelly underrated. I was this whirlwind – a child whose will would not be curbed.

My mother's friends had advised her to crush my spirit but only once, after I had cried for seventeen hours – in my father's version, it was seventy hours – had my mother considered their advice. Instead, she looked into my furious eyes and thought about all the things I might do one day, things she hadn't had the audacity to do. So she decided to let me be a whirlwind, because then I might have the chance to take the world by storm, instead of just dreaming about it.

'And singing about it.'

'Yes, and singing about it.'

In those days, my mother sang only to us and never within earshot of my father. Usually she sang to us while she was cooking supper, but one Friday night, when he was out with his friends at the Passage of Flowers, and the lights were off again, and we were sitting on the balcony, watching the full moon's silver path across the water as it rose in the sky, she sang us her entire repertoire. While she was singing *Stormy Weather* – the song that had become my song, the moment she first set eyes on me, and the song she sang better than anyone in the world, except perhaps for Billie Holiday, who didn't count, anyway, on account of being out of this world, in every sense – I glanced at the garden below, which belonged to our landlords. The grandfather was sitting next to the wall, his face upturned as if to catch my mother's voice, his hands clasped as if in prayer.

He was the only one, besides us, who heard her sing. She'd taken a vow of silence on her twenty-first birthday. She'd been invited to perform at a real blues club, and had turned it down.

'Why though?'

'The club was too far away.'

'You could have gone there in a car.'

'No one wanted to drive me.'

'You could have gone by yourself, then.'

'Not at that time of night.'

'Why not?'

'Well, people can be fresh.'

'Why didn't Daddy help you?'

'Well, even men as wonderful as him can be very old-fashioned sometimes.'

'But that's just not fair.'

'It was for the best,' she said. 'I was getting married in July. And I knew who I wanted to sing for.'

'And who you didn't?'

'And who I didn't.'

Outside the house, amongst people who had never heard her sing, my mother spoke softly and kept her eyes downcast. She ceded to me. I was her translator. I used my ten words of Turkish with the butchers, greengrocers, dry-cleaners, *dolmuş* drivers, and waiters, and my twenty words of French with the Armenian seamstress who lived downtown, right next to the British Consulate. I translated too when we visited the Greek delicatessen owner who sold bacon and butter, a few steps further along, and the marble-skinned lackey at St Antoine's who watched over the candles we lit when we passed by, and the ancient lady of unknown origin at Markiz who served cakes to us children and Viennese coffee to my mother. Even inside, she remained icily and stubbornly demure. Not once did I see my mother so much as lift her eyes to the art nouveau mural of the garlanded, half-naked woman whose name I was able to translate as Spring.

My mother herself had nothing to say to these people beyond *please* and *thank you*. In the street, and even at our own parties, even these words seemed beyond her. She remained on the sidelines, laughing at someone else's joke, or blending into the wall, as if she'd wandered on to a stage by mistake. Most of the college wives had been to college and talked about books my mother knew perfectly well. But she never offered an opinion. Once, she listened until the early hours while my father and a college friend argued about Proust, At the end my father said to his new friend, 'Admit it, you've never read the man.' The friend confessed. My father admitted he hadn't read Proust either. My mother quietly told them she had read every one.

Later, when she told us this story, and we asked why she'd waited so long to show them up, she explained that she enjoyed keeping her own counsel. She might know more than anyone else in the room but she let her thoughts wander and no one was any the wiser.

'So,' she would say, when I got home from school, and we sat down with our linden teas. 'What news have you brought me from the great wide world?' Referring then to the person who would become her dearest friend, and who would remain so, even when the two were thousands of miles apart, she'd ask, 'Have you seen that marvellous woman again? Did she share any of her great thoughts?'

'Just a few of them.'

'Oh, wonderful. It's just what I need right now. Great thoughts from the horse's mouth.'

'She's not a horse,' I'd say. 'She doesn't even look like one.'

'Of course. You're right. The Admiral's wife is a delightful person, and she would be happy if we were more delightful, too. So tell me everything.'

'Everything?'

'Yes, everything.'

I spy

So I began my story from the point where I was halfway up the Twisty Turny, about fifty meters from where the workman lay in wait for my sister. Except we did not know that then.

It was ten to nine with the school bell at the opposite end of our great hill about to ring when I remembered I'd forgotten my boring bologna sandwich. I did not tell my mother it was boring because she was the one who made it for me. Not wishing to upset her, I skipped to the part when I sat down on the low wall where I held my head in my hands and then looked up to see the Admiral's wife leaning out of her kitchen window which looked out on to the road. 'What's the matter?' She asked. 'I forgot my lunch again.' 'Right. You just wait there while I see what I can pull together.' Minutes later she reappeared swinging a small Pan Am bag. 'Make sure there aren't any cars coming, then get ready to catch.'

After school, returning by the same route, I always glanced into her kitchen. Most days she would be darting about as if she was about to leave, but on good days, like today, she invited me in. She baked, she told me, out of habit. She'd always had cookies in the jar when her twins were still at home. She told me they were not identical, though in the photographs, they both had beehive hairdos. The one at Swarthmore *was heading for a career in the diplomatic service.* The other, who had *the probing mind and passionate heart of a true scholar,* was at Smith. While I ate cookies, she read excerpts from their letters, which contained sumptuous accounts of the books they read, the lectures they attended and the thoughts they took away with them. Often these were open questions. 'What is the duty of a pacifist in the face of Soviet aggression?' 'Is there a way to break the cycle of fear that feeds the arms race?' And: 'Is there a way to discuss all this with Dad?'

My mother found it fascinating to learn that we never ate our cookies outside the kitchen. And perhaps because I had once expressed surprise about this rule, the Admiral's wife began, in her quiet way, to offer me instruction in polite living though of course she never put it like that. 'Every family has its own rituals,' she began. Or: 'It is the alien custom to which we must accord the most respect.'

To which my mother said, 'How I wish I could take myself that seriously.'

But it was, nonetheless, from the Admiral's wife that I learned the cookies must never, ever be eaten over a carpet, that it was the duty of the milk-drinker to rinse out her glass before placing it neatly in the sink, and that the proper way to eat grapes was to pull off an entire stalk, because picking them off one by one was not just unsightly but inconsiderate. If I apologised for my ignorance, she pressed her lips into an almost-smile as her eyes slipped away, and said, 'Well, you're only eight, after all. You know a good deal more about manners than some of my husband's colleagues!'

Soon the chance came for me to judge this for myself. I was the one to offer my services at the cocktail party that would turn me into a legend, and in so doing, turn my head.

I suggested it myself, telling her that I had already passed around the hors d'oeuvres at several of the parties for which my parents were becoming famous.

When I arrived at the appointed hour, wearing my olive green corduroy pinafore over a fraying red turtleneck and tights of a different shade of red, and olive green sneakers with holes, the Admiral's wife stifled a gasp.

She was wearing a belted suit that reminded me of outfits

54

I'd seen in old movies, with hair and make-up to match. I later discovered that she had decided, during the early 1950s, to stop pandering to fashion and to confine herself instead to the beautiful ensembles she had already acquired.

'Hmmm,' she said. 'You do like corduroy, don't you?'

'Oh, I love it,' I agreed.

'It might not be quite the look we're after today. A dress might fit the bill better. Perhaps the one you wear on Sundays.'

I shook my head and explained that we didn't wear special clothes on Sundays in our house. Or go to church. I added that my first full sentence had been, 'God does not exist.'

'Hmmmm,' she said again. 'Isn't there a dress you're saving for summer?'

I told her the sad story of the shipment my grandmother had sent us: it had arrived in November and sat in customs for two months, waiting for us to pay the duty, which was more than my father made in an entire month, before being sent back to America. The shipment had included Tang, maraschino cherries, and other things I had learned not to ask for because the Admiral's wife believed in relying on local foodstuffs.

'Oh what a shame. Your mother should have told me. We could have used the diplomatic pouch. But all is not lost,' she said. Was she referring to our shipment or my dress? She found me a blue and red tartan dress that one of her twins had worn, at which point the Admiral came bursting into the bedroom, booming, 'Mother! Your services are needed!'

She shooed him away with her free hand. She spun me around, as carefully as if I were a string of pearls. Then, with a gentle tap on my shoulder, she stopped me. Looking deep into my eyes, she said, 'And let that be a lesson to you. You must run for no man. Always go at the pace you set yourself, and nothng will go awry . . .'

Slowly she led me out onto the terrace, where her husband awaited us. 'Doesn't she look a picture?' she said. He, on the other hand, in his stiff uniform and his smooth white hair and his shiny black shoes, looked like a statue. On the glass table between us, next to his bourbon glass, were his binoculars.

'You like ships?' he asked.

'Not as much as my father,' I said. 'He was in the navy in the war. He had the time of his life!'

'Me too,' the Admiral replied. 'Which is why I made a career of it.'

'Oh really?' I said. 'I thought you were a spook.'

'Hah!' said the Admiral. 'You're a card. Did anyone ever tell you that?'

Our conversation was interrupted by the guests arriving. I picked up my tray. If I stood with my back to the glass doors of the terrace, passed quickly over the carpets, the copper tray, and the ceramic plates that decorated the wall in the dining alcove, and looked instead at the white sofas and chairs and the mahogany tallboys and lowboys and secretaries and coffee tables, I could almost think myself in America, and I liked that.

The party itself was confusingly dull. When people arrived on the doorstep, they just rang the bell and walked inside. There was no raucous laughter as the door swung open, no shouting or back-slapping, no bursting into song as people tossed off their coats and threw them anywhere. Here, the guests handed coats and wraps and hats to the white-coated waiter who waited in the hall. The Admiral's wife uttered hushed words of greeting and ushered them into the dining room where two morose waiters served drinks. I was alarmed to see how carefully the guests held their glasses as they navigated the room, and how slowly they drank from them.

I remained mindful of all I had been taught, standing in my designated corner with my tray or making a round of the room every seven minutes according to my Mickey Mouse watch while not interrupting adult conversation. I stood quietly next to each group until they noticed me. I was to imagine I was balancing a book on my head to achieve perfect posture. I said Sir and Ma'am to all who addressed me, just in case they came from the South.

Returning to the kitchen, I lowered my gaze just in time to

avoid tripping over a discarded high heel. Looking up, I saw a slender creature leaning on the counter, gazing wistfully out the window. Her long brown hair hung loose over her backless black cocktail dress, and she was barefooted, one leg swinging.

10

Our first encounter

Many years later, at the End of the World party, a photographer would catch her leaning on the baby grand in just the same pose, looking for trouble in another black cocktail dress, one bare foot swinging.

But on this, our first encounter, Nella Portishead, wasn't looking for trouble. She just looked lost. When I tried out my good manners on her, asking if there was any way I might help her, and calling her Ma'am, just in case she was Southern, she jumped as if I had slipped an ice cube down the back of her dress. 'Goodness!' she said, as she turned on her toes. 'Gracious!' It was only then that I recognised her as our new school librarian. She'd stepped in the previous week, after her predecessor ran over a pedestrian on the Ankara Road and had to leave the country in a hurry. As she helped me plunge toothpicks into cubes of cheese, Nella explained that she had only been in Istanbul since September. Her husband, whom she had known since childhood, but who had only been her husband since June, was the Admiral's underling at the consulate. And like Nella he was bored out of his skull.

'And you know, if it weren't for Hope . . . Hope is just wonderful. She's been so welcoming and utterly kind. And what a life she's had! Would you believe me if I told you she saved thousands of refugees in the War? Or if I said she has other amazing gifts, all of which she keeps just as secret?' Taking me by the hand, she steered me into the hallway, where she pointed out the line of six ink sketches of a ruin, all unsigned. But Nella just happened to know that the Admiral's wife had drawn every last one, because they both went to the same art teacher. 'In fact, it was Hope who had recommended her.' Nella went on to describe Nuran Hanım and her studio, which was only a stone's throw from the castle, and so close to the Bosphorus that sometimes, when you were sitting around her glass coffee table, surrounded by glass windows, you felt you were swimming in it.

'Actually, I'm an artist, too,' I said.

'Oh really?'

'I like trees,' I said. I was in the middle of explaining why when a man with a lion-like mane of hair poked his head around the door.

'Leaving me in the lurch, are you?'

'Oh, Rex. Have I ever done anything else?'

'State your case,' he said, 'or forever remain silent.'

'Well, the truth is, I've been having the most fascinating conversation with our little helper here,' she said. After introducing Rex as her husband, Nella led me out to the living room. Here, Rex sat me down, asking me to tell him a story or two before he died of boredom.

So I told them about my mother and *Madame Butterfly*. I told them about Dr Abrakadabra, the magician we'd met while travelling along Turkey's Aegean coast that winter. I named the ruins my sister and I had danced in, and the hotel in Konya with all the canaries. Taking them out to the balcony, I pointed out my house. I told them that there was a party going on down there, too. I explained that it would last until dawn, at which point my father and his friends would run down the hill, throw off all their clothes, and hurl themselves into the wild currents of the Bosphorus.

I think the Admiral was close enough to hear this last part, because he was frowning when he asked, 'Aren't you supposed to be helping out?' Jumping to my feet, I jostled Nella's drink, spilling it down the front of her dress. I ran to get some napkins, tripped over a man's foot and went flying across the room. When

Nella picked me up, she was laughing affectionately. She took me by the hand and led me to the bathroom, where she washed the tears from my face. While she went to work on her dress, I kept myself steady with the towel rack, swinging on it to cheer myself up a little, until it came flying off the wall.

'Goodness!' laughed Nella. 'There's no end to the catastrophes!' To hide my hurt feelings, I went out into the hallway to wait for her. I will never know why I thought to use the fire extinguisher as a chair. But I did.

Within seconds it was spewing its chemical foam all over the hall and had drenched me long before I had the presence of mind to jump off. Without me holding it down, it took on a life of its own, whirling in jerks and circles, and relentlessly heading for the living room. Rex grabbed it and rushed it out to the balcony, but only after it had sprayed all the walls, and all the people, and, once it was outside, all the plants lining the terrace. Spent, it finally stopped dancing and fell over.

'Jesus H Christ,' said the Admiral as his guests rushed to and fro with handkerchiefs and paper napkins. His wife tried to calm him. 'It's not the end of the world,' she said. 'It's just a bit of water damage.'

'Water damage? You call that water?' He boomed. He picked up a sodden block of something. 'Damn it, woman! Just look at this!'

'Horace! Please stop for a moment. Consider what you are saying.'

'I'll darn well say what . . . '

Before he could finish that sentence, his words were swallowed up by the commotion of guests trying to help, guests brushing the chemical foam out of their hair or rubbing their clothes with towels, guests insisting that though it was nothing, absolutely nothing, it was absolutely time to go.

It was Nella and her husband Rex who carried me home that night. The party at our house was just beginning. Nella's art teacher, Nuran Hanım, was already there. Nestling in her arm was her almost-grown daughter Semra. Draped with shawls and perched elegantly on my brother's tricycle was the grandmother, who introduced herself as the Divine Hümeyra.

"Whose bunny slippers are those?' My mother asked as she came in from the balcony. 'And whose robe?'

But already Nella had thrown herself into the free chair, crying, 'Ye Gods! Save me from polite society!' Then she went on to tell the whole story, standing up from time to time to stomp around like the Admiral, or to stand firm and erect like his admirable wife, while the mother, daughter and grand-daughter on the sofa laughed in their three startling and distinct ways. Nella had finished with a dramatisation of our retreat from the Admiral's apartment – what she called our Walk of Shame. 'But enough of that,' she said. 'Let's think of something a little more cheerful. Let's see those trees.'

And when I lay in bed that night, still basking in the extravagant praise Nella and the daughter, mother, and grandmother artists had given my tree sketches, and listening to Nella repeat the story of the fire extinguisher to each new wave of arrivals, I heard the Divine Hümeyra say, 'Tell me again how our little darling – and what a sublime creature she is – oh, my heart breaks just to think! Tell me how she sat on it. Was it like this?' There followed a clattering noise, then a thundering rush of feet to the balcony. I reached my parents' bedroom window just in time to see the Divine Hümeyra whirling around and around, on top of what looked like a huge red top, struggling to tame our own fire extinguisher. When it had spewed its last, she threw herself into one of our deck chairs, and roared with laughter. So did everyone else. Rex strode out, mimicking the Admiral: 'Hell and damnation, woman! I'll say whatever the hell I want to say!' And 'God dang it! This girl is not an American, she's an un-American!' Though the Admiral had never said that – about me, about anyone – I knew it was nevertheless true. I had seen too much by now. I had gone too far beyond the horizon. As much as I longed for it to be otherwise, it was true what Lightie and Keenie had already assured my sister: I was no longer an American. This tiny island of love was my only home.

11

The morning after

When I tiptoed into the living room the next morning in my borrowed robe and bunny slippers, I was comforted to see that the party had ended happily, with all now returned to its proper place. The punchbowl was empty – except for the orange and apple slices clinging to its sides – and surrounded by empty and half-empty glasses. Some had cigarette stubs floating in them. In others, baby hot dogs and toothpicks rested on beds of crumpled napkin. The bookshelves were lined with beer bottles that looked as if they were keeping watch. Though the balcony door was open, the air was still stale with smoke. Strewn across the sticky floor were the shawls and clutch bags that guests would come back for later in the day, and there, too, was every stitch of clothing that my father's best friend, Hector Cabot, had been wearing when I'd last seen him. He was sure to be back soon, rubbing his head as he asked me, in a hoarse whisper, if I might also remember where he had left his brain.

Lying with his head under the sofa, was my friend and music teacher, Baby Mallinson. When I put my finger under his nose to see if he was still breathing, he opened one eye. 'I'm not dead yet, am I?'

'I don't think so,' I said. 'Would you like me to feel your pulse?'

'Water,' he croaked. 'Just bring me water.'

But the big water bottle in the kitchen was nearly full. I

couldn't lift it. I went to find my sister but it was too heavy even for the two of us. In the end we gave him half of the *gazoz* we found at the back of the refrigerator. We saved the other half for our breakfast of leftovers. Today it was better than usual, thanks to a forgotten tray of cheese *böreks* in the oven, a bag of tomatoes we found sitting in the bathtub, and a dish of baby hot dogs in tomato sauce that had survived the evening intact except for the (badly stained) white beret someone had thrown into it.

We ate our feast out on the balcony, having found two deck chairs that weren't broken and moved the card table away from the shattered glass, and right up against the railing so that we could see into the garden of the landlords who, according to my mother, had never once complained about the noise.

We went back inside to find the Admiral's wife kneeling over Baby Mallinson and taking his pulse. He was groaning. Artificially, I thought.

As we stood there, silent and unseen, a shard of glass pierced through the sole of one of my bunny slippers. I looked around me, at the brown beer bottles staring down from the bookcase, at the shawls, shoes, and Hector's clothes, and the clutch bags that now reminded me of orphans, at the sticky parquet floor and this ruined man sprawled across it. I had to explain things. I couldn't let the Admiral's wife judge this party by the morning after.

But when she looked up at me, she looked happy, calm, even amused. I saw not a hint of criticism. We might have been back in her kitchen, making cookies. 'If you could grab Baby's feet,' she said, 'I think we can just about hoist him on to the sofa.' After she had sent me off for a blanket and draped it over his legs, she patted Baby on the shoulder. 'I'll see if I can rustle up some aspirin for you. That's all you need for now. But you'll give me a shout, won't you, if you need that undertaker.'

Later, much later, after she had finally taken her leave, and after Rex, his eyes still puffed from sleep, had given the All

Clear, my mother said, 'God! That was something, wasn't it?' My father said, 'I think I need a drink.' Baby, still stretched out on the sofa, cried, 'Bring me one too!' And Nella stood up to stretch her arms. 'I think she's amazing, that woman. Absolutely amazing.'

'Oh, I know,' said my mother. 'But this room does look an absolute fright. I felt her eyes boring into me . . .'

'Are you sure about that?' said Nella. 'She might look stern but actually she's the opposite. She's been around the block a few times. You know she worked in Vienna for the American Friends' Service while her husband was busy bringing troops back from the war? Vienna was a wide open place back then. I'll bet she saw some wild parties!'

'I believe you, of course. But I just can't imagine her like that.'

'Of course not. Because after that, everything changed. She took holy orders.'

'She did?' I said.

Nella laughed as she rummaged my hair. 'What an imp you are. What I meant was, she withdrew from the world to become a full-service wife.'

12

A full-service wife

What had possessed her? How could *anyone* find fulfilment as a full-service wife? This was a question we visited often, Nella and I, but without ever settling the matter to our satisfaction.

We had taken to sitting together at recess, on the bench under the trees. Nella had been asking me pointed questions about the game of Horses and how I felt about it. She'd watch a posse of boys lead away a herd of whinnying girls. She'd wrinkle her nose and say, 'Personally, I find the whole thing disturbing.'

But I was beyond caring. I no longer wanted friends of my own age. They made fun of you if you didn't play Horses. They didn't invite you to parties if you didn't have famous ancestors. They called you names and asked you why you had more books than clothes and told people you had cooties. And on top of all that, they didn't know anything. They couldn't tell you who Fahrenheit was, why salt could melt ice, why the Romans couldn't understand the concept of zero. They couldn't draw from bitter experience, or open new doors. Whenever we went on a school trip – to the Belgrade Forest for a picnic or to a Black Sea beach overlooked by hills bristling with military hardware – I always chose Nella as my partner. One trip was to the Sixth Fleet after it had fended off the marauding forces of Communism in all four corners of the word, and instead of worrying about who had said what behind my back, I could forget myself, and enjoy the vessel's grey decks. I could ask whatever questions came into my head.

On Tuesdays, we would walk together down the Aşıyan to Nuran Hanım's studio. We had begun taking art lessons together. I did not yet know that my mother had given up her own lessons to fund mine.

That spring, we worked on studies. We sat on either side of Nuran Hanım with our backs to her easels and the swirling waters of the Bosphorus in front of us as she took us through her great art books. She sighed in ecstasy whenever she turned the page which revealed a masterpiece she loved. She had huge, sad eyes that looked sculpted when she closed them, and a downturned mouth that faltered at the edges when she had to search for a word. She would scrutinise each masterpiece before tracing out for us the shapes and lines of its composition.

Then she reluctantly extracted herself and returned the book to the coffee table. We opened our exercise books and turned the young woman with a water pitcher into the circles, triangles and squares that defined her and made her beautiful. 'Isn't it mysterious?' Nella would say afterwards, as we walked along the shore. 'Just think. We can find the same lines and shapes in our own faces.'

Nella walked home with me on her library days. 'So what do you have on your dance card this afternoon?' she would ask. 'Nothing? Are you sure? Well, in that case, why don't we drop by on our friend Hope?'

The Admiral's wife never failed to welcome us. 'Oh, what a nice surprise!' she said as she paced about her kitchen, getting out the milk, the glasses, the cookies, plates and napkins. Nella watched appreciatively, her chin propped on her hands. Noticing the flowers in the vase, she said, 'Aren't those the most beautiful flowers you've ever seen?' When the Admiral's wife seemed noncommittal, she asked, 'What are the most beautiful flowers you've ever seen?' The Admiral's wife replied, 'Oh, I've always preferred wild flowers, though there is one small pocket of my heart that is reserved for the glass flowers of the Peabody Museum.' Nella would glance up at the ceiling and say, 'Yes, of course! The glass flowers of the Peabody Museum! Tell me, Hope. Did you ever go there in the afternoon? Did you see how they change when those great shafts of light come pouring through those windows?'

And then, for no reason at all, Nella asked, 'The day they dropped the Bomb – do you remember what shoes you were wearing?'

One day, when we were sitting on the balcony, drinking sun tea, Nella asked, 'So Hope, when you were working with those refugees, did you ever meet a man with seven passports?' And though the Admiral's wife was inclined to monosyllables when quizzed on that chapter of her past, this time she smiled. 'Oh my, that's a very long story.' Something in her tone led me to wonder how long she'd been waiting for someone to pull it out of her.

'Now wasn't that something,' Nella said afterwards. By now, we were with my mother in our own tiny kitchen. Nella called this the post-mortem, though her questions were fashioned to add to the mystery rather than dispel it. Why was it, she asked, that green shoes were off limits for officers' wives in 1945? What sort of man had seven passports? How distressing it must have been to be married during the War – to be walking through the Peabody with your beloved husband, admiring the glass flowers, knowing that in a week's time he might be dead. 'It must have been soul-destroying,' my mother replied as she browned the onions. She smiled, as if a memory had returned to her. We waited to see if she would turn it into a story. And I would wallow in the bliss of being included.

Nella was now a regular on our Saturday excursions – to the Old City, to the mouth of the Bosphorus, to the little restaurants in the little towns of its Asian shore or to the Princes' Islands. Most of the time, Rex didn't come with us, but even when he did, Nella still held my hand, so that my mother had only two children to struggle with, instead of three. Nella called me her little shadow.

At restaurants, whenever I had the usual scramble with my sister about who got to sit next to my mother, Nella patted the chair next to her. 'Mimi! This one's reserved for you.'

Though she was always part of the adult conversation, she never forgot I was there. 'Did you catch that?' she often asked. If I hadn't, she shifted her chair to tell me why the Algerians were so angry or how long ago the Hittites had lived in Anatolia or what Hamlet saw while roaming the ramparts. When we turned back to the adults, there would be a lull when she listened to them as quietly as I did, as if she had forgotten she belonged to them, not to me.

What I now understand was that she was studying them. She didn't understand them any more than I did. So she sketched them, trying to work them out by reducing them to pictures, and encouraging me to do the same. I was still struggling with the lines and shapes at that point. This was easier with the mosques and ferries and fountains that stood reliably still against a background. I could never pin down the people at our table before they ruined the composition by moving but Nella kept assuring me it didn't matter. An artist was not the same thing as a photographer. An artist could choose what to see. Nella always had two sketchbooks with her, one large, in which she recorded every church, mosque and ruin, every caique, ferry and ship, and a smaller one in which she did pen portraits of the other women at the table, sometimes portraits of their faces, but more often their hands, mouths and noses, and the backs of their heads. And when she was done, she would stare at those drawings as intensely as if she was trying to divine some secret they withheld from her.

The wives in particular. She couldn't for the life of her understand why they kept their thoughts to themselves and never talked about their finest achievements. Or why they remained so smug when their lives were deprived of all purpose. One day, I made the stupid mistake of repeating to Nella what my mother had said about her one evening, that she would feel differently once she had a child of her own. A flame of anger crossed her face, but it was gone as soon as it came. She passed her fingers through my hair, laughed and said, 'Why would I want a child of my own, when I have you?'

13

Playing house

Early that first summer, on the night before I left with my family on a train journey that would take us across the northern shores of the Mediterranean and back again, Nella and I had a chance to play house. I got to pretend I was her child, and she got to pretend that being someone's mother could be softer and more companionable than her own experience had suggested.

We began at Nuran Hanım's studio, at adjacent easels. Nella was finishing a view of Ephesus. I was finishing a sketch of the scene on our balcony on the night of the Admiral's cocktail party when I'd rescued Nella and her husband from those deadly dull consular types and taken them along to our party to meet the fun people, like Baby and the Cabots and Nuran Hanım herself, along with her daughter and her mother, the Divine Hümeyra. The moment I'd chosen to depict was the one when our fire extinguisher got the better of us. My Hümeyra was a swirling cylinder holding a smaller cylinder that was gushing water. Rising above her hair, which rippled like fire – I'd put in a peacock feather – the only element in the composition that resembled what it actually was. The rest – the bottles and glasses rolling across the balcony, the dark ship passing safely in the background, the loud cheering crowds – I had stripped of all detail. I had turned them into geometrical shapes, huddled artfully, in deference to the golden mean.

I had just a few details left. As I finished, Nella and Nuran

Hanım put down their brushes and came to look. 'Now that's just wonderful,' Nella said. 'That's just sublime. We're going to have to take this with us tonight. Hümeyra's got to see this. Don't you think, Nuran Hanım? Won't she love it?'

It was decided that Nuran Hanım would take it with her when she went downtown later. That would give it time to dry and gave us a way of managing it, what with all my school things, and my overnight bag. When we got back to Nella's apartment, Rex was waiting at the door. While Nella was throwing on finer clothes, he fixed me a ginger ale with a maraschino cherry. He asked me who I wanted to hear, Sarah Vaughn or Dinah Washington, and while I leaned against a bookshelf to think this through, I knocked over a bowl of alabaster eggs. He told me it didn't matter because they weren't in fact alabaster eggs, but Faberge eggs. I knew these were worth hundreds of thousands of dollars – the weight of this knowledge sent me tumbling backwards into a chair so clumsily that I spilled my ginger ale on the armrest. But not too much. Nothing a paper towel couldn't absorb. 'Can you please stop teasing her?' Nella said, when she came out barefoot to ask Rex to zip up her dress. 'Oh, don't worry about Mimi,' Rex said. 'We've been joined at the hip since birth.'

On the walk down Istiklal Caddesi, I was able to persuade myself that we three had been together forever. That we were a family. It was like closing your eyes on a train and convincing yourself that it was going in the opposite direction. Calling to Rex, just ahead of us on the crowded pavement, Nella said, 'Look! Do you see how *respectfully* they're treating me today? It's because of Mimi. It's because they think I'm her mother!'

At Rejans, I had the seat of honour. There was no question of my sharing a piroshki – as I often did with my sister – tonight I had one all for myself. And a whole chicken kievski too. When I left it half-finished, no one told me that my eyes were bigger than my stomach. No one said I had no room for dessert.

Afterwards, arriving at the Divine Hümeyra's apartment, we could barely make it up the stairwell for the crush of people.

Yet the crowds were happy to make way for us; one woman leaned so far back she almost flipped over the railing. Her two male companions sprang forward to catch her arms. Her drink spilled as they pulled her back in, and she laughed. I was not sure in what language. We walked into a great room and there, in an alcove on the far side of the baby grand, we found the Divine Hümeyra. She had a bright pink shawl wrapped around her shoulders. A green turban served as a nest for her peacock feather. She had struck a fine pose on her antique chaise longue. She was telling a long story to a tense, heavy-set man seated on the sofa opposite. Next to him was a boy of about twelve reading an Asterix comic book with some concentration. When she saw me, Hümeyra threw her arms into the air and cried, 'The great artist has arrived!' There ensued a search for my painting. It was only later that I wondered how she could know I was a great artist when the painting to prove it was sitting behind the chaise longue, still wrapped in brown paper.

It was the boy who located it, with a roll of the eyes, but then he vanished back in to his Asterix and the artist could be indulged. There was the pause as all eyes settled on her masterpiece. The muffled gasps. 'Now isn't this sublime,' said the Divine Hümeyra. 'Just as you foretold, Nella. Just sublime!' Gravely, she traced the shapes with her finger while I told her who was who in my picture, and peals of laughter echoed around me.

I pointed out the rectangle near the oval that had once been a punch bowl. In real life this rectangle was my mother, I explained. The rectangles propped up against the wall were my father and his best friend Hector, and the rod with the screaming egg-shaped face was Hector's wife.

'And this screaming matchstick in the centre with the burning hair?' Hümeyra asked.

'That's you. With the fire extinguisher.'

The Divine Hümeyra threw back her head and roared, so loudly that even the boy with the Asterix looked up. 'Oh, how sublime!' Hümeyra cried. 'How sublime, sublime, sublime!'

71

Lifting up her glass, she proposed a toast to my fine future. Casting the glass aside, she rose from the antique chaise longue to mount my brother's tricycle. She had so admired the tricycle at our last party that my father had insisted she take it home. Tonight she rang its bell to clear her path. 'Give me a tango! A tango now!' she cried. A piano answered back. Through the smoke and the laughter, I could see my friend and music teacher, Baby Mallinson, bent over its keys. Looming over him was the bust of a pouting, wild-haired man later identified to me as Beethoven. Baby brought his hands down so hard that it rocked from side to side and almost rolled over, and many of those who saw this laughed so hard they almost rolled over, too.

A couple began to dance, and now, with Hümeyra's help, they cut a funnel through the crowd. They were the first to sail into the alcove, followed by the Society Photographer with his camera raised and his flash ready, and it wasn't long before every man and woman in attendance had seen my masterpiece. Unless you counted the boy with the Asterix, no one was less than kindness itself. Even when the lights failed, bringing The Admiration to a premature end, even after the Divine Hümeyra had given my masterpiece a title (*Portrait of the Artist Accidentally Spraying her New Friends with a Fire Extinguisher*) and found a place for it on her wall, and the dancing had resumed amongst candles, and the apartment was so crowded that people were leaning out the windows, and were draped over the baby grand, too, and Rex and I were looking everywhere for Nella but couldn't find her – even then, they stared at me in pure delight if I bumped into them or tripped on their feet. Dissolving into smiles, they ruffled my hair and pinched my cheek.

The kindest of them all was the man I would later come to know as Sergei, the ship librarian. But there will still be six months to go before we made the fateful decision to board the *Felix Dzerzhinsky*, so on this occasion he was just a Russian with a gaunt face and black hair that stood up like a brush, who came hand in hand with Baby to adore my painting, and who kissed my hand on discovering I was the artist, addressing me in honeyed tones.

We had a hard time finding Nella because she had locked herself up in the bathroom with the woman I later knew as Dora's mother. Rex had given up. But I solved the mystery simply by knocking on the door. 'We'll be out in a sec!' I heard Nella say. And then, to someone else: 'Listen, if you can't take any more of this, we could just nip out to that bar you mentioned?'

'Oh no, I don't think so,' said a woman with a husky American voice with just a hint of French to it. 'That would be walking into the lion's den. I can't sneeze without their turning it into the war of the worlds. Just pass me a tissue, hon.

'I don't think there is any tissue . . .'

'Oh never mind then. A square of TP will do fine . . .'

'No TP either! Not as far as I can see, anyway.'

'Crisis over. There's some here in my bra.'

With my ear pressed against the door, I listened to this unknown woman blow her nose. 'Now that's better! Could you just duck your head, hon, while I toss this into the wastepaper basket?'

'I don't see one of those, either.'

'Oh shucks.'

'Throw it into the john, why don't you?' suggested Nella.

'How can I? You're sitting on it!'

'Let me move.'

'Why thanks.'

'My pleasure,' said Nella.

'If only everyone else was so accommodating,' the woman said. Over the sound of the flushing toilet, I could hear her sobbing.

'Oh Delphine! You poor darling!'

'It was just so hurtful!'

'Now, now. Daughters can be like that. They don't always mean what they say.'

'I hate to say it, but Dora is like that. She means every word. She really does despise me. She really has sworn never to do *anything* that might send her down the path I've travelled. After all I've done for her. All I've sacrificed.'

'Oh I know, I know,' said Nella.

'But sweetie, come on now. You might think you know, but let me tell you, daughters are a breed apart. One day they're hanging on your every word . . .'

'Well, I certainly know what *that's* like,' said Nella.

To my growing shock and consternation, Nella started to tell the entire story of our friendship as I'd never once imagined it. As something I barely recognised. I was an odd little thing, Nella said, terribly charming in my own quirky way, but oh so precious. I had trouble making friends at school, as quirky little creatures so often did, and at home I was constantly fighting with my sister, and my mother, who also had a toddler to care for and was worn down like a rag. And so she, Nella, had taken pity on me. Which had probably been a bit rash. At least that was what Hope, her husband's boss's wife, had told her. 'But I didn't have anything better to do, and one thing led to another.' Nella then insisted that she did not want to exaggerate. 'In small doses, she is absolutely charming. And her art! She takes it so seriously sometimes I want to yelp!'

'It won't last,' said Delphine darkly.

'God, I hope not. Keeping the illusion afloat is ever more exhausting. Don't get me wrong, though. When I said she was a sweet little thing, I meant it. She just asks so many questions!'

'They all do. But do they ever listen to the answers?'

'I know what you mean,' said Nella.

'Pass me your glass,' said Delphine. 'There's a little more scotch in this bottle, and we have to get through it before we leave the bathroom, or all the bloodhounds in Beyoğlu will sniff it out and come howling.'

'Thanks, just a dot. Hmm. That went down well.'

'There's more in my apartment. It's just across the landing. Maybe we should go back there.'

'I'd happily say yes,' said Nella. 'But alas, I have my little hanger-on with me tonight. She won't leave me alone for a minute with her eyes larger than an owl's observing my every move. She's probably hunting for me this very minute!'

'Yes,' said Delphine. 'Until the day they turn against you, that's what they're like.'

An ashen man with a sad moustache came down the hallway. I pretended to be looking at the Society Photographer's photographs which covered the walls from top to bottom, and which allowed me to turn my head away politely, and so hide the stinging hurt and shame. The man knocked on the bathroom door.

'We're just coming out!' I heard Nella cry.

*

Later, she found me hiding in the darkness of the morning room. Flipping on the light, she said, 'Finally! I was looking for you everywhere. If you don't mind my saying so, young thingamajig, you really had me worried!'

She fell into a chair and kicked off her high heels. Her new friend followed suit. 'God, I don't know why I even wear these things.'

'I don't know either!'

Delphine had mascara running down her cheeks, and her dress – the silken creation I would come to know as her Summer Knock 'Em-Dead Dress, to distinguish it from the velvet number she wore in winter – did not cover much of her long, brown legs. When Nella introduced us, Delphine took my hand and thanked me for letting her 'borrow' Nella. 'I'm afraid she's had to listen to the latest chapter in the infernal soap opera that is my life. Somehow, and very much against the odds, she's given me some hope.'

She asked me how old I was. Then she said what a shame I wasn't the same age as her daughter, who had just turned thirteen.

'If you look out of the window over there, you can see her

for yourself,' she said. When she first pointed ouside the side window, I could see nothing but the night. 'Press your head against the glass,' Delphine instructed. And when I did, I saw Dora in the window opposite, doing the same.

'Don't bother with a smile,' said Delphine. 'She won't return it.'

But she did.

On the way back, in the chauffeur-driven car that had waited for us so long and so patiently, Nella kept saying what an amazing woman Delphine was. 'She's just been through so much.'

'Care to share the juicy details?' Rex asked, lifting her arm and making as if to eat it. But Nella was not sharing. 'That's a story for another day.'

'Can't you at least tell us what it's about?' Rex asked.

'Men,' Nella said. 'What do you expect? It's about men.'

'And women?' Rex asked.

'Okay. Yes. Guess which kind.'

'The kind whose job it is to reflect men back at twice their normal size?'

'Exactly,' said Nella.

'Now why didn't I get one of those?'

'Easy. I tricked you,' Nella said. 'No, it was better than that,' Rex said. 'You lured me into your enchanted lair.'

Later, as they whirled around their living room to Dinah Washington, exalting in her voice, I wondered if there was any truth in her words. Did everybody love somebody sometime?

I shut my eyes.

I smiled so that they wouldn't know what I was thinking.

I wondered how different my life would have been, if only I didn't listen at keyholes. I wondered about the girl in the window. I wondered why she looked sad, even when she smiled. I wondered if her heart felt hollow like mine. I asked myself how Dinah Washington, who'd never met me, could be so sure my time would come.

14

The Mysteries of Travel

She noticed. She must have picked up on it the moment I got home the next morning. But the train was leaving in two hours. There were bags to be packed, and I had to help my sister find her shoes.

She waited until we were marooned in the no-man's land between Turkey and Bulgaria. My brother and sister were with my father in the next compartment. Outside there was a guard who threw a glance at my mother every time he passed our window.

Each time she managed to avert her gaze just in time.

'Is he a Communist?' I asked her.

'This is Bulgaria, so I suppose he must be,' my mother said, but without much interest.

We returned to silence. She looked straight into my eyes, as if to read my thoughts. Finally she said, 'You've not been yourself lately.' I made as if to shrug it off. 'Shall I tell you what I think?' she said. 'I think something happened the other night, when you were out with Nella and Rex. I think you heard something that upset you.'

It all came out.

'I don't think I need to tell you that it's not right to listen to people's conversations through the keyhole,' my mother said.

'I know!' I wailed.

'You're going to have to forgive her. Nella was comforting a maudlin woman in a bath tub. In situations like that, even I would say the first thing that came into my head.'

'No, you wouldn't!' I sobbed.

'You don't know that,' my mother said. 'You don't know what someone is going to do, until the moment arrives. But there is something else you can do, in the meantime.'

She reached for my little satchel, and pulled out Mr Guttman's sketchbook. From her own bag she retrieved a pencil. 'You can sketch that guard.'

It was up to me if I decided to see the world through cubes and cylinders and so erase all his features after achieving a likeness, she said. But if I did, I might think of recording the details of his physiognomy in an appendix.

'Why?' I asked.

'Because. In his face lurks a clue.'

Pencil in hand, I examined the guard's face. His cap shaded his eyes. His lips were sullenly full, his nose blunt, his chin jagged.

'As you're sketching, watch where his eyes travel. Let your eyes travel in the same direction, and you might find out where they've taken our passports.'

I got to work. Soon I had located what I thought might be the telltale room. Through the little window in the sentry box, I could see a bespectacled man leaning over something just out of my range of vision. I drew a broken line and an arrow pointing to it. 'That's good,' said my mother. 'I'd go so far as to call it a bull's eye.'

After the bespectacled man had emerged from the sentry box, and scurried over to the train, and made his way down the corridor, returning each passport in the teetering pile to its rightful owner, my mother said, 'So let that be a lesson to you.'

She went on to explain. Had I crept up to the sentry-box and listened at the keyhole, it wouldn't have gone so smoothly. I might have been arrested, as a spy. And where was the need? I had divined the truth, simply by staying still with my eyes peeled, and examining the evidence to hand, moving my hands only to sketch the surface details. 'Can I count on you to continue doing so?'

I asked her what I should be looking for. 'Follow your instincts,' she said. 'Wherever you look, look deep.'

And so I did, as our train snaked through Bulgaria. I sketched the vendors on the platforms, the horse carts struggling along the desolate and muddy roads. In each I sensed a wordless grief. In Yugoslavia, when the sun returned, and they at last added a diner car to our train, I sketched our waiter against a background of blurry mountain pastures. When I showed it to my mother in our compartment afterwards, she thought she saw a sad secret brimming in the man's eyes. 'What do you think it might be?' she asked.

In a café in Venice, she saw a man at the next table she thought might be a spy. I sketched him, too. We saw a man wearing the same cravat at another café later in the day. 'Do you think that might be a secret sign?' she asked. I thought it might be. He was also wearing pointy shoes. On the train to Barcelona, as we passed through the string of towns all bearing the name of USCITA, I sketched a lady with a wide-brimmed hat, gazing at the empty track from the end of a platform. Following my instincts, I drew a line between my sketch of her and an adjacent sketch of a nearby priest on a solitary bench, gazing at the rings on his hands and looking strangely shifty.

In the plazas of Barcelona, Valencia and Alicante, I sketched men in wheelchairs. Many were missing limbs. My father said they had lost them twenty years ago, in the Spanish Civil War. 'I wonder how many of these poor souls were on the losing side.' But when my mother looked over my sketches of them, she wondered about the dreams they still cherished, deep inside their hearts.

Each artistic flourish in the palace of Alhambra spoke of an unutterable past. Every courtyard we passed in Cordoba and Seville offered a glimpse of a family saga stretching back centuries, and if I sketched it from memory, as soon as circumstances allowed, I could, if I was lucky, capture its essence.

At a hotel on an otherwise deserted cove, some way outside

Malaga, my mother pointed at the headland where my sister and I had got lost the previous afternoon, after my father, hoping for a few hours of peace and quiet, sent us up there with two sticks to search for Roman coins. 'When you were up there, did you see Gibraltar?' my mother now asked.

We hadn't. But my mother assured me that we might have done, had it not been for the sandstorm that had blown up so suddenly across the straits, in Africa. I still had sand in my hair, and I was still angry at my father, who should have noticed from the yellow haze on the horizon, and deduced the sandstorm was on its way, and who ought to have known we'd never find a thing on hard ground like that anyway, not without an archaeologist's trowel. My mother had told him so. My father had apologised most abjectly and had been trying all day to win us all over. But now it was sunset and she was still giving him the silent treatment, and he was sitting at the far table, drinking wine with a young Oxford student and a Dutch conceptual artist. I had sketched them, too. In the background was the headland that blocked the view of Gibraltar.

My mother traced her fingers along its contours. Pointing at the men I'd drawn, so eager and so raw, she said, 'Somehow, miraculously, you've captured their humanity.'

This was something that could never come from words overheard through a keyhole, she informed me. It came only from careful observation. If you set down what you saw – right away or just afterwards, when it was still alight in your mind's eye – you could look at your sketch and see, for example, that your father was an astounding mixture of contradictions. He could feel awful about sending his innocent daughters off into a sandstorm and at the very same moment he could lose himself in a bottle of wine with an Oxford student who thought he looked like Rupert Brooke, and a Dutch conceptual artist who seemed pretty damn sure he was God.

'Do you think they might be spies, too?' I asked.

My mother looked out at the headland, as if in thought.

'On balance, I don't think so. But it will be good to have a record, just in case.'

I had recorded my father's humanity as well as the defining details of his two drinking partners and had just begun the hard and perplexing job of turning them all into geometrical shapes, when I felt my mother's hand on mine.

'Do you think it's wise to erase everything?' she said. What if there's a clue we're not seeing yet, simply because we have yet to name the mystery?' Standing up, she said, 'I have an idea.'

She came back from the hotel kitchen with a straw and bowl of lemon juice, which she had used herself, she said, when she was my age and in need of invisible ink. She showed me how I could use it, for example, on the newly blank shape that was the headland, to record that it was blocking our view of Gibraltar. And in the cylinders and circles of the drinkers' table, I could either draw them again, this time invisibly, or I could jot down all the details that might later turn into clues for the mystery we could not name yet. And for the rest of the summer, that is what I did – on the train across Extremadura, when the conductor drew the wrong conclusion from the title in my father's passport, and took him to see a fellow passenger, who was dying of a heart attack; in the Madrid hotel where my father was bedridden with a nosebleed throughout the week that followed; in Plaza Mayor, where little children ate ice cream watched by sad men who had lost their limbs while on the losing side of a war that had turned brother against brother; in the nightclub where we watched flamenco until five in the morning on the night before we began our homeward journey; and in the Barcelona slum where the taxi driver took us after hours of driving us from hotel after hotel and being turned away from each and every one, saying that his mistress, a prostitute, might have room for us, for a fee.

What I did first now was to sketch the geometrical shapes in pencil. Then I'd fill out the details in invisible ink. In the background, also in invisible ink, I would set down the clues to the mysteries we could not name yet, and the questions that might lead us to the answer we could not yet imagine.

We had planned to board a Turkish ship at Barcelona, but the nose bleed in Madrid and the long search for hotels in the Barcelona, along with the extortionate prostitute, had left us without the money for the ticket. We needed a Bulgarian visa to go back by train, and since the nearest embassy was in Rome, that's where we went next. But the embassy was closed for a Bulgarian national holiday. My mother bundled up my almost two-year old brother in a blanket, because we had just enough money to return by plane if we pretended he was still an infant. My brother then went and locked himself in the bathroom. The man from behind the desk had to rescue him. There followed an unpleasant scene. But in the end, Alitalia took mercy on us and charged us for only three seats, on condition that my sister as well as my brother sat on my parents' laps. We took the money that would have gone towards the fourth seat and went for a celebration meal in the Piazza Navona. It had been days since we had eaten properly.

We each ordered three courses, even my brother, while my parents worked hard to turn our chain of mishaps into something we could laugh about. But still I could not forget how the man at the airline office had disapproved of us, chiding my parents for exposing us children to what he mysteriously called 'infelicities'. 'He only said that,' said my mother, 'because he's hopelessly bourgeois.'

'But he was kind to us.'

'Yes, you're right. We shouldn't forget that.'

'His humanity,' I said.

'He can be as humane as he wants to be,' said my father. 'We won't let him stop us.' He chose this moment to tell us about the trip we would take that coming winter. He was already reading up for it – in fact he'd been reading and dreaming about the ruins of Egypt since he was a boy. He told us about the pyramids, and the Sphinx, and the lost library of

Alexandria. 'There's so much to sketch there, you won't know where to start.'

That night, at bedtime, he recited *Ozymandias* for us.

The next day, as I peered out the window at the Mediterranean from the right side of the plane, I gazed at the horizon, and thought about the dark secrets lurking beyond it.

My satchel was in the hold, but my father tore me off a page from his notebook.

The Mysteries of Travel

1. We travel into the future to find the past.
2. We go in search of great civilisations but find only their ruined remains.
3. The human eye can only go so far.
4. Historians and archaeologists are usually just guessing.
5. If you look at a marble foot long enough, you can imagine the rest of the body.
6. The first words were pictures.
7. If the Egyptians had used cement instead of marble, we would have nothing to remember them by.
8. Would the ancient Egyptians be happy or sad if they could see the Sphinx today?
9. Where does it hide its secrets?
10. Why is it not enough to see the photograph?
11. What truths will emerge when I touch it with my own hands?
12. Since the dawn of time, travellers have left the comfort of their homes and the love of their families to venture into the unknown, driven by a thirst for new experience.
13. When they gaze at the horizon, what do they see?
14. When we reach our final destination, how will we recognise it?
15. How will I know it, when my time has come?

15

The piano party

The day after our return from our great European tour, two college workmen appeared at our door with a piano that had our name on it, and a note from Baby Mallinson.

The following Saturday, my parents gave a party. Baby arrived early, dressed in what he called his cocktail lounge attire. First he tried to tune the piano; then he cursed the college basement from which he had liberated it. They couldn't have tuned it, ever. They must have had the thing pushed right up against a radiator. He did his best to rectify their shameless neglect. Then he ran through his repertoire for the evening, pausing now and again to remind my sister and me that we were to imagine him as a young student with a brilliant future before him, playing in 'some god-awful steakhouse' to earn his keep. He played the same way he did at our school, bending over the keys with his eyes closed, belting out a line of a song here and there, in his beautiful almost-contralto which people without eyes in their heads sometimes mistook for a female voice.

Once or twice he stopped mid-phrase and said, 'So, girls. Do you think this is going to work?'

I had told him about my mother's secret musical history. She herself had spoken with Baby at length about the blues school that she'd attended while working for the shipping company in Manhattan. He had hijacked the piano because he wanted to hear if her voice was as wonderful as I'd said it was. He didn't think she had any right to hide it from a man like him.

While she was out of the room, putting our brother to bed, Baby played his latest song: *My mother, the mystery*. The lyrics were based on things we'd told him. Then he played a few of the others he'd written for us last year: *Never trust a butterfly. The morning after. The new world. If balconies could talk.* 'Which one should I play first?' he asked us. 'Which one will persuade her to give up that damn vow?'

He told my sister and me that tonight (for once) he was going to take it 'slow, dead slow'. 'But mark my words. I'm not giving up. Whatever it takes, and I mean that. If it's the last thing I ever do, I'll get this fine lady to break her crazy silence.'

But for now, Baby was the lone piano player at the god-awful steakhouse. Just before the guests were due, he taught my sister and me how to hush them as they came through the door. When the time came, they wouldn't be tamed, though. One after the other they wheeled into the room with open arms. 'Now isn't this just the cat's pyjamas!' they cried. 'Now doesn't this take you back!' They just wouldn't stop talking. And perhaps my mother was right, perhaps Baby shouldn't have drunk so much of the vodka he'd brought with him. The moment arrived when he brought all ten fingers down on the keyboard in a screaming crash and stormed off to the balcony. My mother went after him, and she was out there for a long time, struggling to capture his humanity.

I was sitting far enough away not to eavesdrop, but close enough for my mother to know that I was there, at the ready, in case she needed my help. So I didn't see Nella till she tapped me on the shoulder. With her hair draped over her shoulder in a single braid and her summer print dress, she looked as young as a college girl. Or perhaps she struck me like that because I was looking into her so deeply. Clutching her arm was Delphine, trembling and swanlike in the green satin number I would come to know as her Dress for All Seasons.

We found Dora sitting straight-backed on the sofa inside,

clutching a canvas bag. Her lank black hair was pulled into a ponytail so tight it stretched her skin. Her face was all angles, as if she had already become her own portrait. Though in jeans and a boy's shirt with the sleeves rolled up, she was wearing a string of pearls.

'I'm glad you're here,' said Dora. 'You're the only reason I came.'

'But you don't even know me,' I pointed out.

'No, but I *have* seen you before.' Had she been thinking about me since our introduction, the previous June, through the twin windows? 'You didn't want to be there – I could tell that much. You looked so sad and lost.'

'It wasn't the party,' I explained. 'It was something I heard.'

'That's the way it is with those parties,' said Dora.

'I shouldn't have been listening, though.'

'What else were you supposed to do, with no one to talk to?'

I asked her if her pearls were real.

'I'm afraid so,' she said. After a long silence, punctuated by the pop of a cork floating in from outside on a wave of laughter, she added, 'It's an heirloom.'

I had never seen an heirloom before. I marveled at its yellow tarnish. 'Actually,' said Dora, 'I hate these pearls, and in fact all pearls. I just wear them to make Delphine happy. And she was so unhappy before we came out.'

Delphine was unhappy, I later heard, because her family was persecuting her most relentlessly. They were Levantines, Dora explained. The family had lived in the city for three centuries, though they still spoke French at home. They were not quite as important as they'd been during the Ottoman Empire, but they were still filthy rich. They had wanted Delphine to marry someone just like them, but she had followed her heart instead, and so they had cast her out. Poor Delphine had been forced to go abroad to make a living. Her long years of struggle in New York had not concerned them in the least because she was out of sight. But now they were up in arms because Delphine had dared to return to her birthplace. Every time she wrote for a gossip page, or appeared in one, they were on the phone, commanding her not to sully their precious name. Even after reading her Reader's Digest exclusive with Her Imperial Highness Princess Soraya of Iran, they'd refused to acknowledge her, let alone give her any respect as a serious freelance journalist. Instead they continued to regard her as a fallen woman. Because as well as making her own living, she'd had the temerity to 'bring a child into this world' without getting some man to marry her. 'Imagine. A piece of paper! That's all they care about.' Dora said. 'They would have preferred Delphine to have had me adopted. Or to have somehow gotten rid of me. So I think you'll understand me when I say I don't particularly care to speak to them.'

We were perched on opposite ends of my bed by now. She was propped up on my best pillows, and leaning against the wall. I had brought in the small cushions from our sofa and had wedged them between the window sill and the metal bed frame, and every time a ship passed, I felt the vibration down my back. If a foghorn was close enough to be heard through the laughter on the balcony, if a searchlight on a vessel rounding the Point of the Wild Currents happened to sweep across my window, Dora would shiver.

'They send the worst ones through at night, you know.'

'Who does?'

'The dogs of war.'

We were sharing her flashlight, each reading under the covers for five minutes at a time while the other made sure the time remained fair and accurate. It was her turn to wait.

'I hate boys,' she announced, a propos of nothing.

I had never met a thirteen-year-old who hated boys. I longed to understand how she had achieved this astounding feat. But I feared running her ragged with my questions as I had done with Nella, so I just said, 'I do too.'

'Nella tells me you hate that stupid game they play at school, whatever it's called. Horses.'

'Yes,' I said. 'I absolutely abhor it.'

'That's good. Because I'll be in ninth grade this year, and I have no intention of playing either. So we can sit it out together. You can be my mascot.'

Was I hearing these words?

She glanced at her watch. 'You don't have a transistor radio, do you?'

I ran into the living room, pushing my way through the crowd of revellers who had gathered around the punchbowl. Spying our transistor radio on the far shelf, behind the piano, amongst the overflowing ashtrays and abandoned glasses, I grabbed it and rushed back to our haven, away from the bright lights and what now seemed to be pointless shouting.

'Baby!' they were saying. 'Baby! Come in and play!'

'Where's that confounded genius gone to?'

'Hell, Hector. Can't you play a tune or two? Why don't you warm up the piano while we're waiting?'

Through the closed door came the strains of a song – something from a musical, drained off all sadness, and to me, tonight, ringing false.

Restored to darkness, I forgot to read as Dora fiddled with the dials of our transistor radio, switching from one ocean of static to the next. Directing the flashlight at her watch, she said, 'Oh well, we've missed most of it anyway.' When she sighed, I did, too.

'Mr Guttman gave us that radio,' I offered. 'He gave it to us the day before we came here.'

'I already know that,' said Dora. 'In fact, I can't think of anyone who doesn't.' She was resting her chin on her flashlight. It lit up her sudden smile but turned her eyes into dark chasms. 'Have you told a lot of people about Mr Guttman, I wonder? Maybe even everyone you spoke to, all last year? My guess is that unfortunately you did. Even my mother's heard about him, you know. And that's not necessarily a good thing.'

'Why?' I asked.

'She sells gossip for a living.'

Crouching over, and putting her hand over the flashlight, so that the light shone right through it, Dora asked, 'Did she upset you, back in June?'

'It wasn't your mother. It was Nella.' I tried to explain but my pain made it hard to finish a sentence.

'Put your pillow here,' Dora said, patting a point on the bed between us. 'Lie down. And do cry, if you need to. That said,' she said, as she patted my head. 'I think you're making a mountain out of a molehill. Whatever you think you overheard that night, I happen to know that Nella thinks the world of you.'

'But how?' I sobbed.

'She said so, tonight, on our way over. And if I do nothing else tonight, I'm going to help you put all this behind you. It's only right, considering Nella's going to be your classroom teacher. Oh, haven't you heard?'

She went on to explain that the teacher who'd been meant to be the fourth grade homeroom teacher had had to leave the country in a hurry after her husband picked a fight with a bouncer outside a disreputable night club. Dora insisted that Nella was looking forward to teaching me, or in her words, 'struggling to keep up' but the prospect of spending a whole year with a woman who was secretly run ragged by my questions sucked all the air from my aching chest, so it was a few dark moments before I was able to ask Dora how she knew all this.

'From Delphine,' she said. She always called her that, never 'my mother.'

'And who – how – where does she glean her information?'

'Oh, from everywhere, really. But mostly parties like this. Don't worry. She would never rat on a friend.'

Outside on the balcony, a drunken chorus was singing *Around the World in a Plane*. In mid-song, their voices faded. 'Hush!' I heard my mother say. 'Baby's woken up. He's in the right mood now. He's going to play.'

After a few minutes of little coughs and scraping chairs in

an almost silence, we heard the first strains of what would, after later, happier rehearsals, become *If I Die Before the Night is Through*.

This time it kept trying, and failing, to take off.

The lights went off. The low cries of surprise gave way to laughter. There was a rush to the kitchen, and then, in the crack under the door, we could see the flickers of candlelight.

Dora shone the flashlight onto her watch. 'It's just gone midnight,' she announced. 'I'm giving Delphine one more hour, and then we're off.'

'Doesn't she mind you bossing her around?'

'To the contrary. She counts on it. We're a team, you see. We have to be. Besides, I'm the one who remembers things. *I'm* the one who's drinking water.'

'Are you the one who remembers the gossip, too?'

Dora looked thoughtfully into the flashlight. This time it magnified her eyes. 'Do you want to know the truth?' she asked.

'I do,' I said.

'The truth is that most of what she hears isn't worth much. There's really no money in it – unless it's about Communists. But here's the thing. Communists just terrify her. That's why İsmet thinks she's not really suited for this business. He's looking for a way to get her out of it.'

'Who's İsmet ?'

'A friend. Well, he started out being a friend of the friend who looked after us in New York but here he's the one who looks after us. Until William can find us something else. But really. I wish they'd hurry. Poor Delphine doesn't understand the first thing about the Communist mindset and perhaps she never will.'

As I fought off sleep, I imagined Delphine in a dark, damp alleyway, staring at the shreds of paper on which she had written gossip about Communists who gave her nightmares because she could not understand their mindset.

I sat up. Dora was sitting up, too, but with the blanket over her head. Through the pool of light I could just make out the shape of a book. 'Dora,' I said. 'Dora!'

She lifted the blanket off her head. 'Aren't you asleep yet?'

'I just need to know something.'

'Well, fire away.'

'Do you understand their mindset? The Communists', I mean.'

'No, of course not,' she said. 'Not yet. But I will. I definitely will. I'm studying them, you see.'

'How?'

'One day, if you come to our house, I might show you.'

16

Pera nights

Everyone seemed to like me more, now that I was under Dora's wing. No one seemed to worry if she might be too old for me. Instead they spoke admiringly of her calming influence. And it was true. I was learning how to behave. At least, I knew better than to run my new friend ragged with questions. I could go for whole hours without asking one. And sometimes, if I shut my eyes, and imagined Dora watching over me – always, everywhere, no matter what the distance between us – I even stopped feeling scared.

That autumn, every Friday afternoon, Dora and I left school arm in arm, ignoring the boys who no longer made fun of me, now that I was the mascot of an older, taller girl who made no secret of her contempt. We would make our way amongst the chauffeurs and the sleek black cars to the one that belonged to Dora's friend and protector, whom I had not yet met, but whose name I knew to be İsmet. Dora always sat on the left-hand side of the back seat, and I sat on the right. Together we would roll down the hill to join the slow procession along the Bosphorus Road, and for an hour we watched the back of the silent chauffeur's head as ships and fishermen rolled past us, and quilt shops and music stores, and greengrocers, fishmongers and butchers, and coffee houses and bus stops and ferry stations and mosques, as well as the wave after wave of moustachioed men wearing tired suits and brown caps who wandered in and out. Just after the Kabataş ferry station and that string of shops that sold sporting goods and replica guns, we swung around a corner that always took me by surprise to climb up into the city proper, along a narrow cobbled road so steep it made the sleek black car buck and scream. Once we'd reached the top of the hill, there were just a few more minutes of creeping past the shoe, fabric, and lingerie stores that clogged İstiklal Avenue on either side, before we each tried to be the first to see the display window with the headless mannequin wearing the wired conical bras that Delphine said were made for Martians.

The headless mannequin's only arm pointed in the direction of Dora's front door. Dora would throw open the car door the moment she caught sight of it. The chauffeur would turn around to chide her, and this was the only time we saw his face.

Delphine would be waiting for us five floors up, smiling broadly and (until the new leaf she had turned for my benefit began to fray at the edges) wearing a white apron. She'd have two glasses of Tang waiting for us, and even as we picked our way through the book towers in Dora's bedroom, we could smell our TV dinners in the oven.

We would eat them on real TV dinner tables, facing the view, though it was hard to see much through the swathes of tarnished scarlet satin that Delphine draped over the sunken chairs and elderly divans, or the dusty sunlight funnelling through the half-closed brocade drapes.

If you stood right up against the great front windows and found a hole in the lacy spirals of soot and looked straight down, and slightly to the right, you could see into the courtyard of the Soviet Consulate. If you looked straight out, you could see as far as the Old City in one direction and in the other direction halfway down the Asian shore of the Bosphorus. You could see the confluence of the Bosphorus, the Golden Horn, and the Sea of Marmara, and the Princes' Islands on the horizon. Until night fell. Then, all you saw were lights.

In Delphine's bedroom was a vast and never-made four poster bed with seventeen bright but tattered satin pillows. Along the inner wall were two wardrobes on either side of a never-tidy vanity table. There were always a few caps that had rolled off on to the floor to join a hastily discarded pair of high heels and tissues with lipstick marks on them. Lined along the far wall were piles of old magazines, some European and American, some Turkish. Strewn across the row of trunks beneath the windows were dresses that Delphine had not yet remembered to take to the cleaners and bras that had fallen short of the laundry basket. Above her bed were three framed photographs: Delphine as a young woman in a strapless gown, gazing up plaintively at a camera that caught her every eyelash and cascading curl. Delphine, our Special Correspondent, outshining Her Imperial Highness Princess Soraya of Iran in a sleek black suit. Delphine on board an aircraft carrier, gazing through binoculars in a tight little sundress.

The bedroom window looked on to an air shaft and offered a clear view into the Divine Hümeyra's morning room, so called, Dora said, because Hümeyra went in there at 11:06 every morning, to mourn her husband, who was and always would be the great love of her life. This despite the fact that she had been the one to shoot him dead, albeit in a moment of mad jealousy, after discovering him to be a trigamist.

The police didn't know this. Or else they did know it and chose to say nothing, out of respect for Hümeyra's father, who had been a Pasha. Dora knew the true story because some mornings, Hümeyra brought the trigamist's last surviving illegitimate son in with her. Judging by their long and winding conversations, she was much closer to him than she was to her own sons by a later union, who were as grasping as they were legitimate, and who sometimes pulled her into the morning room to tell her what they thought of her life, her art, her friends, and anything else they couldn't accommodate in their fat little philistine heads.

And that was just during daylight hours. After dark, people went in there thinking they could hide. According to Dora, there was nothing she had not seen in there, and during the summer months, when windows were left thoughtlessly open, nothing she hadn't heard.

'Oh, how I love our girls' nights in,' Delphine would say as she watched us eat, and that would puzzle me, because as soon as we had scraped our trays and thrown them into a real American grocery bag, Dora and I would be off to see a movie. Sometimes these were ancient B movies from Hollywood, more often they were French or Italian thrillers or farces I watched with little or no understanding. At the intermission, Dora bought me a Frigo ice cream sandwich. On the way back we stopped off at Kulis, the bar that Delphine called her 'office'. At that point she would still be wearing the skirt and twin-set she called her plain clothes. At that hour on a Friday, Kulis would be packed, with Delphine at the bar. 'Chin up, girls! The entire press corps is here tonight!'

While she told Muammer, the bartender, to keep our *gazoz* glasses full, she herself would order another Salty Dog and get back to work. She had picked up a new job of sorts, stringing for a society columnist of her acquaintance, but according to Dora, her contacts at Kulis included columnists with loftier titles, as well as the consular types who drifted through bars like these, and she knew them all. As we sipped our *gazoz*, various members of the press and diplomatic corps came and went, whispering into Delphine's ear and pinching my cheeks as they departed, and, every so often, kissing Dora's hand. 'Time for us to go, too!' Delphine called eventually. Muammer, the bartender, then produced an envelope that Delphine ripped open the moment we were back to the apartment. Pursing her lips, she would nip into the kitchen for another Salty Dog, while we set up whatever it was to be tonight: Monopoly, Risk or cards.

If the phone rang, Delphine pulled the cord as far as it would go into her bedroom. After the call came a spell of silence, punctuated by the click of a powder case. Then Delphine would emerge from her bedroom, radiating perfume in her Winter Knock 'Em Dead Dress. It was so tight that Dora had to zip it up for her.

One last look in the mirror over the mantelpiece. One last touch of lipstick. 'So tell me girls. How do I look?'

'Svelte,' her daughter always said, without looking up.

'I'm just nipping out for a few minutes.' Dora would not look up from whatever game we were playing.

'Dora? Darling? Promise you'll call Muammer the moment you need me.'

And with the harsh edge that she only ever used in her mother's presence, but never when she talked about her in her absence, Dora would say, 'Okay then. If the house is on fire, I'll let him know.'

'Oh, but please. You don't want me worrying all night, do you?'

Tapping her watch, Dora would say, 'I want you back here by two. Do you hear?'

'Two at the absolute latest,' Delphine agreed, 'unless I'm at Hümeyra's by then, in which case I'll knock on the window.' She kissed her daughter on the head before slipping into the stiletto heels that were waiting for her by the door.

'Good night, girls! And good luck!'

As we listened in silence to her clicking and picking her way down the sunken marble stairs, my racing heart threatened to betray me. I had not yet confessed to Dora that I was as afraid of Communists as her mother was. What if that Sergei was lurking in the stairwell, for example? He could have spied on us from Hümeyra's morning room. He could have climbed up from the courtyard of the Soviet Consulate. He could be waiting in the shadows with his hammer and sickle, hungry for blood.

I thanked my stars that Dora was not afraid of Communists but wise to them.

Usually we continued with our board game for an hour or so. Now and again, Dora glanced at her watch. Finally, she'd say, 'Time for our midnight feast!' even though, according to my Mickey Mouse watch, midnight was still hours away.

While Dora busied herself in the kitchen, I crept to the window, to look down, down, down, into the ghost-lit courtyard of the Soviet Consulate, to watch a sentry march stiffly from one corner to its opposite, never once moving his head.

According to Dora, there were people working in that building who had never been allowed outside.

I carried the cups of cocoa into her mother's bedroom while she carried the plate of Oreo cookies that Delphine had procured from the same friend whose PX privileges had brought us our TV dinners. I installed myself amongst the tattered satin pillows on one side of Delphine's four poster bed while Dora went around the room, lighting the candles that would keep us from being distracted if the lights went off again.

'Have you brought your notebook?' Dora waited for me to nod before adding, 'And the invisible ink?'

Because I had now told my mother everything, or almost, I of course told her about the bedroom window in Dora's apartment which allowed us a partial view of the Divine Hümeyra's soirées.

'Is it spying? Because I can see even more than through a keyhole.' I'd asked, because the keyhole business was still troubling me. But my mother had replied, 'Don't worry about it. If Hümeyra wanted privacy, she would have put up curtains. And I for one would be interested to know who turns up there. You might even see your father on his way to the Passage of Flowers.' And once or twice, I did, not that it mattered, because what my mother did not know was that Dora and I were playing for far higher stakes.

Once we had our notebooks ready and two freshly sharpened straws next to our vials of invisible ink, Dora went to fetch her mother's transistor radio which was twice the size of ours. She tuned it to Radio Moscow and I would watch the candlelight flickering along on its metal bands.

The first voice spoke Russian. Dora leaned forward, trying to catch the words because she knew only some of them. Every once in a while, her face brightened and she wrote in her note book The voice then gave way to stirring music followed by an ocean of static which submerged all other sound. When the static receded, another voice, told us, in grainy American English, that people were struggling against the yoke of capitalism all across the world.

The grainy voice ended each broadcast with a list of coded messages about stars rising in the east and fields of wheat rustling in the north wind, while in my mind's eye I imagined marauding bands of Communists all the world over, setting down their hammers and sickles to take heed.

My part in all of this was to sketch the scenes described in the coded messages which Dora was sure came from *And Quiet Flows the Don*. Always we scanned the novel together for references to eastern stars and northern fields of wheat. If we found even so much as a hint, I recorded the page numbers in invisible ink. When we were done, we stood for a while at her mother's bedroom window, watching the edges of Hümeyra's Friday soirée.

Dora would point out the regulars as they came and went: the Tenor and the Translator. The nation's most celebrated Ceramicist, and its most hated Actor who played only villains. The Heir to a newspaper fortune. The wife of the Ambassador to Somewhere, arm in arm with a disgraced Ballerina. Vartui the maid with a plate of *böreks*. Madame Xenia the Accordionist. Doctor Abrakadabra, dressed in a cape.

There, in the corner, was Our Man from the Soviet Consulate. The man whispering into his ear Our Man from Reuters. And here, at last, was the brain-damaged, blankly smiling Society Photographer, snapping and flashing until he'd chased them all away.

Sometimes the room stayed empty for whole minutes. Sometimes a couple came in to embrace or to argue, not knowing that four eyes were watching them beyond the dark window. At two in the morning, Delphine's face would appear, pressed up against the glass, one hand holding a glass, the other waving.

Once a young man appeared beside her dressed in a black suit and with a taut smooth face and eyes like black velvet. I decided he was someone's idea of handsome. After Delphine had waved she tried, in vain, to get a smile out of Dora. Then she gave up, threw up her arms in exasperation and left. But the man lingered on. He wrinkled his nose. Dora relented.

'I thought you didn't like boys,' I said.

Still smiling, Dora turned to me. 'I said *boys*.'

17

School nights

On Wednesday nights, and, if her mother was 'on assignment', on other school nights, too, Dora stayed with us. The sleek black car waited for her as usual in the *meydan* outside our school, but the driver came only to bring a bag of books or clothes, and some PX treat her mother had procured for us. Once he had handed these over, Dora sent him away.

Dora, my sister and I wound our way up to the campus, Dora stopping to buy a *gazoz* for us, and a Toblerone which we split into three to eat on the college terrace. Dora and I straddled the high wall while my sister sat on the bench, which Dora said was safer, and together we watched the ships. For ages. Until we dragged ourselves home.

Baby would already be there. He'd be on the balcony, laughing with my mother. The moment he saw us, he leapt to his feet and bowed and said, 'Baby Mallinson, reformed character, at your service.' He had given up his two worst habits, he told us, booze and older men. Now he was composing again. Even better, he was jamming. With my mother. Each time we caught them together, there was a new tune, a new improvisation: *The Ysteries of Travel. The Enemy Within. I Spy.*

One by one, he sat us beside him at the piano. My sister's lesson was the shortest. Never more than ten minutes. Then it was me. About half an hour. Then Dora for a full hour while the rest of us waited in the kitchen with the door closed. My mother fed my brother and prepared our supper while Dora played. My sister went through a ream of paper, drawing a stick figure on each sheet before discarding it. And I read.

Finally, the announcement came. 'The coast is clear! You can come back now!' and we all trooped back to the piano. Dora ceded her place to my mother and Baby played the opening chords of *I've Been Around the World in a Plane*, my sister's song. By the time Grace performed my song, *Stormy Weather*, her voice was warmer and her emotions deeper and more passionate. The anguish more deeply felt. I understood that. My sister didn't. 'Better than vodka!' Baby declared when my song was over. 'Better than smack and weed combined!'

'Now, now,! Remember our promise.' my mother said.

'Please accept my most sincere apologies, ma'am. It won't happen again.' Although sometimes it did.

Once, he told us a thing or two about the operatic heroines we were named after.

Mimi, the consumptive seamstress, coughing herself to death.

Violetta, the consumptive courtesan, dying in her lover's arms.

He did not have to tell me what consumption was. I knew already and it chilled me to the bone.

I could tell it chilled Baby, too, even though he was half smiling. 'What the hell did you have in mind, girl?' he yelled at my mother. 'How could you do that to your own daughters?' And my mother replied, 'Well, actually, Mimi and Violetta didn't die, because they were actresses. After the curtains went down, they left the stage, stepped out of the tragedy that had produced such beauty, and went on to fabulous feasts, to be feted by suitors and sycophants. They escaped from their grasp to sail off to sing other operas, in the other great cities of the world.'

'Now that's what I call fancy footwork,' Baby said. He made as if to take off his hat in deference, but without leaving the piano bench. Because it was time for my song now. And then, if my father was still not home from work yet, my mother would sing the song she had assigned to Dora.

101

If ever my father came home early, all music ceased. My sister and I took turns being the look-out at the kitchen window, in case he came walking down the hill. But if he came home only to go straight out again, to nip down to Bebek for a paper, and also, though he never admitted it, for a quick beer at Nazmi's, Baby continued, playing all his steakhouse specials, and then maybe something he'd been working on in his spare time, and then, if we were very good, he'd play an aria from each of our operas, always beginning with the drinking song from *La Traviata,* because that was my sister's opera and she was the youngest. Our mother sang, on and on, until we heard footsteps in the hallway and Baby hissed, 'Quiet!'

My father walked in knowing perfectly well that he had been left out of something. 'So you've had your lessons?' he asked us. Then he turned to Baby. 'Was that you singing just now?' and Baby replied, 'Oh yes, massa. It surely was.' And I nudged my sister to remind her to keep quiet while she did her best to stifle her delight at our conspiracy. My mother smiled blandly, but when she got up and walked past us to get my father his beer, and Baby his soda water, she'd roll her eyes or distend her nostrils, and then it was all over for my sister and me. We just couldn't keep the laughter inside.

Dora just sighed. Because she worried for my father. She didn't like leaving people out. The charade troubled her so she found another way to involve him. She was as interested in the news as he was, and knowing that my father had read the paper at Nazmi's, Dora would scan it too and at supper she and my father would discuss the most disturbing reports.

After supper, Dora helped with the dishes and I took my homework into the kitchen so that I could listen to them talking. Some of the stories my mother told Dora were ones my sister and I knew well already, but with added details and asides I'd never heard before, and there was more talk about what she had done at Dora's age and how hard it was when you were the only thirteen-year-old in the whole wide world who hated boys.

On Wednesday nights Dora read my sister her bedtime story to give my parents some time alone on the balcony. Afterwards, she joined me in my room, where we sat on opposite ends of my bed reading until she was ready to go to sleep in the spare bed in my brother's room.

There were never any arguments on the nights Dora stayed. She had, everyone agreed, a way of lightening the atmosphere, even though she herself could be so very solemn. No one quite understood how – with her charming but nevertheless alarming loose cannon of a mother – she had come to be so understanding, so quietly astute and effortlessly generous. Perhaps, people said, she'd inherited these virtues from her father – whoever *he* was.

She was not just the perfect house guest. She was also a revelation in the classroom. She was effortlessly fluent in French as well as English, reading so widely in those languages, as well as secretly in Russian, that her teachers were forever on tenterhooks, worried that she might upstage them. That's what Nella said, anyway. One afternoon, when I was inside reading in the only language I knew well enough, and Nella and my mother were on the balcony, I heard Nella say that Dora was a credit not just to her mother but to our *collective ethos*. Instead of being hemmed in on all sides as Nella herself had been at that age, Dora was genuinely free to let her mind roam. But her far-ranging intellect did not stop her from being one of the kindest, wisest creatures Nella had ever met. 'The change she has wrought in Mimi is quite extraordinary,' I heard her say. 'Age difference notwithstanding, we couldn't have done better if we'd designed her from scratch. She does seem to be the perfect friend.'

I, too, thought her perfect. As perfect as a snow peak. She was a calming influence, just like Nella said. I returned from my sleep-overs at Dora's with all the wrinkles ironed out. I might pick a fight with my sister, but later, when I said sorry, I would review the more considered thoughts that Dora had put into my mind: that I should indulge my sister's charming if also preposterous stories about Lightie and Keenie since it was patently clear she had invented them for no other reason than to infuriate me. That sibling rivalry was natural but that we would outgrow it. And that I would hate being an only child. Dora told me that even if I could not see my sister's redeeming features, it was my duty, as the eldest, to keep looking for them.

Dora's instructions on the care of the adults in my life were similarly compassionate, though I struggled to put them into practice. She said that our elders might not be our betters, that all except my mother were blind to things that only we could see, and that somehow we had to protect these fragile unfortunates who were not really meant for this world. These propositions terrified me. My mother assured me that Dora, too, would be weighed down by difficult thoughts. 'Which is why she likes being here with us. If there was ever someone who needed to air out her brain every once in a while . . .'

'Is that why you let her hear you sing?'

'I just want to take her mind off things. This urge she has to understand everything . . . Girls her age should be having fun.'

'You still think she's a good influence, though.'

'She is most certainly,' my mother said. 'She's an absolute saint. Just think what it was like for you at school last year. But now, with Dora watching over you, reminding you of everyone's good qualities . . .'

And it was true. I could hear Dora's kind if stern injunctions even when she was a classroom and two closed doors away from me. When I sat at my desk, listening to Nella speak with some authority about gears or photosynthesis, I would try to acknowledge Nella's kindness and high spirits, and the care with which she now approached me, after all these months, still making amends for the unfortunate affair of the keyhole.

But it was hard to think about Nella's virtues now that I knew her to be a recipe for disaster and riddled with contradictions. When I confessed this to my mother, she explained that Dora was better able to cherish friends and

104

teachers, warts and all, for no other reason than that she was older: she had been studying their behaviour, and capturing their humanity, for four years longer than I had.

So, in time I, too, would accept Nella as a delightful young woman with a divided soul. I would understand she was a carbon copy of all those college girls that my mother and Dora's had met when working in Manhattan: young women who wanted to be free but who also needed a man in tow to hold the doors open. Nella, like them, had thousands of bright ideas but not the stamina to stick to a single one. And she was dangerously naïve. On the day before she left America, she had actually gone to her local drugstore and asked to buy a thousand condoms.

I had never even heard of condoms before Dora told me this story, or of their horrifying purpose, just as I had never heard that the Admiral's wife, for all her fine ways, had conducted a secret affair with a Communist refugee – the man with seven passports – while working in Vienna soon after the War. Or that my art teacher Nuran Hanım went about sighing because her husband was in prison in Ankara, accused, Dora thought unjustly, of publishing Communist propaganda.

And had I not heard of the tragedy that had brought Baby Mallinson, our beloved friend and music teacher, to these shores? Had I not wondered why a musician of his calibre had fled America, just as his star was rising? It might just have something to do with the colour of his skin. And also with what Dora called his Proclivities. But the truth was he'd also been a card-carrying member of the Communist Party, if only until 1956. He'd torn up his card in disgust after that 'debacle in Hungary', but by then he'd been well and truly blacklisted, and razed from the national memory.

'Yes, that's the sort of country we come from,' Dora mused. 'If you can count me at all.'

But who was to say we could? People like Dora belonged nowhere, and the same could be said about both her mother and Baby. They might be on different poles when it came to politics, but in the real world they were condemned to the same fate. The same was true for almost everyone in our midst. They had been labelled different and the world had shut the door on them. That was why I was not to judge these people about whom I now knew more than I wished to know. Dora was furnishing me with facts that might help me step out of my shoes and into theirs. So if Baby sighed when he saw an American flag, I could have some inkling of the turmoil in his heart. And if Delphine or the Admiral's wife or Nuran Hanım shivered when they saw those Soviet ships creeping up the Bosphorus by night, I had to understand that those ships' slippery shadows returned them to lost dreams and lost loves.

In other words, they saw only their own ghosts, Dora could not think of a single adult in our midst who was not thus afflicted. Even Nella suffered from this ailment, despite her young age. And Baby, in spite of everything. My father, too, for all his bold denials. And maybe even my mother, though she was harder to read. 'She might be whistling a happy tune' Dora said, 'but remember only you and I can see things as they really are.' We drank water. We kept our minds open. We looked under the surface of things. We did not fear Communists. We sought to understand them.

Which was why, when the inevitable happened, and life as we knew it came to a sudden, cataclysmic end, she and I were the ones who were best prepared.

It was a cold, sunny January afternoon when Dora told me that. We were sitting on the wall of the college terrace, just the two of us for a change, sharing a Toblerone. As a small white liner rounded the point, Dora sighed and said, 'So I hope you make the most of it.'

She went on to inform me that when I left for Egypt with my family in a fortnight, I would be travelling on a Soviet ship not unlike the one that was passing beneath us. 'You lucky thing,' said Dora. 'I'd kill for a chance like that. To see them in action, with my own eyes. To see through the Soviet shell right to their humanity. Well, you'll have to take notes. In invisible ink, of course!'

She advised me to prepare myself because this time, I was going on more than just a journey. It would be a great adventure and would change me forever. For once, I would not be coasting past the lives of others, imagining their stories. I would be living and breathing the story, and clinging to its very heart.

But I should also prepare myself for the rough waters ahead, Dora warned. For at times I'd feel as if I had utterly lost my bearings, tossed this way and that by churning waves too towering to see. 'And then, one day, you'll open up your eyes and see you've come full circle. You'll be home again. But will it even look like home, after all you've been through?'

I kept my hands hidden inside my corduroy jacket because they were trembling.

18

Bearings

Perhaps it was because she could not see my trembling hands that she continued with her chilling and bewildering predictions. A crisis was brewing, she informed me: a crisis that could bring the world to its knees. Yet she refused to tell me what it was. With terrifying smugness, she called it classified knowledge. Her informant would be in big trouble if it ever got out that she had breathed a word.

'But never mind,' she said. There was no need for me to know more than the general shape of things. For I could be sure my father knew the rest, and it was a credit to him that he had not breathed a word either. 'In any event, he is sure to be under strict instructions to maintain radio silence.'

About what, though?

'Well, I really shouldn't be telling you this, but it will probably help for you to know that we're talking about the No Camp.'

The No Camp?

'Let's leave that for another day, shall we? The last thing I want to do is overload you. Then you'd lose your bearings, and where would we be then?'

I walked home very slowly, keeping an eye out for every bump and crack that might take me by surprise and cause me to lose my bearings. Whenever one did, and a bolt of horror passed through me, I steadied myself with visions of the home that would welcome me when I swung open the door: my mother browning onions. My sister drawing stick figures at the table next to her. My brother at her feet, knocking two spoons against a bowl. My father at his desk, clearing his throat.

But that afternoon he was studying the map on which he plotted our itineraries.

He had drawn one line between Istanbul and Athens, and another between Athens and Alexandria. Alongside each he had written the words, 'Felix Dzhershinsky'.

Which sounded Russian to me. Which meant that yet again, Dora was right.

Later he sat my sister on one arm of his favourite chair and me on the other and opened the map to test us. I knew what was coming.

'Show me where we went last winter.'

Izmir, Antalya, Alanya, Konya, Ankara, and back again, by ship and by train.

'Show me where we went last spring.'

Rhodes, Nicosia, Famagusta, Haifa, Izmir, here.

'And now last summer.'

Another full circle: Venice, Marseilles, Valencia. Alicante, Grenada, Cordoba, Seville. Madrid, Barcelona, Rome, and home.

'And now our next trip.' He pointed to the lines across the sea, and into Egypt, and up the Nile, and down the Nile again, and back across the Mediterranean to Beirut, Damascus, Aleppo, Antakya and beyond.

'So now,' he said. 'Which of you can identify all the cities on our route?'

First we found them. Then we practised saying their names. Then, at supper, we took turns closing our eyes and trying to recite the whole list, and that was hard because so many of them were new to us.

'Try imagining them in your mind's eye,' my mother said, when my father was back at his desk again.

But how could we when we'd never been to them?

'That's easy. Just close your eyes.'

Our journey would begin, she said, in the vast grey customs

109

building that I hated so much. Once on board the ship, we would see the domes and spires and minarets and towers of the city that had claimed our hearts. We would wave farewell to them as they vanished into the mist. Then we would pass once again across the Sea of Marmara to travel through the Dardanelles. We would pass the small town of Gallipoli and observe a minute's silence to honour its dead. We would enter the Aegean to pass islands too dark to be seen by the naked eye. By morning we would reach the ancient harbour of Piraeus. We would jump on to a small and smelly train to Athens, and after we had seen the Parthenon, the Caryatids, and Zonar's, we would return to Pireaus to sail through the calm waters of the Sardonic Gulf, before returning to the treacherous deeps of the Mediterranean. We would be at sea for two nights and a day, and on the second morning the great city of Alexandria would rise from the mist. Behind it, but still hidden in the sandy folds of the desert, would be Cairo, and the Pyramids, and the golden remains of Tutankhamen's tomb, and the waters of the Nile, shaded on both sides by palm trees of the most luxuriant green. This snaking ribbon of life would lead us to the jewel that was Luxor, and the miracle of ancient engineering that was the Valley of the Kings, where we would behold secrets that had lain in wait, undetected, for millennia. Now, at last, the codes could be cracked. The ancients would speak to us, through the winds of history. They would tell us where to go, and what to do, and why.

But only if we kept our eyes peeled, our mother warned us. Only if we delved deep. We would take our time, she said, imprinting each new marvel in our memories. And then, with hearts that were heavy not from sadness but from the weight of our new treasures, we would begin the second leg of our journey, via Cairo, Alexandria, Beirut, Damascus, Aleppo, Antakya, until we had completed yet another full circle.

Until we were home again, the five of us, as good as new.

19

The Red Threat

It was as simple and as beautiful as that, she assured me. There was nothing to fear, beyond fear itself. That was until Delphine dropped by our house that Saturday evening, on the arm of a bachelor who taught English Prep, arriving at the tail end of a dinner party to which she had not been invited. Dora had told me to expect her, to brace myself, and to take everything she said with a large pinch of salt. 'Or better still, don't listen to her at all.' But Dora's instructions only encouraged me to discover what Delphine had to say that was so terrible that her own daughter wouldn't tell me. In preparation, I returned to my old hiding place in my parents' bedroom, behind the reading chair, next to the door. As I pushed it open, creak by creak, I heard Delphine in the kitchen. 'Grace dear? I think we're ready for that new bottle of Kanyak.' There was a hush while my mother poured. There followed the gentle buzz of after-dinner conversation, tapering now and again to a single voice that got lower and lower until it slid into an exclamation point I could almost see, and an explosion of raucous laughter.

Then, during a lull, Delphine asked her question. 'So I hear you're off to Egypt?'

'We most certainly are,' said my father. He had his back to me so I could not hear his answer but it sounded like he was telling her about our itinerary.

'And whose idea was it to fit this Soviet ship into your programme?' Delphine now asked.

'I'm sorry,' interrupted Baby, 'but I cannot for the life of me see how that's your business.'

'It's my business because there are children involved.'

'Forgive me if I've missed something but last time I checked . . .'

'They might not be my children, but since their mother seems unable or unwilling to keep them safe . . . well . . . I think you'll agree that it's my duty to step in.'

'You know,' said Nella. 'Maybe we should tread carefully here, Delphine. Maybe we should remember that some people – not me, but some people – worry that you yourself . . .'

'I'm sorry but I'm just not having that!' Delphine yelled. 'I might not be the most perfect mother in the world, but I don't pretend to be! I don't go around playing the meek and sweetly silent paragon, before throwing all caution to the wind! I'm not reckless like some mothers I won't mention at this precise moment. I don't put my own selfish desire for adventure first!'

There followed a scuffle. 'Take your hands off me,' I heard Delphine say.

'I'll take my hands off you,' said Baby, 'when you have apologised to our hostess.'

'Well, that I can do with an open heart because really, Grace, I didn't come here to insult you. I came here to reason with you. I'm sorry it all came out the wrong way.'

'Fine then.' This was my father. 'Let's hear her out.'

Once again silence descended. I opened the door a little wider, stopping it just before the place where it squeaked the loudest. Craning my neck, I could see Delphine holding her head in her hands, and grimacing. Then she sat up straight. 'I know your story, Grace. And it's beautiful, it really is. I know how much effort you invested in making your wish come true so that now, against all the odds, you're here, leading the life of your dreams. And God only knows that's well nigh impossible for a gal to do. But somehow, you pulled it off. You walked off the edge of the earth and you landed on your feet. And still with a band on your finger. And three beautiful children to boot! So hats off to you, pardner. Honestly, hats off. But Grace, my dear, there are lines you shouldn't cross. And risks you shouldn't take. There are things lurking beneath the surface of this rotten world that you are far too nice and innocent to begin to understand. So I beg you . . .'

My father brought his fist down on the table.

'This is just preposterous,' he said.

Delphine leaned forward, pushing her face right up to his. 'Are you going to hear me out, or not?'

'You have one more minute,' he said. 'I'm timing you. Get to the point.'

'Okay, then. Grace, my point is this. If this was about adults boarding this ship and if you were leaving those darling children of yours at home, then maybe, just maybe, I could see the point of the foolish venture. But to take two impressionable young girls and a *toddler* . . . to drag them with you into the *monster's lair* . . . why, they could be *eaten alive*! I'm talking to you now,' she said, swinging around to jab a finger at my father. 'Is this little adventure of yours worth the risk you're taking with their lives?'

'I know it might be hard for someone like you to believe this,' said my father, 'but some of us aren't snitches. Some of us don't earn our keep selling cheap gossip to the highest bidder, or waste our lives looking for reds under every bed. Some of us just want to get to Egypt to see the goddamn sights.'

'Oh, I believe you. Thousands wouldn't, but never mind. But I'm not talking to you anymore. You can go to hell in a hand basket while I talk to Grace. And Grace . . . I can say this in all sincerity . . . because I know you have nothing up your sleeve. For you, it is really all about getting to Egypt. To see its beauties. To share them with your children. But dearest, let me assure you. You really need to think of another way of getting there. You simply cannot take your family aboard this ship.'

'Why the hell not?' Baby asked.

'Because you can't barge right into the heart of the Cold War and come out the other side unscathed,' she cried. 'There will be consequences! And they could be dire! Don't ask me how I know, but I do!'

113

'Hark,' said Baby. 'The oracle has spoken.'

Thrusting herself to a stand, Delphine lurched around the table to take my mother's hand. 'Poor, poor Grace,' she said. 'Now you are confused. And upset.'

A strange thing to say, I thought. From where I was, my mother looked like she was smiling. But what could she be smiling about in this smoky room full of angry people? She looked as if she had already flown off somewhere else, and couldn't see them. Sometimes she could do that.

Now they were all talking at once. And a ship was passing; the floorboards had begun to hum. The pictures and the copper plates made such a clatter that I was unable to hear what Baby said that made Delphine lurch across the table to grab his collar. All I could hear was Delphine's chair falling, and her voice rising.

And then it was Baby, saying that he hadn't known she was a card-carrying member of the John Birch Society. Then the man she'd brought with her, the one from English Prep, spoke for the first time and called her a card-carrying ignoramus. I did not know what that meant either. Delphine bustled to the door in a flash of a red coat. She threw it open. She turned around to brandish her fist at my father. 'I'm talking to you now!' she said. 'I am warning you one last time! If you love your children at all, you will not put them at risk to further the ends of this infernal No Camp.'

What was a No Camp?

They were asking the same question at the table. And: 'What's got into that woman?' 'What's *possessed* her?'

No one seemed to know. So I went back to the window. When I pressed my nose against the cold picture window, it was humming again, but I couldn't see the ship.

All I could see was a shadow blacking out the lights on the Asian shore as it slipped around the point, until a flitting searchlight gave me a glimpse of a long white deck. A ferry blew its horn – twice, as if in panic – and the great ship replied, with a single blast, as if to warn me:

I was not in safe hands.

20

The plan

The original plan had been for just the six of us to go to Egypt – my parents, my sister, my brother, myself, and Baby Mallinson who had come up with the idea in the first place. But Delphine's tirade in our kitchen had so outraged the Cabots and Nella Portishead that within minutes of her departure they too had declared themselves 'in', if only to 'prove the point.' The sole dissenter was Nella's husband, Rex, but he chose his words carefully, entering the conversation only when there was a lull in the righteous anger. 'You do realise just how tense relations are between us and Egypt right now, don't you?' and 'At the end of the day, a ship is a ship. Soviet or not, it will get you from A to B. Nella, has it occurred to you how this might look to our friend, the Admiral? I just can't see how I am going to play this one at work.'

'I thought I married a man who wanted to see the world,' said Nella softly. 'But all I see now is another cog in the machine.'

'Dearest! Don't you think that's a little harsh?'

His voice was slurred, as was hers when she said, 'Oh drat! I suppose it is. But, pumpkin, you're not going to stand in my way, are you?'

'How could I? You're a force of nature.'

'And damn right, too,' she said.

'The Admiral's not going to like it,' he warned.

In a harsh voice I'd never heard before, Nella said, 'Then

you'd better make damned sure you speak to them before Delphine does.'

That proved impossible. As Nella herself told me just a few days before our departure, when she sat down on the bench next to me at recess, Delphine had certain advantages like pretending to be a foreign correspondent: 'You might not get the bylines, but you have plenty of free time for making mischief. You should hear the disinformation that woman is putting out about us. You'd think we'd all signed up to the Red Army!'

She lit a cigarette; she'd given up a year previously but these events had made her start again. 'After the treatment I got at the consul's residence on Friday, I'm going on strike,' she continued. 'Even Rex was appalled by the things that so-called Admiral saw fit to bleat at me. And where exactly does he get off, lecturing me about the evils of Soviet rule? I mean, has he even bothered to *go* there?'

It alarmed me when my father said almost the same thing over supper that night. He described his own unpleasant exchange with the Acting Vice President of Robert College after the faculty meeting. 'The poor man had his facts all wrong, of course.'

To which my mother replied, 'Well, of course he did. He'd been briefed by a journalist!'

'Amy Cabot's getting cold feet, I understand.'

'Oh, she'll come round,' my mother said. 'There's no way she's going to let Hector get on that ship without her.'

'Well, fair enough,' he said. 'But it worries me that this is going to be a bridge too far for Rex.'

'You mean he shouldn't let Nella go alone?'

'I wouldn't like to be the one to tell her that!' my father said. 'At this stage, wild horses wouldn't stop her.' There was a note of admiration in his voice. I remembered it the next day when Dora informed me that my father was carrying a torch for Nella. So Delphine said, anyway. 'Like everyone else,' Dora added. 'So I wouldn't worry too much. It's just one more thing to add to your list.'

116

As I clung to the corner of my pillow on the eve of our departure, silently reciting Dora's list, I practised the deep breathing techniques the Admiral's wife had taught me, in happier days, to use in case of emergency. My mother, who must have heard me, came in to sit on the edge of my bed. 'Mentioning no names,' she said, 'but people have been putting ideas into your head again, haven't they?'

'How do you know?' I asked.

'I know everything,' my mother said. 'I have binoculars at the back of my head.'

What a relief it was to hear that. 'So you know about the Jupiters?' I asked.

'I can't say I do,' she said. 'Are you talking about the planet, or its moons?'

'Neither,' I said. And then I told her what Dora had told me only that afternoon, on the solemn promise that I would breathe a word of it to no one, and most especially not my mother. But I had to tell her. How could I not tell her?

No one would ever know I had told her about the Jupiters because now she had promised not to breathe a word of it to anyone else, and most especially not my father.

And so I told her about the big fat missiles that went by that name, offered to Turkey many years ago by our own great nation. 'Except now the Kennedy Cabinet is about to change its mind.'

'How interesting,' my mother said. 'But tell me. How does Dora know all this?'

'She has her finger on the pulse.'

'She most certainly does. But Mimi, I assure you, none of this concerns us.'

'Not even if Mr Guttman's college roommate has a brother in the cabinet?'

'Which cabinet?' my mother asked. I told her. She laughed, fondly. 'Now who told you that?' she asked. Without waiting for an answer, she added: 'Darling. Listen. There are a lot of people in this town who could weave a rumour out of a cobweb.

Any time they see something they can't understand, they make up a story to explain it. But the real story is this: they can't understand us. And you know what? They never will.'

'Why not?'

'Because we go where we want to go. We see what we want to see, when we want to see it. Don't you remember? We're on a quest.'

A quest for what, though?

'Beauty,' she said. 'As you already know.'

She squeezed my hand. 'And how are you going to see anything at all if you're starved of sleep? Why don't you tell me your worries, one by one, and then I can hold them for you while you rest your weary head?'

So I closed my eyes and listed the facts that Dora had passed on to me: the names of the spies who'd be watching us on board the ship. The ruthless butcher it was named after. The Greeks who might board it, bearing gifts for Nella, which she should should on no account accept, even if they looked like normal packages, wrapped in brown paper.

The torch that my father might be carrying for Nella.

'Oh really now. How interesting.'

The No Camp.

'The *No* Camp?'

I explained. 'Oh for goodness sake,' she said. 'I sometimes think these people need to get their heads checked.'

'And *you*,' she said. 'You need to clear your head of every bit of nonsense they've packed into it.'

One by one, she brushed the last remaining worries off my forehead: the bridge we'd soon be crossing, if it wasn't too far. The wild horses that might try to stop us boarding the ship. My father's loose lips, which might sink it.

I chose not to ask why, on a night as dark as this, my mother had to struggle not to smile. Instead I asked, 'Can you warn him about his lips, at least? Can you remind him about discretion?'

'Of course I can,' she said, smiling broadly now. 'I haven't let him go off the rails yet, have I?'

All night, I dreamed about rails, and going off them. I would wake up in a sweat and when I closed my eyes again, it would be to recall my mother's carefree smile.

And then I reminded myself of the postcard I had given the Admiral's wife to send to Mr Guttman via the diplomatic pouch. If all else failed, Mr Guttman would vouch for us. He would prove to the Admiral, or whoever asked, that neither he nor my father had ever even heard of a No Camp and that neither of them had so much as listened to those refugees at NYU or Fort Monmouth.

I pictured him getting my postcard: sitting in America in his favourite armchair, eyebrows raised, as he deciphered my Pig Latin. Now he had taken his glasses off, now he was swinging them back and forth, like he always did when we had a problem. That's what he would say at times like this: 'Ladies and gentlemen, we have a problem.' Only to add: 'But for every problem, there's a solution. If you pause to think, that is.'

I pictured him thinking. And with that picture, I drifted back to sleep.

Waking up the next morning, I remembered something else Mr Guttman had told me about honesty always being the best policy. And what the Admiral's wife had said about children sometimes knowing better than adults what was right and good.

It could only be right and good not to leave it all to my mother this time. My father might not take her seriously, if only because her voice was so soft. I had to warn him myself and make sure he listened. And do it seriously.

But there was no chance to speak to my father before we left home. We had to turn the house upside down to find my sister's shoes, or rather, I had to, and the louder my father barked his orders ('Have you looked under the beds? Well, look under them again. How about the under the sheets? Why don't you do a thing unless I specifically ask you to?') the more I felt the desperate, acid desolation that would define my adolescence. I felt the deadening indignity of having to obey adults who knew less than I did.

In the taxi, a silence fell over us, following the usual argument between my parents about the passports. My father liked to carry his own, whereas my mother, who did not trust him around ships, insisted that she kept all our passports in the bag she was clutching on her lap. As she always did.

Now, I thought. Now or never. This was my last chance to find out what my father knew, and what he didn't know. And to warn him. And make him listen. I tapped him on the shoulder. 'What is it now?' he asked.

I told him that there would be someone on the ship who would want to talk to him about the Jupiters.

'There's just one Jupiter,' he said.

'I don't mean the planet,' I said. 'I mean the missiles.'

'And what missiles would those be?'

'The big fat ones Kennedy wants to put along the Black Sea Coast of Turkey to protect us from the nuclear threat. Except that half the Kennedy cabinet is panicking now, which means the whole thing could unravel.'

'Well then let it,' said my father. 'It sounds like a crazy idea, anyway.'

'Is that what you really think?' I gasped.

'Of course it is. The more the arms race escalates, the greater the danger to us all.'

'But . . . but . . . what if Turkey is angry? What if they generals really, really need those missiles?'

'Then let them ask.' said my father. 'What the hell does it have to do with us?'

'Well, the Russkies don't want the Jupiters in Turkey either so they're hoping you can help them.'

'Oh really? How?'

'By making overtures.'

'Overtures.'

'I mean, by bringing them a message of peace and solidarity from the No Camp.'

'Oh, for God's sake. Not *that* again. What the hell *is* it, anyway?'

120

He looked genuinely mystified. It was with huge relief that I explained what the No Camp was rumoured to be. 'But they're wrong, aren't they? You don't know anyone in the Kennedy Cabinet, do you? And even if you did, you wouldn't take your innocent family on board an enemy ship, just to help the No Camp forge a back room deal. Would you?'

'For God's sake. What are you talking about? Who the hell do you think I am?'

'It's not what I think,' I said. 'It's what they think. They could make a rumour out of a cobweb, you know.'

'They. Who are they?'

'The KGB,' I gasped. 'But, not just them. Some of our guys think the same.'

'Our guys.' I could hear the sarcasm in my father's voice.

'I mean,' I said, 'I mean, I'm not really sure. Dora just said to be careful, and oh yes, the whole ship will be bugged. And watch out for the ship's librarian! His name is Sergei. You'll probably recognise him from Hümeyra's parties. Baby Mallinson is madly in love with him, by the way. Dora says he's putty in his hands.'

'Oh really,' he said. 'How interesting.' His voice sounded menacing now. His arms were tightly folded as he stared at the road ahead. 'So tell me, where does Dora get her information?'

When I didn't answer, he said, 'Yes, I thought so.'

Turning to my mother, he said, 'I think I know now why Delphine had to flee New York in a hurry. She was escaping from a lunatic asylum.'

My mother, still furious about the passports, gave him a gorgeous smile.

'Does that woman know no bounds?' my father persisted. 'Will she stoop so low now as to use her own daughter as a conduit?'

'Just because Dora hears too much gossip,' I said. 'That doesn't mean she's wrong about everything, does it? That doesn't mean you shouldn't be careful! And it's not just Dora who says so! The Admiral's wife thinks so too!'

'Oh Christ. Don't tell me *she's* in on this.'

'She's not against our going, you know! She thinks there is nothing more important than meeting a stranger and seeing the light inside him. She just wants us to be careful, because of this KGB guy who's going to be on board! And this man called İsmet will be there too, to make sure you don't talk to him, and at least a dozen Egyptians!'

'Oh, for Christ's sake.'

'I'm not saying we shouldn't go,' I pleaded. 'I'm just saying you should watch your step. They'll all be trying to pull you into a back room, but you mustn't go, and you shouldn't even talk to them! Especially when the ship docks in Pireaus. A Greek might be there bearing a gift. We'll need to foil the approach.'

'The *approach*. What an elegant turn of phrase. Tell me. Was it the Admiral's wife who taught you that word, or was it Delphine and her poor, misguided daughter?'

'I don't think it's fair to blame everything on them. And there's another thing. You should worry about Nella. You shouldn't let her twist you around her little finger!'

'If you're so worried,' my father said, through clenched teeth, 'why come with us at all? We could turn up the hill right here, and take you straight up to your wonderful friend, Dora, and the two of you can spend your whole winter vacation gossiping about innocent people who've done nothing wrong, and staring at the courtyard of the Soviet consulate through Delphine Giraud's binoculars and sending your reports through to the Admiral's wife. And leave the rest of us in peace.'

'Darling! Please!' my mother pleaded.

'Don't you get involved in this,' my father said. 'What I'm telling Mimi is important. That Dora has too much power over her. That woman too.'

'Then why do you want to take me there?' I cried.

My mother chimed in, to ask the same question. 'You'd think you were trying to throw her away,' she said.

'Oh, for God's sake,' my father said. 'Don't twist my words.

I just want Mimi to think clearly. And lately, she's just signed her mind over to this new friend of hers. And that's just not right.'

'Dora is a very lovely girl,' my mother said.

'She's also four years older than Mimi. She might be lovely, as you say. But there's something about her that's just not right.'

'Darling! What a thing to say!'

'It's the truth.'

'I beg to differ.'

We went the rest of the way in silence. Struggling to remember what was right and good, I practised my deep breathing.

I was still practising on our way into customs when I felt my mother's hand on mine. Planting a kiss on my ear, she said, 'We're in this together, remember? You can be my eyes and ears. You can help me foil the plot.'

What plot?

'What I mean, darling, is that you can keep me abreast of all the bad things that might happen, before they happen, and then we can make sure they don't.'

But what about Nella?

'Nella in particular,' my mother said. 'Let's keep a close eye on her and that torch.'

But how?

My mother looked up, as if to consider the stormy seas ahead. Then her face lit up. 'You two are friends again, aren't you? Doesn't that give you the perfect cover?'

I stopped to consider it, but my father was calling from the door of the customs hall and my mother had to set off. 'What's keeping you? Hurry up!'

I stayed where I was, just to see if she noticed. But she hurried on through the door with my sister and brother, and without a backward look in my direction.

21

The Temptress

The Temptress was the last to arrive at the vast grey customs hall. She was wearing a coat I had never seen before, with the same cut-off tights and ballet slippers she wore every Tuesday to Nuran Hanım's studio. Her hair was in a chignon kept in place with a wide fawn-coloured hair band – the type you saw on models in fashion magazines if they were lying on deck chairs in white towelling robes with cucumber slices over their eyes. And like them, she was wearing no lipstick.

She hurried over, swinging her two matching leather suitcases. 'What's up, doc?' she asked.

In spite of everything, I almost told her: I am alone in the world. No one loves me. No one listens. Even when I'm trying to save them, they just laugh. Even my mother. She's as reckless as the rest of them! And selfish, even though she pretends she's not! She sees only what she wants to see. And all she cares about . . . all she wants . . .

The terror that swept through me extinguished the thought. It wasn't true. It couldn't be. It wouldn't be, ever. And also. In the meantime. There was reason to hope. We might not be boarding this ship after all. The same stray wind that had landed us in this quandary might just end up saving us.

'So where is everyone?' Nella asked. I showed her where they were: Baby Mallinson, stretched out on a bench, staring up at the ceiling. On the same bench, my father's anguished friend, Hector Cabot, and his livid wife. Beyond them, standing on the pier, my mother. She had my brother in one arm, and on the other was the bag with all our passports. My sister was clinging to her legs. The ship looming over her looked like a vast white wall.

'So,' said Nella. 'What's gone wrong here?' I told her the story. At about ten o'clock, immediately after the Customs Man had marked all our bags with chalk, we'd lined up at the little table where that man in the grey jacket – my mother had whispered that he might be the Grim Reaper – sat stamping passports. He'd noticed that Amy Cabot's passport had a photo of her with two children sitting on her lap. Amy had insisted that the children had been removed from this document and issued with their own, until Hector, hitting his head with the palm of his hand, remembered that he'd plumb forgotten to stop off at the consulate the previous afternoon, *even though it had been at the top of his to-do list*. So now Amy was standing rigid, arms crossed, glaring at the vast grey wall, while Hector sat crumpled beside her, cradling his head. Meanwhile my father . . .

I could not finish the sentence. I could not bear to lead her to him.

But already, Nella was staring over my head. 'Poor Amy. How does she ever manage? Honestly! You couldn't trust that husband of hers with a can opener.' Her voice was low, but Hector heard it, and when he gazed up at her, his anguish melted in a way I had never seen before.

Or had I?

Nella was already on her way over to Passport Man. I observed her, because I had to. Gracefully, she placed her bags on the floor before him, placed her hands on her waist and looked him straight the eye, smiling as she addressed him in Turkish. When the stunned man complimented her on her command of his language, she waved her hand with delighted laughter and insisted that she knew 'so very little' as she launched into a second full sentence. He beckoned her into his office. So that's how she worked her charms. It was so obvious.

125

Why hadn't I seen that she had done the same with me?

I left the great hall for the narrow, dismal pier, and the dark decks of the *Felix Dzerzhinsky*. The lower deck was lined with Soviet seamen; the upper with the masses. The ship was juddering, and the gangplank was raised halfway up, so that the lowest step was flush with the highest porthole. And that was where my father had planted himself, standing, arms crossed, chin jutting, on the lowest step. My mother, who was standing just below him, on the edge of the pier, was pleading with him to come down.

Time stood still. The gang plank did not. Every time my father so much as cleared his throat, its lowest step shuddered, banging against the side of the ship. Finally, Nella emerged from the Grim Reaper's office, a small, triumphant smile on her face. She shouted up to my father but he was so absorbed with being angry that he didn't register it was Nella. Not at first. He said, 'Flake off. I'm not budging an inch.' Then he looked down, saw who it was, and almost lost his balance.

Aha, I thought to myself, as the gangplank began its slow and noisy descent. Aha. It's true.

When he stepped on firm ground again, it was as if he had forgotten he had a family. Almost. He was so busy smiling at Nella. 'You're saying help is on its way?' my father asked her in a strange high-pitched voice.

'Yes, I managed to reach Bob.' Nella said smoothly.

'Bob in Passports?' my father asked, his voice breaking. She nodded, but her eyes were travelling beyond my father, up to the top of the gangplank, to the man standing there. I recognized that gaunt face, that black bottle brush hair, those alarmed and appraising eyes.

The ship's librarian was wearing a tweed jacket and cleaning his glasses. When Nella called up to him in Russian, he fumbled and almost dropped them.

'Don't be too impressed,' Nella said to me as the man hurried down the gangplank. 'You've just heard everything I know.' But what did it matter that she had no more than twelve words of Russian because once again she was sparkling with laughter and accompanying her words with strategically targeted smiles. 'Oh, my!' she said. 'A gentleman of the old school!' And then: 'And you know what they say. One good turn deserves another.' At which she put out her hands, as if she were wearing a swirling crinoline gown, and made the deepest of curtseys, as if she had never seen a man introduce himself with a bow, or clicked his ankles together as he kissed her hand. 'So pleased to meet you, sir!' And then she gestured at the grey pier and the dark, juddering ship looming over us, and let out a great peal of laughter, as if to say: 'Who would have thought it! In this, of all places!'

Of course Sergei spoke English. In honeyed tones. He and Nella were still conversing when Bob-in-Passports came dashing out and ran along the quay side.

Nella did the introductions. 'Bob, meet Sergei. Sergei, meet Bob. Sergei is the ship librarian, Bob.' Two customs men arrived carrying a small table. Two others followed, carrying chairs. Bob put his satchel on the table, and snapped it open to reveal an assembly of stamps, seals, pens and forms. He created brand new documents for Amy's children Chloe and Neil, and stamped a statement that officially removed them from their mother's passport. Then he turned to the photographs in the old passport and drew two X's over their faces. What disturbed me most, I think, is that they were still smiling.

By now, the ship was rumbling vigorously, churning the waters caught in the narrow strip between the ship and the pier. But Nella wasn't finished. Back she went into the customs hall to charm the Grim Reaper into stamping Amy's newly defaced passport. My father was already climbing back up the gangplank. We clambered up after him. The gang plank rose the moment the last foot touched the deck. The masses who now surrounded us on deck were speaking in a language I had never heard before, and our new friend Sergei had taken charge of our luggage, and was using his honeyed tones to clear a space for us along the railing so that we would watch the departure. As we pulled away from the shore, and the hills of Pera came into view, I sought out the spires of St Antoine, counting the buildings to its left until I had found the window where Dora had promised to be standing. But all I could see was a blank, black frame.

It was an overcast day. Istanbul was as grey as the clouds. We watched the city erase itself until where there had once been domes and towers and minarets and hills piled high with sighing windows, there were only greying, fading lines.

I felt a tap on my shoulder. 'See?' my mother said. 'It all worked out in the end, didn't it? Just like I said. So why not take your sister and get to know the ship? It's a good time to play that game of yours, don't you think?' I must have given her a look, because she leaned over and whispered into my ear. 'Just keep to the plan.'

She put my sister's hand in mine and walked away across the deck. 'Don't get lost!' Nella called after us.

22

Getting lost

I had to prove our innocence to Sergei, and anyone else who
might have been watching and listening. There had been a
colossal misunderstanding which now hung over our party, and
there was a chance we would all end up in jail, or, even worse,
we would be deported to the Soviet Union, where life was hard.
It was up to me to sort it out. I would follow my father
everywhere, and take notes, and if we ended up in court, they
could use my notes as evidence. They could even cross-examine
me. I would be ready, with chapter and verse. I would save
my father's skin by persuading the judges that we were on that
ship because we loved to travel and not because we were spying
on people or carrying packages for them. And (having been
expressly told not to do so by the Admiral's wife) we were not
holding secret meetings with strangers carrying lights inside
them in the middle of the night. It was all a huge misunderstanding.
We had boarded the ship for no other reason than to see the
world in ruins.

I led my sister from the deck to a foyer where a giant nautical
map was pinned up. I traced our itinerary with my forefinger,
testing my sister on the names of all the places we would visit.
After I had corrected her pronunciation, we recited the list
together: the Sea of Marmara and the Dardanelles. Gallipoli,
and Pireaus. The Parthenon, the Caryatids, and Zonar's. The
Sardonic Gulf and the Mediterranean's treacherous deeps. The
great cities of Alexandria and Cairo. The Pyramids of Giza,

the waters of the Nile. The temples of Luxor, and the Valley of the Kings.

Violet tracked my finger, from north to south. I was not sure how much she had taken in. Nor was I sure if I'd spoken loud enough for the walls to hear me. The walls had to hear me. So when I explained the rules of the game we were about to play, I raised my voice.

Lost and Found was a game my mother had invented for my sister and me during our short journeys on the Turkish Maritime Lines the previous year. The purpose was to wander from deck to deck, from corridor to corridor, until we had no idea where we were. Until we were lost. Each new door led us to a corridor that looked identical to the one we had just left. But – and this was the whole point of the game – we had to find a way into First Class, and come back with a memento to prove it. In the past we had managed to sneak in through the cinema and out of the back door. If that failed, we would have to try the boiler room, the bakery, the orchestra pit, or the door behind the shuffleboard, until finally we found the swarm of ladies wearing ostrich feathers and coasting past ice sculptures of swans, like we had on the ship we'd taken from Famagusta to Haifa last winter. On that occasion, we had been chased away before we had a chance to seize a trophy, but I had drawn a good sketch of the feast and the fine ladies whose necklines had in my mother's opinion had left nothing to the imagination.

We set off, but no matter how many doors we tugged open, and how many corridors we walked down, we couldn't find first class. Not only that, all roads led to the lounge. There was no escaping it. Every time we emerged, we discovered a new tableau. First there was a lady with Cleopatra hair, gazing out the window and smoking. Next time, she had been joined by a heavy-set, glowering, grey-haired man. On our third entrance, a boy had joined them, sprawled on a chair, an open newspaper covering his face and heaving chest.

130

The next time – and by now we were exasperated with the cunning design of the ship – there was a fourth member of the party: a younger, sharply dressed man whom I recognized when he looked up and I saw his dark, velvet eyes. It was İsmet, Delphine's protector, and Dora's friend. Having been warned by Dora not to acknowledge him, I was confused by his warm welcome: 'Look at these girls! What a sight for sore eyes!' Tapping the newspaper that the boy was hiding behind, he said, 'Sinan! Come and meet these two beauties!'

I fled. Out of the door. I ran for the safety of the anonymous corridors, dragging Violet with me. And then I kicked myself for showing my panic and fear. It had been a big mistake to run away like that. It had given them a clue.

I told myself that from now on I had to act like the carefree child I no longer was. I was not to give anything else away. I had made one mistake. There were to be no others. I pulled at a the next door that we came to and walked into a cabin stacked with bulging baskets and enough room for just one Communist in a brown suit. He chased us down the white corridor, spluttering menace, shaking his fists.

We made a dash for the lounge – again – and found a hiding place behind the heavy curtains. Through a gap, I saw that İsmet, the lady with the Cleopatra hairdo and her grim friend had all left. Only the boy was still there, sitting up straight, his face covered not by a newspaper, but by a book.

The angry Communist – who had followed us – called across to him. The boy kept reading. Throwing up his hands in exasperation, the Communist growled a few last words, and left.

The boy kept reading. Slowly, softly, Violet and I crept across the room. Not once did the boy move, not even when Violet tripped over a chair leg. Not even when we were standing right over him, and Violet coughed.

I was close enough now to see that the book's title was in English, but upside down . . .

I tilted my head. WHITE FANG.

'Do you speak English?' I asked the boy. Or rather, the book, and the hands holding it.

No movement. No response.

I persisted. 'Why are you reading that book upside down?' Slowly, he lowered his book. We saw his dark, dark eyes. Of course, I thought. I've seen this boy before. He was the one who was reading Asterix at Hümeyra's soirée, the one I went to with Nella, the night I listened through the keyhole. He had been rude and supercilious. Now here he was reading a book upside down.

'You're hiding from me, aren't you?'

The hands on the book twitched.

'I'm right, aren't I? You're hiding from me, because you don't want me to recognize you. But I know who you are. I even know where we met before! So it's too late,' I said, in a voice that still sounded braver than I felt, even though there was a little wobble in it. 'Yes, it's too late, because we've rumbled you! So you might as well give up, and surrender.'

He lowered the book. In his mouth were plastic fangs. He let out a low, wet growl, and lunged.

'Run!' I screamed to my sister. 'Run for your life!'

But there, blocking the passage, was the ship's librarian, brow furrowed, eyes narrowed and burning bright.

23

In the ship's library

Eight tumultuous hours later, when I was sitting in the ship's library, attempting Sergei's portrait, trying and failing to capture the humanity I had not seen in his eyes earlier but saw so clearly now, a new possibility flashed through my mind.

What if Sergei was neither black nor white but a mixture of light and shadow like my sketch of him? What if he was a good man caught inside a cruel plot? What kind of retribution might be visited on him by his masters if he failed to claim my father as his prey?

It was almost midnight by my Mickey Mouse watch but I had not filled in the lower half of Sergei's face – because the eyes still bothered me. I kept erasing them and starting over. So now, at Nella's suggestion, I was doing a series of quick studies which together might cast light on the mysteries his eyes concealed.

The first showed Sergei coming to our rescue in the lounge that afternoon, despite our best efforts to stop him. He was picking me up when my knees buckled, picking up Violet when she wouldn't stop playing dead.

The second showed Sergei delivering us to the bar where the grown-ups had been all along, one that looked third class even if it wasn't. In this study, I portrayed myself telling the grown-ups that we had failed to find any sign of a first class bar, and Sergei was the only one who wasn't laughing.

My third study was of our tiny cabin. My sister and I were

holding our noses, because it stank of ship's paint. In the doorway, framed by a shaft of golden light, was Sergei in silhouette, delivering us an invitation in the name of the Soviet People's Republic which, he was saying, cherished children above all others. For did we not hold the seeds of the future? Could we not accept the hand of friendship and solidarity on a higher, airier deck? He was talking about the nursery, the subject of my fourth study.

It showed a rough floor plan of the nursery to which he had moved us: six dormitories, two bathrooms, a kitchen and a dining alcove. The nursery had a large playroom with a rocking horse, a train set a tricycle and a great chest overflowing with wooden toys.

My fifth study showed Sergei dropping by the nursery at cocktail hour, to make sure we had all the vodka we needed. I'd drawn myself perched on the window seat, and behind me, in clumsy miniature, the view through the plate glass window: the tragic hills of Gallipoli, caught between the tarnished waters of the Dardanelles and the darkening sky. I'd put my mother with my brother and sister on the bumpy grey linoleum, next to the toy train track, and the rest of our party at the low table, hunched over their vodka glasses, looking so very silly in the little chairs. Sergei was looking hurt because Baby had just snarled at him.

The sixth study was of the dining room with its starched linen tablecloths, its glistening samovar, and its waiters straight out of posture school. Near the far wall: six identically dressed Egyptian officers. In the corner: White Fang, and the sparkling lady with the Cleopatra hair whom I assumed was his mother, as well as her two male escorts. In reality, they had gone out of their way to make a show of ignoring the whispered jokes, smothered giggles, and fumes rising from our table, but I'd taken the creative liberty of dispensing with their masks. In my study the Egyptians and the Cleopatras were glaring at us, open-mouthed, while Sergei stood at the entrance, clutching his chest.

My seventh and last study was of the after-dinner fiasco. It had taken place in the lounge. The orchestra my mother had dubbed the Lugubrians had stepped down to welcome Baby to the piano to play solo. Sergei had just whispered a request in his ear to which Baby had replied, 'Oh fuck off, you queen. Sit down and let me do my thing.' Which turned out to be a smattering of *Porgy and Bess*. Except that he'd stopped mid-verse, and stood up to ask my mother to sing: *What the hell is the point of having a voice, you impossible woman, if you keep it under lock and key?*

When my mother refused him with that infuriating new smile of hers, he crashed his hands on the keys. My study caught the moment when he said: *I guess it's just me, then! Little old lonesome me! Singing for my supper as usual. Singing for all our suppers! Whaddyou want next, Comrade Sergei? A dash of Billie, with a spot of Ella for good measure? A few of my own?* The Red Threat, *perhaps? No, of course you don't want that. You want this!*'

This was his imitation of Paul Robeson singing the *Internationale*.

And now, to deepen our disgrace, there was this ugly scene in the ship's library. I was sketching this, too, even as it played out before my eyes.

It had begun in a spirit of friendship and solidarity, with our host bringing out his best vodka glasses for Nella and my father, and another warm apple juice for me. Seeing my sketchbook, he'd expressed a polite interest in my work and looked through my drawings. Sergei then consented, in fact expressed pleasure, to my sketching his portrait. It was at this moment, while sitting still, that Sergei chose to apologise for having no books for me to read but I could borrow the ship's copy of White Fang when the boy had finished it. 'It is by Jack London, and it is, in my view, one of the greatest achievements of American literature.'

In my view, too, I said.

My view was met by silence. My father filled it by apologising for Baby.

'Please!' Sergei protested. 'We understand. The vodka has gone to his head!'

'You've met before, I take it?'

'Oh yes! On several occasions, in fact.'

'At the Consulate, I presume?'

'There and elsewhere. I am, as are we all, in thrall to his genius but . . . as to his destructive streak . . . it's such a pity, isn't it? Such a pity he's a homosexual.'

'Why do you say that?' my father asked.

'Isn't it evident?' Sergei cried, opening his arms wide. 'He is a hostage to the animal urge. He can never know an honest woman's love.'

'Oh please. Do you have any idea how many honest women, as you call them, fall for this man? He could have them all if he wanted. But he doesn't. He wants men. And they want him. So where's the pity?'

'I would have thought that a family man like you . . .' Sergei gestured in my direction, his eyes crazed with fear on my behalf.

'Don't worry about Mimi,' my father snapped. 'She understands all this, possibly better than you do.'

'Though perhaps we have jumped to conclusions,' Nella offered hastily.

But my father had already turned to Sergei and was asking, 'Exactly what do you think about homosexuals?'

'Oh,' said Sergei sadly. 'That is a very long story indeed.'

'Then give me the short version.'

The short version was that homosexuality did not exist in the People's Republic. A tense discussion ensued, giving way in time to a different topic that proved equally contentious – car ownership. Sergei declared that the fabricated desire to own a car was an immoral attempt on the part of Capital and its gnomes to dazzle workers with the lust for material goods while at the same time chaining him to massive debt. I'd heard my father make exactly the same argument but now he folded his arms and jutted out his chin, insisting that workers actually wanted cars. Why was he changing his tune? Did he have a motive, or was he just being ornery? And why was he dragging me through this? Did he have no milk of human kindness? I tried to concentrate on my portrait but raised voices kept calling me back. Sergei was talking about John Steinbeck and the dustbowl, or Paul Robeson and the oppression of the Negro race. My father and Nella were explaining why Jack London was considered a children's writer in America, and therefore did not number amongst the greats. This news plunged Sergei into a further bout of gloom which I could not help but share.

And maybe this was why I lay my head down on my sketchbook. And dozed off, but only for a minute. I woke up to find my father leaning forward, his fist and his jaw clenched. Nella had her hand on his shoulder, as if to restrain him.

'You've plucked his name out of a hat,' my father was snarling. 'You're fishing.'

'In fact, I have no need to fish.'

'There must be thousands of men with the same name.'

'In Berlin? In 1945?'

'He was nowhere near Berlin,' my father insisted.

'Of course, in those days, he worked for the OSS.'

'He never had anything to do with the OSS. Or what followed.'

'If he had, do you think he would have been foolish enough to tell you?' Sergei leaned forward. 'My friend, I know this certain someone sent you here. And my dear man, it is for the best. This insane escalation of weapons! The future of mankind is at stake. But – if we can join our hands together – if we can harness science, in the name of peace . . .'

'Don't think you can fool me with your talk of peace.' My father brought down his glass with a crash. I must have stirred because Nella was saying, 'Now look what you've gone and done. You've woken Mimi.'

Back in the nursery, swaying in my dark bed, I had no trouble staying awake for my parents' return and my father's blow by blow account of the ensuing argument.

'Frankly,' my father told my mother, 'Frankly, it was like

being in a play. He kept prompting me, as if I'd forgotten my lines. He actually seemed to expect I had a message for him. And, Gracie, who on this earth would stoop so low as to implicate *Leo Guttman*? Hasn't the poor man suffered enough?'

'What exactly was Nella's position in all this?' my mother asked.

'Why not check with that special bodyguard you sent along. She was practically taking notes!'

'You should be glad you had a witness.'

'I'll be glad when we've left this ship.'

'Oh, I will, too,' my mother said, 'but until then, there's nothing they can do, can they? Sooner or later, they're going to have to accept that.'

'Accept what?'

'That we're going to Egypt, come hell or high water.'

24

tttt

In the early hours of the morning, we docked in the still waters of Pireaus. But for me there was no peace. The waters running deep in me were turbulent and troubled, because of the mysteries that could turn into serious problems if I didn't manage to sort them out. I was tired, too, and that made me even more nervous, because I knew I couldn't afford to miss a trick. Because our safety depended on me keeping my eyes peeled. Because I was the only one keeping track.

But how was I to know what was important, and what was not? Why didn't anyone understand what a strain it was to sit on the naked, windswept steps of the Parthenon while struggling alone to do the right thing, and then getting into trouble for it?

I hadn't wanted to be mean to Violet, not for a second. I'd only shouted at her – in extremis – to stop her scribbling over the notes I was adding invisibly to Mr Guttman's sketchbook and completing the lists of suspects and suspicious acts that would, when passed before a flame, reveal the true culprits and become the key that would get us out of jail.

My efforts at salvation, though, were causing anger and irritation. At one point, when I was hiding behind the Caryatids trying to think, I heard my father ask my mother: 'What is wrong with that girl? We drag her halfway around the world, show her things you and I could only have dreamed about – like now, feasting our eyes on the Parthenon, and what is Mimi doing? Sulking.'

'She's so mean to me, so mean,' I heard my sister sob.

And my mother said, 'Oh, I know, darling. I know.'

'I want you to talk to her,' commanded my father. 'Knock some sense into her.'

'Just give her time,' my mother said. 'When we get to Egypt, she'll calm down. She'll go back to being the girl we know.'

'She's always mean to me,' my sister said. 'No matter which girl she is.'

My father shook his head in despair. 'She keeps looking at me like I'm some sort of villain. As if I've angered the gods or broken some divine law by daring to show her the world. She's beginning to remind me of your mother.'

'Oh darling,' my mother said. 'Don't be hurtful, please.'

'I'm sorry,' said my father. 'She's not the daughter I thought I knew, that's all.'

'You leave it to me, then,' said my mother. But still she avoided me.

Athens was cold enough to give us frozen breath, and the sky over the Acropolis was a hard and flawless blue. The marble we walked on was pockmarked and uneven, but smoothed by thousands of years of people walking there into shapes that reminded me of coral. When Nella sat me down next to my sister, beneath the least eroded Caryatid, it was hard to stay still. By now I was anguished. 'How about this, then?' Nella said. 'Why don't you sketch the scene behind me, while I sketch you? Try and find the golden mean.' I tilted my head and closed one eye. The Parthenon teetered against the sky, defying gravity.

When we left the Acropolis, my mother handed my sister to my father but she did not give me her free hand as we wended our way through the tangled streets of the Plaka. I walked beside her, as close as I could manage.

At one point, when we were a long way behind the others, she touched my shoulder and said, 'I'm sorry your father kept you up so late. I'm sure that's why you're cranky.'

'I did fall asleep.' I said. 'But only for a minute and I didn't miss anything.'

'It doesn't matter,' she said. 'You were there, and that is the important thing, because just by being there, you kept everything on track.'

I wanted to tell her I wasn't so sure about that. Instead I said, 'I wrote everything down.'

'In invisible ink, I hope?'

I nodded.

'Well, that's wonderful. You know, you really deserve a prize.'

She spoke as if all danger was now behind us. So I said, 'Don't forget the Greeks bearing gifts for Nella.'

'Oh goodness. Thanks for reminding me.'

'When do you think they'll make their approach?' I asked.

'Who knows?' my mother said. 'Perhaps they've given up on the idea altogether.'

Maybe it was the way I gripped her arm at that moment, because she seemed to change her mind. 'You're right. It won't hurt to keep your eyes peeled. You've done a sterling job so far. Who knows what you'll unearth next?'

We had reached Syntagma, which looked so white and grand that day, so different from the seething, sun-baked square I would come to know in later years. Our first stop was American Express where (for the first and last time) the cable from our American bank was waiting with my father's salary. From there we went to Eleftherodakis to stock up on books as we would do every summer after this one until I left home. Afterwards, laden down with books, we walked to Zonar's where an elderly waiter served us ice cream sodas in tall glasses that nested in ornate metal cradles like those in which we'd been served tea that morning on the ship.

Our mother was wandering after our brother, who was winding amongst the other tables, pretending to be a cement mixer. The other adults were in their red leather booth, hunched over their Tom Collinses. This was my chance to case the joint, to survey its length and breadth: the glittering display cases and its brass-lined counters, the hushed array of wedding cakes with grooms who wore the same jackets as waiters, the marble floors, the fur-lined ladies sipping coffee and the rows of empty tables on the pavement outside, lit up by the winter sun.

I sneaked out to collect as much information as I could.

25

The Sardonic Gulf

When White Fang came into the ship's dining room that evening, he walked past the Egyptian officers without so much as a nod. The officers feigned the same indifference, little knowing that I had made a note that they had been in secret conversation outside Zonar's only hours earlier. White Fang's mother seemed equally insouciant, meaning she had no idea I had seen her heading towards the Ladies Room at Zonar's, holding a package that might well have been *the* package. But when I glanced through the plate glass window, I gasped with the tell-tale shock of recognition because there, staring straight at her, was a man in a camel hair coat.

At Zonar's, she had been wearing a white fur coat and matching kidskin ankle boots. Tonight she was wearing a suit with a matching jacket, red and tailored, the kind you'd expect to see worn with a pillbox hat. Her performance at the table was a repeat of the night before. The poses, the cigarettes, the smiles that were not reflected in her eyes. The little silent jokes with her son.

The waiters bending from the waist. The borscht. The vodka. The pregnant pauses. The expectant glances.

It was as if they were all waiting for a sign.

What was it?

I wrote this question in the remaining blank space in the sketch I had completed at Zonar's (locating and numbering each sighting of a package or a camel hair coat). Then I returned to my sketch-in-progress of the dining room. Peering over my shoulder, Nella said, 'That's excellent. Truly, everyone has to see this. Look, guys. It's like a stage set. Look, she's sketched in the full cast and we're all frozen with shock, because those crazy people have rolled in – and here's the clincher – those nuts don't know their lines!'

All eyes were on us again that night. Even the adults noticed, but they were not going to let the stares stop them from having one hell of a time. Instead, Amy Cabot launched forth. 'Goodness. We *are* making a spectacle of ourselves.' To which Hector replied, 'Well, if we're going to make a spectacle of ourselves . . .' He leant forward to whisper a joke, too fast for me to follow, until the punch line: 'Is that damn nun in here again?' As his fist came down, peals and fountains of laughter exploded. Heads and chairs tipped back. Baby pushed his chair too far and fell over backwards. The room fell silent while he righted himself. Having poured himself his eighth or ninth or tenth vodka, he slurred, 'Nuns. Where'd we be without them? Bless their little cotton socks.'

My father turned to Nella. 'By the way, I never thought to ask you . . .' And Nella replied, 'No I'm not a Catholic, as a matter of fact. I'm what your daughter tells me you call a rock-jaw WASP.' Amy Cabot bridled, as she always did when my father called anyone a rock-jaw wasp, until Baby muttered something smooth and light that featured rocks, jaws, wasps and nuns that made Hector Cabot slam his fist on the table and say, 'Why Baby! That's spectacular!'

Nella wanted more stories, and the men obliged. Most I had heard many times before. There was the one about their friend Old Cal who woke up in Vienna after a bomb and thinking that he had broken a lot of glass during a blackout bender, had offered to pay for everything. And there was the one about the punch bowl that broke and sent a river of eggnog down the cobblestones into the missionaries' garden. And story after story about Bunny Evans. These began the usual way, with Baby saying that he wouldn't be surprised to see Bunny Evans walking through the door, and Nella predictably responding with, 'But who *is* the real Bunny Evans?'

'Oh my,' said Amy. 'Where to begin?'

But before they could decide, the ship lurched to one side so violently that Hector and Baby both fell off their chairs. Baby was making a habit of it.

When I remarked that we must have just reached the mouth of the Sardonic Gulf, they all burst out laughing.

I pretended not to care.

I saw my mother watching me.

26

Stormy Weather

It was not until after supper, when my mother was tucking my sleeping brother safely into his makeshift bed at the edge of the lounge, that she shared her thoughts with me. I had wandered over to be near her. 'I know I've said this once today already, but I think you need to hear it again. I truly appreciate your help in keeping this show on the road. I know it's been hard and I know that no one but me has noticed or appreciated your efforts. But thanks to your tact and courage, we've managed to head off the gravest danger of all,' I didn't have time to ask my burning question before she continued, 'So, anyway. I want to give you a token of my gratitude.'

What was it?

'A surprise.'

How would I know it?

'Oh, you'll know, when the time comes.'

When? When will I get the token?

Instead of answering, my mother gestured towards the dance floor and said, 'You were worried that we would offend the others, weren't you?' She said 'others' with a special intonation. 'Or cause an incident. But look at what we've done instead. Who would even know that our two countries were at war?' I had to admit that she was right. The chill I had felt so keenly in the dining room was no longer there. The storm, now entering its second hour, had melted the ice, softened expressions, produced smiles, brought the two sides together in communal defiance of the elements. They were playing a waltz. My sister was dancing with one of the Egyptian officers with her feet on his shoes.

A second officer was leading Nella to the dance floor.

The Cabots were dancing the Lindy Hop.

The floor was swaying along with the dancers, though sometimes in the wrong direction which sent them flying. I was gently holding my brother's foot and watching waves splash up against the windows when I felt a tap on my shoulder. It was White Fang's mother. She placed herself next to me.

She said her name was Sibel and asked for the story behind my own name. She asked about my 'beautiful brother' and told me how sorely she missed the days when her own son was that age.

I was tempted to commiserate.

'Our Sinan is quite the little devil now, isn't he?' she said as she lit up a new cigarette.

'You still manage to love him, though,' I said.

She let out a ghastly laugh. 'That seems to be my fate in life. To love, and to be betrayed.' She took a long drag from her cigarette and watched the smoke rise. I watched her diamonds catch the light.

By now, the others had started singing. First Baby. 'Just a few things I pulled together in the early hours, before the damn hangover hit.' The first song was *The Red Threat* which everyone seemed to find funny, perhaps because they were drunk. I took pride in having provided him, over supper, with his other new titles: *The Approach. In the Belly of the Beast. The Package.* And, to the happiest applause, *The Sardonic Gulf.* Then, at Sergei's request, Baby played something from *Porgy and Bess.* Without sending it up. When he launched into *Some Enchanted Evening*, Nella jumped up to sing along but her harmony was way off pitch. Why did she always plunge into things she couldn't do? Perhaps accepting her foolishness, Nella put out a plea for reinforcements. So now it was Amy Cabot clutching the microphone, washing that man right out of her hair. Hector Cabot joined her, to ask about that doggie in the window. And when he was through, he took the microphone out of its holder and walked over to my mother, got down on his knees and said, 'I beg of you.' Baby called from the piano. 'Me too!' Though she demurred at first, I knew that she had made up her mind and I witnessed the change, from mother to songstress, as she made her way across the tilting floor.

She cupped her hands around the microphone. She looked across the room to find me smiling at her. She nodded, to tell me that she would be singing for me, and me alone.

The laughter tailed off, the ship lurched so violently that Amy Cabot put her hand to her mouth and screamed. We watched in frozen silence as a troop of orphaned bottles rolled across the dance floor and then came rolling back. The few peals of laughter turned into a cheer as my mother sang the first words of *Stormy Weather*.

Her smile didn't falter as she became silent once again and waited for the cheering to stop. When she began singing again, from the top, hearts melted and, one by one, my worries melted away.

Her voice had never been so beautiful, nor the song so sad.

I could see my father weeping. Sergei too. Even White Fang was transfixed. His father and İsmet were frozen. When my mother sang the final words, the Lugubrians jumped from their seats and rushed to grab my mother's hand. The loudest applause came from Sibel. 'Bravo!' she cried, clapping so loud that my ears rang. 'Bravo!'

Sergei had fallen into a chair. He was staring at my mother, and clutching his heart.

The orchestra burst into a waltz and Nella and Hector went spinning across the floor.

When the waltz was over, my mother picked up the microphone and lamented not singing, not ever, not even after going around the world in a plane. Then she launched into the second verse and Sergei staggered to the place where she sang in the middle of the swaying dance floor, fell to his knees, and clasped his hands in prayer.

'Just look at that!' said Sibel. 'Such spontaneity. How happy you all are. How carefree. How I envy you. I envy you so much I could cry my heart out.' She then asked me how we had found ourselves on this 'godforsaken ship'. When I told her, she chuckled. 'Imagine that!' she said. 'To travel to Egypt, in the middle of winter, just for fun! To be on this ship, and rocking in this storm, for pleasure! To sing – to be allowed to sing – for pleasure!'

She laughed tragically as she lit another cigarette.

'I used to sing once,' she said.

'For pleasure?'

'For that and more,' she said. She sounded so sad. It was then that the ship hit the side of another big wave. The ship listed sharply, sending a chair against the sofa where my brother was sleeping. I waited until the ship had righted itself before pulling the chair upright.

When I glanced over at White Fang's mother, it was as if someone was shining a light on her.

I looked up. There was Nella. 'Why hello there. Are you going to introduce me to your friend?'

By bedtime, everyone had met everyone. Each of the Egyptian officers had danced with each of the women. White Fang's father and mother had done the cha cha. We had all done the limbo, even White Fang, and İsmet of the velvet eyes had won. Baby had played us Chubby Checker's latest and Sibel had shown us how to do the twist, partnered by her morose and reluctant son. Then Sibel had pulled Nella on to the dance floor to show her. Then Amy Cabot. Then my mother. Each time the tune faded, Sibel raised her arm and cried, '*Encore*, I say! There is life in us yet!'

The rest of us had a hard time getting the hang of this new dance. Sibel excelled. No matter how low she twisted, and no matter how far the ship lurched, she never lost her balance. With each triumph over gravity, her laughter grew more raucous. Towards midnight, her two male escorts took her to one side to whisper and persuade, but from the churlish and emphatic way she shook her head, it was clear that Sibel wasn't ready for bed yet. She broke free and strode back to the dance floor, casting aside her little red jacket. 'I wish for another vodka!' she cried, raising her arm. 'Another vodka, for my soul!'

It was one in the morning but only the children were removed to the cabins for sleep.

'It will be fine,' our mother assured us. 'After all, The People's Nursery is only a hop, skip and a jump away from the lounge'. All I had to do was open the door a crack, and I would hear their voices.

I must have opened that door to their voices at least a dozen times, but finally, when my Mickey Mouse watch said twenty-three minutes past three – I opened it to silence. And I knew at once I'd been a fool to let my guard down.

I stepped outside in my robe and bunny slippers, and caught the first poignant notes of *Stormy Weather*. First my mother sang alone. Then other voices joined in.

I struggled down the swaying white corridor to the lounge. I passed the ship's library. Behind the glass door, Sergei was conversing with White Fang's father, who looked livid, and with İsmet, who looked grim.

The song was ending. Someone was clapping. 'Bravo!' I heard Sibel cry. 'Bravo! My hat is off to you. My girls, that was sublime! We are going on tour together. The four Sirens! We shall take the world by storm! No man shall stop us! Least of all ours!'

I walked into the lounge. The only light came from the waves splashing against the windows.

Though the blackness came an explosion of sniggers.

'Yoo hoo! We can see you!' That was Amy Cabot.

'Come out, come out, wherever you are!' That was Nella.

'Is that you, darling?' That was my mother.

And this was Sibel: 'There are no darlings in this darkness! Only my jailers! But let me tell you two, my new friends, that after the night, comes the morning. You have no power over me, and you never will. So you can go shit yourselves! Your prisoner has broken free!'

27

The prisoner

When I woke the next morning, the ship was rolling, rolling, rolling, and I was on the floor, wound in a blanket.

Outside the windows of the nursery's great play room, waves were smashing against the plate glass windows from a sea that was an angry, swelling grey. The sky was the harshest white: the kind that would, in a familiar world, augur snow.

Only my father and I made it to breakfast. The only other person there was Nella, and she looked as grey as my father did.

'What's the latest?' my father asked.

'Mixed,' she said, grimly.

'Is there anything I can do?'

'Hard to say.' From the way she bit her lip, I could tell she wished I wasn't there.

I couldn't bear that. 'What's happened?' I said.

'Oh, nothing,' she lied. 'It's just the storm. A true test of character, as it turns out! We three are the only ones upright.'

'Unless you count the Soviets,' I said.

'Yes, of course,' she said. 'I guess it helps to be in the navy.' Giving me a quick glance, and perhaps sensing an unwelcome question, she turned to my father. '*You* were in the navy during the war, weren't you?' It triggered the story I had heard many times before, about when he'd signed up and how old he'd been, why he'd trained as a frogman, how he'd narrowly missed being involved in a battle somewhere in the Pacific where all but one frogman died, how he'd ended up travelling through Burma, all the way to China. Nella nodded brightly, but I could tell she was hardly listening. Patting me on the head, she said, 'This must be so tedious for you. Listen. Let's go and find some people and you can do their portraits.'

I explained that I had yet to finish Sergei.

'Well then. We shall see to that pronto!'

Sergei seemed overjoyed to see us, but his eyes darkened when I told him my mother was seasick. He lurched to his feet. 'Is there anything . . .?'

'No!' Nella said, too emphatically. 'Honestly. There's nothing!'

Then she was off again, leaving me with Sergei. 'There's just something I need to check.' This was the drill for the rest of the morning, though I could just not understand why they were all in such a hurry, with not a moment to spare. If it wasn't Nella racing off somewhere without a word of explanation, it was my father. If it wasn't Sergei dashing off after my father, it was Sergei trying to catch up with Nella. I had to draw his portrait from memory, and then check against his real face when he came back, but then he was usually gone again before I'd finished erasing my mistakes.

Once he came rushing back into the ship's library, out of breath and clutching his heart. 'And how is she now, your sainted mother? Still poorly? Oh what a catastrophe!' He sat in his chair and gazed vacantly at the ceiling, sighing heavily, and shaking his head. Nella returned, and the two of them sat there, wordlessly, not a vodka glass in sight, until Sergei pointed through the door and said, 'Oh look, Mimi. There's Sinan. Why don't I ask Sinan to show you around the ship?'

That's how White Fang and I ended up sitting face to face in the lounge, which was grey and grim and heaving. No place for a party.

For a long, long time, he wouldn't speak. Instead he examined his fingers.

Then suddenly he looked up and stared hard, straight at me.

'These games you play with your sister. They're very childish.'

'She's only six,' I said.

'But you are . . .'

'Nine.'

'Nine. That's a bit old to be playing *Lost and Found*, isn't it? Let alone *I Spy*.'

'You play that, too, though. With your mother. I saw you!'

'Why are you raising your voice? It's so childish.'

'Everybody keeps saying that, and it's so unfair.'

'And also boring.' He did a theatrical yawn, and said 'But I digress.'

'I don't think so,' I said. Desperate to let him know the meaning of the word. 'You know, you can't go off the subject unless you have one to start with.'

'Shall we play then?' he said.

'Play what?'

'*Lost and Found*,' he said. 'But this time, no children allowed.'

'Do you know how tired I am of hearing that today?'

'Then pay attention. Listen to what I am saying.'

'What are you saying then?'

Reaching into his pocket, he retrieved a spent tube of İpana toothpaste.

'Only an hour ago, this tube was full. Would you like to see what became of it?'

'Only if you stop calling me childish.'

'That would take all the fun out of it. Don't you think?' He headed across the lurching lounge. He pulled open the door. Outside, great waves were crashing on to the deck.

'Don't worry,' he said. 'I'm right beside you. If a wave comes too close . . .' He clamped his hand around my arm. 'I'll save you, like this.' He gestured at a white line that made a stripe down the deck. It was made of toothpaste.

'If you like, you can step on it. I don't mind. I don't care! You can make as many footprints as you like. However, you could live to regret it.'

I made my way down the howling, swaying deck, steering clear of the toothpaste, racing beside the waves and the great clouds of spray.

Back inside, I saw the toothpaste trail stretching out before me. One white-marked corridor led to another. 'It's just like *Lost and Found*, isn't it?' he said. 'Except, more interesting.'

By now we'd come to the end of the trail. I turned around but White Fang had vanished.

Just ahead, I could hear a woman sobbing, and another whispering behind a propped-open door. I crept towards it. I peered in.

Nella was kneeling on the floor, with her back to me. In her hand was a ball of cotton wool. Standing over her was an anguished İsmet, holding a bowl of water. With every new wave, it sloshed on to a different part of the floor.

On the bed was White Fang's mother, whose arm had a bright red gash in it, whose lips were swollen and purple.

28

In the shadows of Egypt

The next morning we left the ship for the bright, flat shores of Alexandria, but Nella was not with us. In a voice as bright as the landscape, my mother explained that Nella had caught an early train to Cairo, having promised Rex to report to the embassy 'first thing'. To me, that seemed a pathetic excuse, but I had learned how to eavesdrop with discretion and said nothing. I knew precisely how far away to place myself – on the coach, in the roadside cafeteria where the coach stopped for lunch, and in the stuffy dining room of the Swiss Pension in Cairo. I bowed my head over my drawing in order to keep my bearings and to protect myself from being tossed by the waves of doubt that Dora had described as too great to see. I erased myself, except for my eyes and ears, while I waited for the adults' conversation to drift my way.

Mostly they were trying to remember the Storm Party. Mostly they couldn't.

'Oh, Grace, put us out of our misery. Won't you please tell us what we did?'

'You were all wonderful,' she said finally. 'It was the party of the century. Everyone joined in. You all had the time of your lives.'

'So when did it get ugly?'

'Who said it got ugly?'

'None other than your esteemed spouse.'

'Actually.' My father cleared his throat. 'Actually, I can't remember much either. Everything I know, I know from Nella. And even she . . .'

'Discretion! Please!' This was Amy, who went on to indicate in sign language that *A Child Was Listening*.

The next morning, there we were again in the same stuffy dining room at Swiss Pension, only I was marooned at a separate table with my sister, pretending not to care about being put out of ear-shot. 'Hi, kid. What's that you're drawing – a table leg?' came an unfamiliar voice.

I glanced up and saw beside me the man I would come to know as Mr Wakefield. A look in his eyes made me fear for my invisible ink. However, he said nothing. Just patted me on the head like everyone else, a gesture meant to tell me that I was only a child. 'Keep up the good work,' he said.

At the adult table, there was a great scraping of chairs followed by nervous greetings. Once seated, the man leaned forward, and so did the others. His voice rose and fell and I could only catch some words: *unfortunate, ruckus, wild card, a sensitive moment in negotiations, not wishing to alienate our allies, which is why they've called me in. To be perfectly frank with you, lickety split, without treading on any toes. But meanwhile. Our friend Sibel. In the hands of the best doctors, making a full recovery. Yes, I know her well. And a fine woman she is, too. Her husband, well that's more complicated. Yes, I'm afraid you're right there, one hell of a temper. But we can make things right for her. If we proceed with caution.*

And after harsh whispers from my father: *Well, obviously. I certainly see your point. That said, his Excellency is a staunch ally, indeed, an indispensible ally. And our friend Nella here, some very serious allegations, very serious indeed. So it would help to know if any of you people intend to support her.*

The man sat back with folded arms and looked at each adult in turn. Each in turn, they bowed their heads, as if they were not adults but children.

Well, you see, William . . . This was Baby. I couldn't catch the rest of it.

The man waved his arm. 'Oh, listen. We all know how to paint the town red. But you people walked right through the very heart of the Cold War and spat at it. You had your party and now we are asking you to clean up the mess you made and help us deal with the fallout. As much as I care for Sibel, and I care for her a whole lot, she will not thank us if we let this get out of hand.'

Now my father spoke up. 'I'm not sure I like where this is going.' The man interrupted, but my father kept talking over him. 'In fact, I was not the only one to see that brute of a husband hit her. One of the Egyptian officers was with us so don't think you can get around that. I can even give you his name. Mubarak. Whatever he says now, I can quote him verbatim from that night. He said . . .'

My mother interrupted him. 'Be that as it may,' she said. 'I may be the only one at this table who remembers every detail because, as it happens, I was drinking water. And William, I can assure you that nothing untoward happened. In fact, a splendid evening was had by all . . . No, that can't be possible. I mean Nella and her new friend . . . Did you say her name was Sibel? She had a wonderful time, too . . .'

After the man left, Baby said, 'Now what the hell was that about?' My father turned to my mother: 'You don't actually believe that crap you said, do you?'

Her voice was as composed as ever. 'I told him what I know. As for Nella, we'll have to wait until we can ask her!'

But when Nella did turn up, halfway through our third day in Cairo, my sister and I were the only ones awake.

*

It was siesta time. We were back at the Swiss Pension, having spent the morning with Tutankhamen's treasures. I was trying to get back my bearings by giving up on questions which were unspeakable. Why did my mother lie to Mr Wakefield, when she knew from me – her eyes and ears – that Sibel had suffered ugly red and purple injuries?

Although I said nothing, my mother read the question on my forehead. Which was why she sent me downstairs to help Baby work on his new number, *Mayhem on the Mediterranean*. She promised me that music would soothe my overheated brain. But then Baby vanished in search of 'light refreshment' and left my sister and me pounding on the piano in the dark, overstuffed sitting room and infuriating the manageress, who kept flying through the door and begging us not to disturb her guests' siestas. 'So would you be so kind?' she said each time. And we'd say, 'Nokay!' which seemed terribly funny.

We were staggering around in circles when I spied Nella, asleep in a red velvet chair.

'Nella!' I said, tugging her arm. 'There's something I need to ask you!'

But the question stuck in my throat.

'So tell me,' Nella asked, feigning nonchalance as she redid her ponytail. 'What have you two rascals been up to?' I told her about Tutankhamen's disappointing mummy. 'And the Pyramids?' Continuing to feign childish boredom, I dismissed them too. 'Would you like to see them again?' she asked. 'With me?'

I feigned delight at the suggestion. My sister pretended to check with Lightie and Keenie. I remembered to take my notebook. Once it was agreed, off we all went at Nella's usual speed. Not until we climbed in to the taxi did she hesitate. 'Oh God, I should really have left a note,' she said, but did nothing.

At Giza, she stepped out of the taxi as if in a trance. Ignoring the three great pyramids, she walked straight over to the Sphinx. Having removed her camera from its brown leather case, she charmed a guide into photographing the three of us sitting on the Sphinx's paws. And there we stayed, eating our way through her stash of oranges and chocolate kisses, until suddenly she stood up and stepped across to the nearest of the pyramids. Her ascent was fast, but only to the ninth step. An hour later, she was still there, and I was adding the finishing touches to my sketch, including the guides and camels and trinket sellers

159

gathered at the foot of the pyramid, and Nella on the ninth step, and the two more distant pyramids reduced to shadows, and the sun disappearing from a sky thick with invisible notes.

'So. Tell me,' Nella said afterwards. 'Have they sent the wolves after me?' I shook my head, perhaps too vigorously. I made a second attempt to ask her about Sibel but again the question stuck in my throat.

We returned to the city in silence. Nella dropped us off at the hotel, claiming a forgotten errand. I ran straight upstairs, my sister trailing behind me, but the door to our parents' room was locked. Nor were they in the parlour. I took hold of my sister's hand, and headed for the door while I battled with the knowledge of what had really happened. Our parents hadn't just forgotten us this time, like they often did. No – they had been abducted. Nella, treacherous Nella, had spirited us off to Giza to clear us out of the way. It had been a plot.

It was the hour of prayer. The streets were covered with carpets and kneeling, bowing, chanting men. We stood at the entrance of the Swiss Pension, staring out at the world. I felt my father's grip before I saw him. 'What the hell do you think you're doing?' he yelled. My mother scooped up my sister, then she turned to look me up and down as if I were a stranger.

Back in the hotel, when my father was spanking me, and my mother watching on in silence, I told myself she must be putting on an act. Even when my sister stuck out her tongue at me, I maintained a dignified silence. That night, after she fell asleep, I kept my sketchbook under my pillow. Just in case.

But my mother didn't come in to thank me, not that night, nor the next, nor the next.

We had moved on to Luxor. It was the third dark night of my soul. I was leaning against a French door with the adults outside, whispering in the desert night. Under the table was a bottle they'd purloined from the ship.

My mother was telling them the latest on Nella. 'You're not going to believe this,' she said. 'But she's gone and made a scene at the Turkish Embassy.'

'Why would anyone do that?' This was Baby.

'She must sincerely believe there's a cover-up.' That was my father.

'Be that as it may,' said my mother. 'There's something we shouldn't forget.' She described the package that Nella had agreed to carry for someone, or deliver to someone.

'Who told you *that*?' This was Amy.

'No one,' my mother said. 'No one needed to. All I had to do was use my ears and eyes.'

Though she must have heard my sob and anguished fleeing footsteps, my mother did not come after me. It wasn't until the next day, on the great ramp leading to Queen Hatshepsut's temple, that she took me to one side.

'I'm sorry you had to hear all that last night. It wasn't for your ears.'

'I am your ears,' I said, brushing off hot tears. 'I'm your eyes, too, and you don't even thank me!'

'Of course I thank you,' she said, wrapping her arm around me. 'In fact, I don't know where I'd be without you. But here we are, at long last, in the Valley of Kings.'

She paused to gaze out at the distant mountains. 'No one wanted us to get this far,' she said. 'Every step of the way, they've tried to stop us. If you hadn't been there, identifying bad things before they happened, who knows what might have transpired?' She paused as if to conjure up searchlights and killer dogs.

'What's happened to Nella?' I asked.

'Don't worry about Nella. She'll be fine. Once she decides what she wants out of life, she might even be happy.'

'How old were you when you knew what you wanted out of life?'

'I think you know that,' she said as she squeezed my arm.

Then she told me a few things about the Queen Hatshepsut – how she'd ruled wisely and without opposition for twenty years, only to have her stepson successor order that her name be removed from public records, and all depictions of her effaced, except in this, her final resting place, which had itself sunk back into the earth. How she'd gone from presiding over a great empire to hiding in the shadows of history, robbed of her name and all detail, like almost all the great women of history, before and after. 'But then, at last, her temple was rediscovered, with all the writing on its walls intact, and now here it is, open to the sky once again, and how happy that Queen would be if she knew you were here basking in her ancient glory, and sketching in her name . . .'

'Why would she be happy, if she never knew me?'

'Because,' my mother said, 'she would know just from your grave manner that I have entrusted you with the task of recording our great adventure for generations to come.'

She pointed at the row of columns above us. 'There's some nice shade over there. Wouldn't that be an ideal vantage point?'

'For what?'

'For sketching a small patch of this beautiful place, on this beautiful day, which should never be forgotten. *For embracing beauty*.'

She pointed at my sketchbook, now swollen to bursting with invisible questions. I could see my father approaching, my brother on his shoulders, my sister hanging on his free arm.

My mother's last words were, 'Nobody must know we had this talk.'

Now why would she say that?

Arriving at the ideal vantage point, I gazed out into the middle distance as, one by one, the clues floated across my field vision and, one by one, fell into place.

I steadied myself against a column. I looked down the ramp and beyond to the chalky hills encircling us. I lifted my eyes to the pale blue sky, and closed them, and felt the sun on my eyelids. All the time, the clues shimmered in their new-found completeness and unity. The transistor radio and Mr Guttman's sketch book. The witch hunt at Fort Monmouth and my grandmother's dark thoughts. The Admiral's wife and her care packages and her cryptic warnings. Delphine's ugly campaign.

Dora's grand predictions. My mother's determination to keep to the plans, come hell or high water. The ship's librarian and his odd questions and my father's answers. Baby's tantrum. The storm party. All the things my mother pretended not to care about: Sibel's bruises, Nella's pleas, my heart.

It was not a butterfly but a mission that had brought us here. It was initiated not by my father, but my mother. She had carried us through the storm, and I had helped, by being her eyes and ears.

I alone knew she had come here to foil the war-mongers, to refuse their plots, to show the way. Hadn't she done just that on the *Felix Dzerzhinsky*? Hadn't their hearts melted at her voice? Had she not shown them what was possible, if weapons were replaced by beauty? This was my mother's secret mission. She had brought us here and still propelled us, but now there were two of us who knew.

The others thought she was just a mother. Just a charming wife. She and I would continue to let them think that, until the time was right. When the right moment came, she would give me a secret sign and out I would go in search of a gallery that was worthy of her. One by one, I would pull out the drawings recording our journeys. We'd pass a flame over them, but not too close. I'd watch my words emerge, faint at first but slowly browning. We'd send them to be framed and when they came back, I'd arrange them in chronological order. Between them we'd have panels, one for each chapter of our story. When the sun was low in the sky, and sending down slanted rays of golden light, and the punch bowl was ready, and the waiters lined up, and the orchestra primed, and the first cold drops falling from the ice swans on to the delicacies sent by the world's greatest chefs, my mother would nod and I would throw open the French doors to a grateful and astounded world. And together we would raise our glasses to celebrate her glorious feats.

29

Questions and Theories about Beauty

It took time to adjust to my new faith. The musings I collected at the back of Mr Guttman's sketchbook, under the heading *Questions and Theories about Beauty*, attest to this. Where had it all started? Did my mother act alone, or in concert with others? Did she dream alone, or had she shared her dreams with fellow travellers? Where had she met her first free spirits? Was it at the blues school? Did her soft exterior hide a steely determination, and perhaps also solid combat training, just in case?

I looked at my mother's handbag, swollen to overflowing with bottles and spare diapers, and I imagined – just imagined – that it owed its bulky shape to a secret pocket with a flashlight that converted into the revolver that she had hidden, ready for the eleventh hour, if persons unknown conspired to block our way.

I imagined her at shooting practice, fixing her eye on the cardboard Khrushchevs on the far side of the lawn before peppering each bald head with bullets that never wavered.

How close I'd come to blowing her cover. But now I knew the score, she could count on me to be her eyes and ears until Nella decided what she wanted out of life, and stopped blocking us at every turn.

One evening, in our hotel in Luxor, I peered into a wedding reception and thought I saw Nella in the flesh, just behind the belly dancer. At breakfast, I noticed a man slip an orange into his pocket. He could be taking it to her. He could be her handler. That white napkin I could see amongst the palm leaves – perhaps Nella had tossed it from her window?

In Alexandria, I thought I saw her behind the great bouquets in the open carriage in which Nasser and Tito were waving at the stampeding crowd that nearly killed us. In Beirut, I thought I spied her in the shadows of a hotel balcony.

When I felt my spine tingling at Baalbek, I pictured her behind the great fallen columns, longing to return to us. I saw her again in the Damascus souk; the veil which half-covered her face did not disguise the familiar suffering in those tragic eyes. She was there again, sighing down on us from the parapets of the fortress in Aleppo. And in Antakya, near the famous mosaics, I didn't see her, but I heard her sobs. I duly recorded all of these occasions, together with the number plates of every vehicle that had offered a glimpse of a profile that might have been hers.

Suspect Number One, I called her. Or SNO for short. Who had turned her?

*

On my first day back at school in Istanbul, Dora brought me the first perplexing answers. She could not tell me where Nella was, but she knew all about the Storm Party and its aftermath – having spoken to none other than Sinan who turned out to be some sort of relation. And – just in case I had been encouraged to think otherwise by overprotective grown-ups – she assured me that the bruises and cuts I'd seen on Sibel's face were put there by her husband, and not for the first time. Sibel's protectors would soon have their pound of flesh. Discretion was of the essence, Dora insisted, but sadly, it was too late for Nella who was still in a huff and would heed no one.

Nella, apparently, had gone straight from the ship to the US Embassy in Cairo to inform on a Turkish diplomat who had assaulted his wife on board the *Felix Dzerzhinsky*. She had demanded swift and decisive action. It had not occurred to her that the US envoy might not be very interested in the personal affairs of an important ally just then, when Nasser seemed hell-bent on giving the Soviets a foot-hold in North Africa.

Nella should have thought of that before causing a furor in the foyer of the Turkish Embassy. What would have happened if Mr Wakefield had not materialised to put things right? He had been Delphine's boss, Dora said, as far back as the OSS days and had remained their friend and protector in New York. After Cairo, he'd stopped off in Istanbul, which was how Dora knew he'd seen me sketching in the Swiss Pension.

Mr Wakefield was based in Washington now, but he visited Turkey often, *to look in on the store*, as he put it. He would be paying another visit soon: there was a lot of cleaning up still to do. 'The double dealing over the Jupiters was bad enough already,' Dora said. 'But the Storm Party and Nella's one-woman crusade have put the entire US-Turkey alliance in jeopardy.'

'But we didn't mean anything like that to happen!' I could not help but cry.

'My poor little mascot, I know you didn't mean it! But you must have noticed that the others were hell-bent on making a scene. Never mind, though. What's done is done. And there are things that matter far, far more. The real question is . . .what were they *like*?'

'Who?'

'The Communists.'

Dora was trawling my eyes in search of answers, but where to begin?

How relieved I was to see Nella, holding the school bell. We filed back into our separate classrooms. Nella had written a list of facts about friction on our blackboard, accompanied by cartoons of Archie and Veronica. In the thought bubble above their heads was a question: *But what would life be like if there were no friction at all?* Nella opened up the discussion. 'So Mimi. What's the first image that comes to your mind?'

The ship, of course. The bottles, rolling over the lurching lounge floor. But I could never say that. Not in front of all these classmates who would laugh at me, and call me stupid, and say it served me right, for going on that enemy ship. So instead I said, 'We'd all be slipping around. 'Our desks, our chairs, everything.' To which the class troublemaker said, 'So what are we waiting for? I'm bored sitting here anyway.' Whereupon she flicked a spit ball that landed smack in the centre of Nella's desk.

For a few tense moments, Nella stared at it. Then she looked up brightly. 'You've just earned yourselves another pop quiz, I'm afraid!'

After I had filled a page with my description of a world where nothing could hold on to anything else – where cars started and never stopped, and babies drowned in the bath because their mother's couldn't get a grip on them, and pencils slipped to the floor to roll off to infinity – I looked up at Nella and the pile of untouched workbooks on her desk.

She reached for her Raybans. She was still wearing them when she joined me outside after school. The class troublemaker, whose father worked for the consulate, was on the tetherball court with the gang of younger children she called her slaves. When she saw us on the path, she said. 'Okay guys! All together now!' And her slaves began singing *She'll be Wearing Red Pajamas Cos She's Red*.

I heard Nella's sharp intake of breath. After we had crossed the *meydan* together, skirting the black cars and the chauffeurs standing smoking under the plane tree, she said, 'I wonder what happened to that girl to twist her so.'

It was a sunny day, and there was spring in the air. We took the cobblestone lane that ran along the upper castle walls, side-stepping the horse and donkey turds, waving sticks at the dogs, and ignoring the boys who ran after us, crying, *Hello, who are you? Will you suck my cock?* Here and there, we saw a woman in a headscarf leaning from the window of an unpainted wooden house.

At the lowest point in the road was an old plane tree and a fountain. Stopping in front of it, Nella put her hand on my shoulder and said, 'Isn't that just the prettiest thing you ever saw?' The sadness in her voice alarmed me. Had she come back only to say goodbye?

The lane looped up to meet the castle's southernmost tower. From here the cobblestones followed the wall of the Aşıyan cemetery to the Bosphorus. We turned onto the shore road, passing an outdoor *gazino* with its large posters of the fleshy singers who performed there by night, and then took the path that led to Nuran Hanım's studio, which appeared so close to the surface of the Bosphorus that it was sailing on it.

The tankers hummed, the ferries hissed, the caiques puttered and the canvas on Nuran Hanım's easel trembled. The fishermen called to each other. The currents swirled, blue on blue on blue.

That afternoon, Nuran Hanım was wearing her green smock with her hair pulled back under a red silk scarf. Her forehead was as high as the ones she'd shown me in her Dutch masters, and her large brown eyes as sad as the ones in her Modiglianis.

She leafed through the new pages in my sketchbook, passing her fingers over the contours of the shapes I had emptied out to make room for my invisible scribbling. 'I like the texture,' she said. 'These indentations provide such intriguing new dimensions. Don't you agree?' she asked Nella. And Nella nodded absently. Pointing at my first sketch of the pyramids, Nuran Hanım commented on the white squares that were draped on their lowest steps – my brother's diapers, placed there by my mother – and the bent rectangle reclining next to them – me.

I described how I had felt, stranded on the lowest step with the diapers because the higher steps were almost as high as I was. How, as I had watched Amy Cabot and the others scale those steps so effortlessly, I had felt myself a prisoner in a child's body.

Nella and Nuran Hanım exchanged looks.

'Let's look at yours, now,' Nuran Hanım said then. But instead of obliging, Nella stood up with a deep sigh, stopped at the window, and began to weep.

Nuran Hanım went to her and put her arm around her. 'It can't be helped, my dear. Some things can't be helped.'

Nella pulled away. Bunching up her fists, staring down at the floor like a willful child, she said, 'I'm sorry. But I just can't accept that.'

Why was Nuran Hanım crying too, as she rocked back and forth with Nella in her arms? Why was everyone succumbing to dark intrigue again? Why couldn't they put it behind them, like my mother and I had done?

I asked her when we were on the balcony that evening, and she agreed that it was a terrible shame. 'But time heals,' my mother said. Maybe I could suggest this to Nella myself, when she was calmer.

But the next morning we heard that Nella had left Rex. She never came back to our school.

30

Fallout

I was worried that Nella might have defected to the USSR but my mother assured me she'd gone back to America to sue for divorce. 'And if that's what she wants, then so be it.'

I nodded sagely, even as I wondered how someone who didn't know what she wanted out of life could be sure about a divorce.

'I wouldn't be at all surprised to see her back here very soon,' my mother added. 'Her heart is here, after all!' Then she smiled to herself in that private way I was learning to tolerate now she had let me in on the most important secret – her covert quest for peace.

She tapped the arm of her chair. 'Until then, it's our lovely Dora we need to think about. Seeing as her mother's in a cast . . .'

This was how I heard of Delphine's unfortunate fall into a pothole outside Kulis. It happened during an altercation with Nella only hours before Nella's departure.

That first Friday after our return from Egypt, and after Nella's departure, Dora and I walked down to Bebek to find her car parked outside Özsüt. The driver jumped out to open the door, but Dora waved him away as she led me into the pudding shop.

İsmet was sitting at the table by the window, staring at his idle hands. 'He wants to talk to you,' Dora explained. But at first it seemed he just wanted to buy us puddings. Once we'd been served, he asked after my sketches. He told me that in Turkey people called children like me honest and hard-working. Then he told me he was just back from four years of study in America, which he 'sorely missed'. Dora shifted in her chair, inching her hand across the table, until it was almost on his. Moving it aside, he looked straight into my eyes. 'Now I wish to apologise to you,' he said. 'You saw things on the ship that no child should ever see.'

'Nice try, İsmet. But wouldn't you agree that it's far too late for that?'

This was Sinan, who had slipped into the chair next to me.

According to Dora, he wanted to ask me something, too. But before he could begin, Dora added that Sinan was hoping we could help him find his mother.

'I didn't know she was missing,' I said. 'I thought she was fine.'

'She was,' said Sinan. 'Until she vanished.' He went on to explain that she had gone missing on the same day as Nella.

'So the link should be evident. Could you two tell me if you hear anything?'

'How could we tell you,' I asked, 'if we don't even know where you live?'

He shrugged his shoulders. 'Where I live most days is neither here nor there.' All we needed to know what that he spent the weekends with his uncle – just down the road, in the third house after the Egyptian Consulate – we could find him at Özsüt at this hour any Friday.

And so we did. If it was sunny, Dora and I walked to Özsüt. If it was raining, her driver took us. Sometimes, we'd find İsmet with him. One Friday, Mr Wakefield was there too, in the back of the room. He overturned his coffee cup as soon as it was empty but instead of looking for his fortune in the grounds, like the customers at the other tables, he scraped it with his spoon, while Sinan waited.

Finally, he said. 'I thought you'd want to know we've tracked them down.'

'They're in Paris, aren't they?'

A half nod from William.

'I knew that's where she was calling from,' Sinan said. 'Why did she lie?'

'This is just a flash in the pan, Sinan. She'll be back by summer.'

'How can you know that?'

'We've spoken.'

'What good news,' said Sinan joylessly. 'And what of my butcher father?'

'He's not a butcher,' said Mr Wakefield. 'He was under a lot of pressure that night.'

'He chased her away.'

'It will all blow over,' William Wakefield assured him. 'You watch this space.' Nodding in İsmet's direction, he said. 'So. How's my Man Friday treating you?'

'Is that what you call him?'

*

That spring, Dora and I visited Sinan often at his uncle's grand villa, three houses down from the Egyptian consulate. I was the only child: the others were all teenagers. But Dora made sure they were all kind to me. Some Saturdays, if the sun was warm, the older cousin would take us out in the speedboat that one day he would drive into the rudder of a ship. With us he was careful, even gentle.

Sometimes, if we were not in the mood for Özsüt, we went to the teahouse by the mosque. Here the boys played backgammon while Dora and I watched. Sometimes İsmet joined us, sitting next to Sinan and offering him advice in Turkish, until Sinan threw the board in the air. İsmet chided him while he picked up the pieces. Setting up the board again, he'd say, 'So Sinan. This is when you find out who's boss.' If İsmet lost, he punched his forehead: 'Undone again! Undone by the great master!' Dora would poke him, and İsmet would clutch his stomach, feigning pain.

In mid-June, I looked up and saw Mr Wakefield, in the suit he'd worn to Dora's graduation earlier that afternoon. We followed him out to the quay behind the mosque, where the Hiawatha was waiting. We did the full tour that day, following the European shore to Sariyer, and the Asian shore to Üsküdar, turning towards the Golden Horn, and then following the European shore back to our mooring place.

Along the way, Mr Wakefield took pictures while he talked to Dora about the French *lycée* she'd be attending from September. He talked to Sinan about the island, by which he meant his mother's summer house on Büyükada. Did he want to go out there anyway? From this I guessed that Sibel was still in Paris.

The diplomatic storm seemed to have subsided. Slowly, but oh so surely, beauty was melting it away. The Jupiter missiles had finally been deployed. They were keeping us safe now, all along the Black Sea coast. Today, on the Hiawatha, Mr Wakefield and İsmet agreed to disagree as to the wisdom of this measure. Speaking haltingly, almost paralysed by deference, İsmet said he was certain that the Jupiters would keep the Soviets in check, while Mr Wakefield feared that they might push Khrushchev to desperate action.

In fact, it had already happened. Khrushchev had already stood on the shores of Yalta, and looked out over the Black Sea. He had already raised his fist at the Jupiters casting their long shadows over the horizon. He had already said to his confidante: If the Americans can put nuclear weapons on our doorstep, then we can do the same to them.

Had Mr Wakefield anticipated Khrushchev's move? Was that why he trained his binoculars on each Soviet vessel to cross the Hiawatha's path?

'That's a big one,' he said at one point. 'That's definitely something to write home about.' Yet in his voice there was also assurance that this menace, too, would pass.

We went straight from the Hiawatha to the Mehtap, where Delphine was waiting with the Admiral's wife at a large round table at the water's edge. It was there, soon afterwards, that Sibel walked in and kissed her son's head before slipping into the seat beside him.

Conversation was stilted, as it must always be when one is attempting reconciliation. Sibel would ask her son about his studies, his weekends, his reading, his friends, and Sinan would answer in monosyllables, gaze down at his idle hands, and pout. From time to time he would glance up at his mother, as if to make sure he still had her attention. Sometimes, he did, but when a lull lasted too long, Sibel turned away, her silken hair flying, to converse with Delphine in rapid French. Mr Wakefield alerted Delphine to a secretarial position at the consulate that might be just the thing to tide her over. Delphine didn't think much of that idea. 'I'm a doer, not a sitter. I'm a professional freelance journalist, god damn it! I just need one big scoop.' Mr Wakefield had eyes that could take in a whole room without moving. I saw him watching Dora, as she sidled closer to İsmet, and İsmet grabbed her wrist to say, 'No, Dora. No.' He watched a little longer, as Dora moved away in mock anger, and İsmet chided her, most gently.

'So where are you off to this summer?' William Wakefield turned his attention to me. 'Still sketching away with your invisible ink?'

In the car going home, he and the Admiral's wife spoke in code about Baby Mallinson, though that was hardly necessary since I'd been at our End of the Year party the previous weekend, when Baby and Sergei had argued about the animal urge. I was the one who had discovered Baby afterwards, in the bath of red water. I still couldn't understand why they'd had to fly Baby to another country, or why Sergei thought Baby was an animal. I couldn't see how he could be one, if he could light up a whole room with his music. Or why, even if he was an animal, he had wanted to die. I let it all go. I had other things on my mind.

'That's a fine woman,' Mr Wakefield commented, after dropping off the Admiral's wife. When the car bumped back down the cobblestones, Mr Wakefield mentioned that he'd had a long talk with my 'friend' Mr Guttman.

'What?' I gasped. 'Really?'

'Yes, really,' he said. 'And a very good talk it was, too. He was glad to hear news of you. He's been a little worried, actually. He says he's hardly heard from you.'

'My father is just terrible with letters,' I explained. I told him about the one he'd been given by the secretary at Fort Monmouth and forgotten to put in the post box for a whole year, by which time the cousin to whom the letter was addressed had died.

'That's very funny,' said Mr Wakefield. Though he did not laugh.

By now the car was standing outside my house. As he walked me to the front door, he asked me how often I saw the Admiral's wife. 'Not as often as before.' I replied,

'It's only natural,' he said. 'You're just a kid, after all. But remember that Hope is utterly discreet. If you ever want to tell me something, you can trust her to make sure it reaches me without anyone being the wiser.'

That night, as I listened to the ships, it occurred to me I should have asked him how exactly he'd met Mr Guttman. So I got up and went out to the balcony to ask my mother what she thought. I still told her everything. When she thanked me, and told me what a good set of eyes and ears I had, I felt the comfort of knowing how much she still depended on me.

'I've always wanted to go on the Hiawatha,' she said. 'I'd like to sail along this coast on that boat and look up at our hill and contemplate its mysteries from the outside.'

That reminded me that Mr Wakefield had taken a picture of our hill from the Hiawatha. 'Do you think he was looking for the mysteries, too?' I asked her.

'Oh, I'm sure he was. But I doubt he'll find them.'

31

A corner of a foreign field

The next day it was summer, with more ships to take us far away, as far as the Greek Islands, where, with the few words of summer Greek I acquired after a few weeks of playing *Red Light Green Light* with the girls in the *plateia* in Naxos, I became my father's mouthpiece as well as my mother's eyes and ears, especially in Athens, when we had to wait ten days for our money to arrive at American Express while we lived on burnt corn. Every morning, my sister and I would act as scouts until the angry man at the reception desk in our dingy hotel on Omonoia Square left his position long enough for us to sneak past, without his asking us when we intended to pay the bill.

During our long wilting days in the Royal Gardens, I managed to get along with Violet so that even after the money came through, she and I still played *Sorry* together in the afternoons in the little restaurant attached to the windmill that we had rented on the island of Skiros for the entire month of August. That was where we were when Marilyn Monroe died and all the Greek men cried, while I worried again about poor Baby and his wrists. Even so, when I woke up the next morning and saw the sun rise, I could begin to understand why some people believed in heaven.

Later, when I asked my mother if heaven had been invented by a group of simple shepherds, who had watched the sun rise, she said, 'You may be right there,' but she sounded absent-minded. She was lost in a book, and although my father was too, he looked up to remind me that heaven was not something that the ancient Greeks had worried about, even if they were only simple shepherds. 'The Elysian Fields were the best they could hope for.'

'Or immortality,' I said.

'Yes, that, too. But they never fooled themselves into putting all their faith in an invisible and omniscient force of goodness, which is, if you ask me, the greatest con ever invented.'

My mother did look up from her book as my father returned to his. She studied his bent head as if she were about to sketch it.

I thought about heaven again when I went out with the windmill family to gather salt on the rough-hewn islets in the bay. At sunset, the sky was a blood-red bowl, its jagged edges locking perfectly into the black mountains that protected us.

The next day a storm blew up that lasted a week, and when the sea was almost calm again, the daughters of the windmill family invited me to visit their grandfather's farm on the island's most remote promontory. We went by sea. We returned in the evening, in a caique laden with melons and peaches and grapes. I sat on the prow, my feet dipping into the water with every wave, and my eyes on the darkening mountains of the shore. By the time we got back to the windmill, I'd seen the sun set seven times.

It would have been the next day that I went on that long and scorching walk with my father, in search of Rupert Brooke's grave. The poet had died of septicaemia on a World War I hospital ship that was moored in a bay on the southwestern corner of the island. Before departing for Gallipoli, Rupert Brooke's shipmates had buried him under a stone cairn, carving on to it an inscription that broke your heart, my father said, if you paused to consider that of the five fellow soldiers assisting at that small makeshift funeral, three would perish in the catastrophe to which they were headed:

Here lies the servant of God, Sub-lieutenant in the English Navy
who died for the deliverance of Constantinople from the Turks.

We were in the vanishing shadow of a very hot olive tree when he quoted those lines for me, confessing that his own impatience to join his own world war had been no less grandiose. Later still, when we were at last forced to accept that we'd walked along the wrong coast of Skiros and had reached the wrong bay, which at least offered beautiful water for a cooling swim and larger olive trees with longer shadows, but no sign of a tragic grave. That was the point when I couldn't hold back the sorrow inside me – about Baby and Marilyn Monroe and now this poet, who had once been dubbed the most handsome man in England, had been brought down by an adverse reaction to a mosquito bite acquired in Port Said.

To cheer me up, my father recited the first lines of Rupert Brooke's most famous poem, now inscribed on the fine marble grave paid for by his mother – a replacement for the stone cairn, after the war was fought and won:

If I should die, think only this of me:
That there's some corner of a foreign field
That is for ever England . . .'

'Did he believe in heaven?' I asked.

'I certainly hope not,' my father said.

On our walk home, he told me that Rupert Brooke would have written less glowingly of England and its lovely little corners had he lived longer. 'Even a week longer, had he lived to see Gallipoli, and this, I hope, will be a lesson to you. Men are drawn to war like moths to a light, and their way is paved with grandiose illusions. But I've been to war. I've seen what it does to people, even if it's a good war, a war that had to be fought, like mine. You can't go through a war and come out of it believing in God.

'Not the Christian one, anyway,' he added. 'Greek gods in the plural, yes, perhaps. Gods who are forever warring with each other and can't be trusted.'

As we rounded the next bend, he asked, 'Your mother hasn't been trying to get you to believe in God lately, has she?'

'No,' I said. I did not add that we did light candles at St Antoine when we went downtown, because I'd promised my mother not to tell him. Perhaps he knew about it already, because as we struggled on, me with two hastily fashioned walking sticks because my legs were hurting so much, he reminded me that he was a physicist, who could tell me about all manner of grand designs that actually existed on our planet, and in our universe, and that had been discovered through scientific enquiry, through questioning and doubt, whereas religion, and most especially the sort of Catholicism from which he had only narrowly escaped, and just in the nick of time, just by the skin of his teeth, which metaphor I was not to take at face value.

'What I am trying to say is that wherever you have an organized religion, you have a band of pompous old men telling you how to think, and then, because they've fooled you into respecting them, you vote them into office, and there lies darkness, there lies the insanity of war, all war, even this cold one. Most especially this cold one with its weapons that can wipe a city off the map, in a matter of seconds.'

He asked me if I'd managed to read *Hiroshima* yet. I reminded him that we'd intended to buy it at Eleftherodakis, but then, when the money finally arrived, we'd forgotten to go back to the bookstore. 'Well, let's not forget to buy it for you next time,' my father said.

For the next few bends, he talked about the book, which he said wasn't perfect, but did put the reader right there when an unexpected and never-before-seen flash had ripped across the sky. He told me about the doctor who'd been heading down

179

a hospital corridor, just inches from a window. Those standing in front of that window were killed instantly, while the doctor, only inches behind, was spared. He told me that at exactly the same moment, he himself had been in a small town in China, near the Burmese border. He explained that history was never straightforward: the Bomb, the greatest evil known to man, had probably saved him from an early death. 'My chances of survival in a small outfit assigned to Chang Kai Shek were slim. It was the Bomb that got us disbanded, and so you could almost say that without the Bomb, you wouldn't even exist.'

For the next few bends in the road, we thought about this in silence. The sun was low in the sky by now, and I could trace the peaks and valleys that had given me my seven sunsets. 'So that was what gave you the idea,' my father guessed.

'Yes, and also sunrise,' I admitted.

He spent the next few miles explaining the science behind the miracles of sunlight.

He told me about the skies he had seen in the navy, in the Pacific, from the gunner's nest, shooting at Japanese aircraft, on the top of a train cutting through the jungles of Burma, and in bombed-out, burnt-out Hamburg at the end of the war.

His ship was taking soldiers home, and on one journey, it was mostly Japanese Americans who'd had no news of their families during the time they'd been fighting for their country in Europe. It was on the ship that they were finally given their letters and so discovered that their relatives had been interned for the duration to keep them from collaborating with the enemy.

'That's when I really started thinking,' my father said.

When we got back to our beach, we stopped for a drink at the restaurant attached to the first windmill. 'What a wonderful day it's been,' my father said, as he downed his first beer in almost a single gulp. 'You ask such good questions.'

'We should do more of this,' he said. And: 'You might enjoy studying physics yourself one day.'

He had to carry me the last hundred yards or so, because

my legs gave way. My mother brought out a pillow and drew up a second chair so that I could keep them elevated. That night, I was allowed to have as many *portakalades* as my heart desired. We had finished our omelets and fried potatoes and were working on the salad when my father announced that I might have it in me to be a physicist. My mother demurred. My father was flabbergasted, disappointed, and deeply hurt.

When I woke up in the middle of the night, they were still arguing. I heard my father say: 'You're telling her she can't do it, before she's even had a chance!'

And my mother: 'While you expect her to do things that would be difficult or even impossible for someone twice her age!'

'You can't say she didn't enjoy it. I told you about her marvelous questions. Didn't I?'

'Yes,' my mother said. 'But can you hear the questions she doesn't dare ask?'

'She knows she is free is ask whatever question comes to her.'

'Oh really. Then I hope you will afford me the same privilege. Why set out on this twenty-mile trek and take so little water?'

'I've walked halfway across Florida with less.'

'Mimi is not a man. She's not a soldier. She's a ten-year-old girl with eyes that are bigger than her stomach.'

'Is that your excuse for locking her into a life of submission?'

'I just want her to be happy,' my mother said.

*

All summer my mother had been trying to wean me off portraits because they were frustrating me. There was so much in people's eyes I couldn't fathom. At her suggestion, I'd gone back to doing tableaux of imagined arrangements of real people and real objects in familiar locations. There was one of my tenth birthday party with my new Greek friends on Naxos. Another was set in the café in the Royal Gardens in Athens where we'd eaten our burnt corn. A third was of the windmill and its restaurant, with lobsters crawling amongst the diners' feet and lanterns blowing in the wind. There was no electricity on Skiros; according to one of the old men who had cried at the death of Marilyn Monroe, it was because the island had sided with the Communists in the Civil War.

My last tableau of the summer was *A Corner of a Foreign Field*, by far the hardest. I started it on the day my father set out for Rupert Brooke's grave again, this time with two students – two more lookalikes, my mother said – from Oxford. They left before sunrise, without telling me, taking with them the map that I could have used to catch up with them, if I had alternated walking with running.

My mother suggested I imagine the grave I would never see. She thought it would calm my raging tears at being left behind. 'You could also draw it. There's still plenty of room in there,' she said, nodding in the direction of my dog-eared sketchbook.

I wasn't sure. 'How can I imagine a whole *place*, if I've never seen it?'

'Is it so hard to imagine a corner of a foreign field that is forever England?'

'I've never been to *England*.'

'Yes, but think how many English books you've read. So many with lovely illustrations . . .'

An hour later, she came to check on my progress. I had depicted three men kneeling, not praying, before a grave that didn't have a turban on it. 'That was a good decision,' my mother said. 'This gravestone really could be in any corner of the mother country. But why leave your father and his two fine friends to enjoy this high moment alone? How about drawing the rest of us there, too?'

When I hesitated, she said, 'Listen. Just give it a try. Give us a chance to be there, in spirit if not in life.'

'I never get the shadows right with people who weren't really there,' I said.

'Oh, I know, I know. Verisimilitude requires such precision, such finesse, but you're getting better every day, you know. I think you should try it. Put us in there, and see how we look. You can always erase us later.'

'Don't forget the beauty,' she said around lunch time. Towards evening, she added, 'If you have room, see if you can fit in the sound and the fury too.' I did. In the finished sketch, my father and the two Rupert Brooke lookalikes were joined at the graveside by a group of old men weeping over Marilyn Monroe, whose likeness was draped over the grave. In the sky was a large mushroom cloud, inside which you could see my mother and sister and brother and me as well as Hera: I'd thought long and hard about which goddess would share my rage about being left out of an expedition of such significance, and after trying out several poses, I'd opted for Hera shaking her fist. Athena stood on a far hill, looking wisely over a sea criss-crossed by large black ships.

32

Sultry in October

The glow of summer remained a few weeks later, when I sat down on our balcony in Istanbul to plan what would become my final, and most compressed, series of tableaux. There were now only six pages left in Mr Guttman's sketchbook, but after the rapturous reception I'd enjoyed at the windmill in Skiros for my sketch of Rupert Brooke's grave which had brought smiles even to the men who had been moribund since the death of Marilyn Monroe, my mother assured me I was a good enough artist to work in miniature, so why didn't I do a series of panels, three or four to the page, in the manner of the great Hogarth, whose engravings we had been admiring just the other day? If I followed his august example, making the most of each page, I would not just capture the humanity in life's details, I would, through compression, evoke the spirit of our age. 'You could even call it *The Rake's Progress*,' she said.

'Wouldn't Hogarth get angry if I used his title?'

'He can't. He's dead.'

'But what about his children, and his children's children?'

'You can state your indebtedness to the master next to your signature. And next to that you can put "Istanbul: circa 1962".'

My mother suggested I devote my first panel to the scandal of the moment: Nella's return to Istanbul as a footloose woman. Some weeks had passed since our first sighting, and I still felt shocked. In mid-September, we had gone with the gang to Kilyos, on the Black Sea. Towards sunset, we had found Nella and Sibel lounging louchely in the bar of the beach hotel. They had, they informed us, been hired to 'sing with the band' and had introduced us to their new manager, who, according to my mother and Amy Cabot, looked like some sort of gangster. On the way home, my father and Hector Cabot had chastised them for their '*hausfrau* sentiments' and called on them to muster 'some fellow feeling.' Sibel and Nella had been pushed 'beyond the pale' by their irresponsible husbands. 'How would you like it, if we did the same to *you*?'

In the first panel of my final series, I depicted the shock encounter at the beach hotel, with Nella and Sibel perched on their bar stools, with the wreaths of smoke rising from their cigarettes fashioned into halos. My father and his friends were kneeling at their feet, while the gangster, now enhanced with a narrow mouth and protruding shark-like teeth, looked on, and the band waited on the stage, slump-shouldered, and the wives sat in alarmed seclusion, clutching their children. Behind them was Baby, whose thought balloon said, 'Now Sibel, *she's* got something. But Nella? That girl can't hold a tune!'

My second split panel depicted the argument in the car and the great silence that night at home with my father frowning squarely in his arm chair, and us children huddled on the sofa with our mother beneath thought clouds dark with question marks.

The third panel showed my father and Hector Cabot racing around town with a headless chicken. The fourth portrayed what was supposed to be going at just that moment, as we sat with my mother on our balcony on that sultry Sunday afternoon. *High Noon at Nazmi's*, I'd called it. Because it was at Nazmi's that my father and Hector had arranged to have their preliminary meeting with Nella's soon-to-be-ex husband, and their very definitely ex-friend Rex. To this I had added a few banners: *You goddamn hypocrite! Cough up the money or else*!

And now, as we made the most of the warm sun on our beautiful balcony, I began planning my fifth panel, which would depict the trip we'd make the next weekend to Sibel's summer house in Büyükada. The purpose was to stand guard while she and Nella brokered some kind of deal with their exes.

I was searching for the golden mean when I spied the familiar white ship sailing down the Bosphorus. My mother had already seen it, and it was at her suggestion that we jump to our feet and wave at the stick figure who might be our friend Sergei, the ship's librarian.

The stick figure did not wave back, and neither did the one with the submachine gun at the bow. As I watched the ship sail on towards the point of the wild currents, I scanned its decks for other signs of life, and that was when noticed how low it was in the water.

I said nothing, but my mother could see a question forming, just by looking at my forehead. She sat me down, to give my tired legs a rest. She told me to shut my eyes so that I could feel the warmth of the last sun of the season. I kept my eyes closed as I drank my linden tea. I let the sea breeze ruffle my hair as I waited for the rowboats that would spread out across the water in just a few hours, each one with a father and a son and a lamp and a net for catching the *lüfer* that would be racing down from the Black Sea after sunset, as they'd always done, every October, since the beginning of time. I waited for the blue in the Bosphorus to darken and the sun to set fire to the windows lining the Asian shore.

I did my deep breathing, while in the haze beyond the brown and rolling Asian hills, I thought I saw the faint outlines of a mushroom cloud that had the same shape as Khrushchev's bald head, until it, too, faded into the haze.

Still my breathing wasn't right, and I could feel my heart racing so I limped into the kitchen. I stood there until my mother turned around to ask, 'Are you feeling better now, darling? Is there anything else I can do?' I cleared my throat. I lowered my head, and asked her to tell me the story. 'Which one', she asked. 'The one that brought us here', I said. And Violet chimed in.

There was a sigh before she relented. A glance out the

window. She put down whatever dish she'd been washing, while, out on the balcony, Violet and I pulled our best deck chairs to the far edge, saving the one with the most cushions for her.

I could feel my heart warming, melting even, as she joined us on the balcony, and thanked us for the ottoman we had furnished for her tired feet, and gazed for some minutes at the patch of Bosphorus that had just turned from pink to silver, and smiled at the haze on the horizon, which did not look at all like a mushroom cloud, or indeed Khrushchev's head, at least not to her.

And after she had told us the story that had brought us here, she treated us to what would be our last private concert: first my sister's song, and then mine. As the last notes died away, we heard a strangled whimper from the cobblestone street below.

We peered down to see Sergei, shivering inside a striped towel. Silently, unsmilingly, my mother inspected him. Then, she waved for him to come up.

When I opened the door, Sergei's head was bowed, and his hair damp. Beneath the striped towel I could see a sopping wet suit.

'Oh Sergei. Just look at you. Girls, go run this man a hot bath.'

He followed her into the living room in his squelching shoes. His head was still bowed and his teeth were chattering when we returned from the bathroom.

'Girls, I think we need to make this man a hot toddy, to warm his bones.'

'With whisky or without?' I asked, and Sergei said 'Please! Please! I must not trouble you.'

'Perhaps he would prefer vodka,' I suggested.

In the end he accepted a linden tea.

We watched him take his first sip. And then another, and another. He looked up at my mother, who was as far across the room as the room would allow, sitting demurely with her hands folded and her eyes downcast.

'Am I dreaming?' whispered Sergei. 'Is it you I see, oh fair lady?'

'Actually,' I said, 'You should be able to see all four of us.'

Sergei extended a damp hand to pat me on the head. He retrieved it to hit his forehead. 'I am lost!' he cried. 'We are all lost!'

'Perhaps you'd better explain to us what happened,' my mother said.

'Did you not see me, on the ship? Did you not wave? In fact beckon?'

My mother's only answer was a slight tilt of the head.

So I spoke for her. I said, 'We did see someone, but we weren't sure it was you. We waved just in case.'

Rolling his eyes to the ceiling, joining his hands as if in prayer, he moaned, 'Just in case? I have risked my life, my limb, and the motherland, just in case?' He began to sob. In the background, we could hear the bath running.

'The ship,' I said.

'What of the ship, my little one?'

'It was low in the water.'

He nodded heavily.

'Were you hiding something?'

Another nod.

'Were there weapons under the deck?' I asked. 'And marauding bands?'

He hung his head. 'It seems that you already know everything.'

'Nonsense,' said my mother. She went into the bathroom to turn off the water. On her way out, she stopped in the doorway with her arms akimbo. She told Sergei that his bath was ready in almost the same voice she used for my brother. 'But first why don't you tell us what you came here to say.'

He was still in the bath when my father returned from Nazmi's. My mother took him straight out to the balcony and kept looking over her shoulder, as if to make sure we children weren't listening. By then I was perched on the window pane in their bedroom, concealed by the curtain, except perhaps for my feet.

I didn't hear much of what my mother said about Sergei's strange tale until my father raised his voice, to shout, 'He said what?'

'What he *said* . . .' my mother's voice had a familiar steely edge. 'What Sergei said in actual fact was that he was already suffering from a crisis of conscience.'

'So he didn't actually throw himself overboard and swim to shore, risking an international incident, because he's madly in love with you.'

'Darling, please! I mean, honestly. How could he be madly in love with me? The man's a fruitcake.'

'I don't like you using that word.'

'Why not? Everyone else does. Even he does.'

'I still don't like it. It's . . .'

'Just not me?'

'Don't put words in my mouth,' my father snapped. 'Just tell me what the fruitcake said.'

She lowered her voice. I didn't need to hear this part, having heard it already. Even so, I hoped she was leaving out the overtures. Sergei's declaration of undying devotion. His eternal respect for her marriage vows, her fine husband, and her saintly children. His awareness of his own base nature. His shame and despair at knowing that my mother, a paragon of innocence and virtue, knew how often and how basely he'd succumbed to the animal urge. My mother's protestation: 'That's no way to talk about Baby.' Sergei's slamming of his hand against his forehead. 'No. As always, my sweetness, you are right. That is no way to talk about Baby. It is my own animal urge that I'm decrying. It is from the depths of my innermost heart that I shall now speak.'

I hoped my mother wasn't repeating that part. I hoped she'd skipped to when, after again declaring his undying devotion, he'd told my mother and by default the rest of us, that his heart, in response to her pure beauty, had instructed him to betray his sacred motherland. And now he was embarked on a dangerous course.

Yes, this was the part my mother must have jumped to – the part when Sergei laid out Khrushchev's secret ruse in some detail: the number of ships heading for Cuba, and the number of missiles. The troops – 40,000 in all. And the arctic outfits in which they were now roasting below deck, just to put us Americans off the scent.

'He told you *that*?' my father bellowed. And then, 'Why the hell did this fruitcake tell you that?'

'I imagine,' said my mother, 'that he wanted me to pass on the warning.'

'The warning.'

'Yes, well, as he said, President Kennedy is going to be very unhappy indeed, when he hears about it. So . . .'

'Let me just get this absolutely straight.' My father cleared his throat, always a bad sign. 'Going back to the top now, this clown is so besotted with you that he jumps off a ship to warn you about the secret troops it is carrying to Cuba, and – do stop me if I have this wrong – he is also suggesting that you now pick up the phone and warn Kennedy.'

My mother coughed lightly, another bad sign. 'Actually,' she said, 'that was not the name he mentioned.'

'Oh don't tell me he asked you to pass this on to Leo Guttman. Did he? Oh for God's sake. Why can't they just let go of that name? Where did they get it from in the first place?'

I cringed, thankful that they couldn't see me.

'The moment this fruitcake gets out of the bath, he's leaving. He can't stay here,' my father announced.

My mother, sounding haughty now, and said, 'I couldn't agree more. I hope you can understand that I did nothing to invite this.'

'Let's hope that's true,' said my father. He asked her if she'd spoken to 'that woman', by which he meant the Admiral's wife. 'Let her handle it. For Christ's sake, it's her job. If this man is trying to defect, then he should be going to them, not us.'

'Actually, I did suggest that,' said my mother. 'But Sergei wasn't having it.'

'Why the hell not?'

'He's not trying to defect, you see. He's just trying to make contact with something called the No Camp.'

'Did you say the No Camp?'

'Yes, that's what I said. The No Camp. I'm sure that's what he called it. Yes, I am. Apparently, there is a No Camp in the Kennedy cabinet. They keep themselves to themselves, no traitors there, but apparently they never wanted Kennedy to send the Jupiters, which are missiles, I think, to Turkey last year, and if he hadn't, Khrushchev wouldn't have fixed on this wild idea of sending his missiles to Cuba, and we wouldn't be in this mess today. That's what he said, anyway. He said you knew all about this No Camp. Do you?'

'Only from the fruitcake himself,' said my father grimly.

'And did he also tell you that Leo Guttman is related to someone in the No Camp?'

A slamming of a fist. 'Oh for Christ's sake! He's not still carting around that same pile of shit as last winter!' Standing up, and jabbing his finger at my mother, he said, 'We can't get mixed up in this. It's insanity. You call that woman up right now. Tell her to come down and take this fruitcake off our hands.'

I heard a creaking floorboard, and when I parted the curtains, I saw Sergei, who was standing uncertainly in the doorway, gazing out at the balcony and who did not look too impressive in my father's oldest and most wrinkled corduroy suit.

Wordlessly, with just a nod in the direction of my parents, he asked for my take on the scene outside. I shook my head. He stepped back inside. I was back behind the curtains when I heard the front door open and then close again.

The next day, when I asked my mother what was happening, and what were we going to do now, to foil this new plot, she just said, 'Nothing.' When I asked, but what about Sergei, what about his secret, and shouldn't we be telling our great president before it was too late, she just said, 'It's really none of our business.' I had often made a phone call on her behalf if she was dreading it, and now I offered again. I could speak to Kennedy's secretary and hand the phone over after she put us through to the wise statesman. At this she sighed, and cupped her fingers around her face until she'd recomposed it. 'The moment I know something, darling, you'll be the first to know but in the meantime, I am asking again for your understanding, and your silence.'

And my ears, she conceded later. And my eyes. And my very, very fine hand. 'Remember. You are not just the artist of our grand adventure. You are our scribe.'

There was something in her voice, though. Something listless, or agitated, or just fed up with saying the same thing to me over and over.

Why was she sitting there, instead of taking action?

Why was she shutting me out?

33

The Summit

For days, nothing happened. Then, on Friday night, my father came home to announce that we were not the only ones planning to visit Nella the next day in her hide-away on the island of Büyükada. Now everyone knew she was holed up in Sibel's summer house there. And tomorrow her 'soon-to-be-ex-husband' was heading out to see her with his 'full phalanx' of spies.

'Nella has asked me to get out there as early as possible,' my father said.

'Just you?' my mother asked.

'Naturally I told her it would be all of us,' my father said. In a sterner voice, he added, 'Do you honestly think I would leave you and the kids alone with that fruitcake still at large?'

I couldn't hear what my mother said next. But her voice was firm.

'I'm sorry,' my father replied. 'But can you imagine how I felt when . . .'

'Hush,' said my mother. 'Hush.'

What were they not telling me?

I found out the next morning. Our ferry was pulling away from the Galata Bridge, and passing beneath Topkapı Palace and Aghia Sophia and the great mosques, when suddenly there was Dora, sitting on the bench next to me. At first she wouldn't explain why she was there. Then she announced that she and her mother (who was out on the deck, smoking a cigarette) were joining us for lunch. 'Actually, we weren't invited,' Dora admitted. 'But we decided we were needed. It's going to be tense! Nella's already calling it a Summit!'

Then, in a hoarse whisper, Dora brought me up to date, telling me a lot of things I didn't want to know about Sergei because, frankly, I felt the same way as my mother: the more days that passed without our hearing his name, the better.

Except now I found out that my mother had been hearing his name plenty of times. According to Dora, she had even seen him. Or rather, Sergei had seen her. Early that Thursday morning, he had planted himself in St Antoine's, as he had been doing every Thursday morning, with the knowledge that my mother regularly went into town on a Thursday, on the pretext of buying bacon, but really to pray in secret to her God. Having guessed correctly, and caught Grace in the act, Sergei had followed her out to the street, only to lose her in the crowd. He had then hijacked Dr Abrakadabra's magic truck and pursued my mother down the entirety of İstiklal Caddesi, proclaiming his devotion over the megaphone, and promising to do everything in his power to dismantle the Cuban missiles and send them back to where they belonged – or bust. But then – right in the middle of a sentence – he had fallen silent, and that was the end of it. He might as well have vanished from the face of the earth.

'Good riddance,' I said.

To which Dora replied, 'Goodness! If I didn't know you better, I'd say you were taking this a bit too personally! People are allowed to fall in love with Grace if they so wish. She's a beautiful woman, and why shouldn't she bask in the sunshine while she can? You father doesn't own her, you know!'

She smiled, superciliously. I tried to smile back as, one by one, my unspoken words exploded: Don't you dare smile about my mother! Don't you dare utter her name! My father may not own her but he loves her!

But already Dora was on to her next news item. 'Don't tell anyone,' she whispered. 'My source said not to breathe a word but apparently Kennedy knows all about the missiles. He finally put two and two together a few days ago, and now Washington is on red alert. Behind closed doors, at least. We're on the brink of a nuclear holocaust. I just thought you'd want to know.'

As the deck trembled beneath my feet, and the tips of my fingers froze, I knew that I wanted my mother to know, too. Somewhere, somehow, we had to find a phone. And call Kennedy. And tell him to stop this madness. There was no time to lose.

But already we were turning around the point. Already my father was on his feet, with my mother standing behind him, my brother in her arms, and my sister hanging on to her skirt. When I tapped her on the shoulder, she just said, 'Please, Mimi. Not now.'

'But it has to be now!'

She must not have heard me, with all those engines rumbling and seamen shouting over each other as they rolled up the gangplanks and tied the ropes.

When we were on firm ground again, I tugged at her sleeve. 'Darling, I meant it,' she said. 'Use your eyes, for once!' There was something hard in her voice, something I wasn't expecting, and it hurt me to hear it, and it was to hide that hurt that I turned my eyes away from her, and towards the ferry, just in time to see the spies walking down the gangplank in single file. First the Admiral, then Rex and Mr Wakefield. Then İsmet. And bringing up the rear, Sibel's husband (or was he an ex-husband by now and what was he doing here with us, if he was still the Ambassador to Egypt?). Next came Sibel with her taciturn son. I did a quick count. With Dora and Delphine, and the Cabots, and Baby, that made seventeen of us heading up to the house together, pretending we were all great friends.

At least, the women did. It unnerved me, to see how good they were at pretence.

Delphine was enthusing about trees that still had leaves on them and the sun poking through the clouds – as if these things were startling. Smiling brightly at nothing in particular, she

195

remarked, 'We could end up with a very fine afternoon, at this rate!'

Amy agreed that there was nothing more wonderful than a warm afternoon in October and my mother exclaimed in agreement before turning to Sibel to ask after Nella's health. As if she cared.

And though she must have known my mother was just pretending, Sibel still said, 'Poor, dear Nella. She has suffered so, but she is strong, maybe even too strong.' After which, Delphine was hypocritical enough to sigh. Had she forgotten her fisticuffs with Nella outside Kulis the previous winter?

Now Sibel linked arms with Dora. 'And how is your new school?' she asked.

'Oh, it's okay, I suppose,' Dora said.

'And love?' Sibel asked. She dug her elbow into Dora's side. Dora giggled.

The men, at least, had fallen into silence. Why was my father's corduroy jacket so wrinkled? Why were Baby's and Hector Cabots equally crumpled? The spies looked expensive in their sleek black overcoats. Why had all five chosen to dress in black? Were they in mourning for the world already?'

White Fang kept reading while he walked, until he bumped into me, accidentally on purpose. 'So,' he said. 'The great artist returns. The chronicler of our times. So tell me: have you moved on to microfilm?'

'Who gave you that idea?'

'I just wondered,' he said. He closed his eyes to yawn, which was why I was the only one out of the sixteen who noticed Nella lurking at the entrance to a side street, almost incognito, in a trench coat that accentuated her hunched shoulders. Her hair was concealed under a tight red scarf. She was wearing dark glasses and glaring at her galoshes as if they held secrets.

As I passed her, she reached out and grabbed me by the arm. I opened my mouth. She slapped a hand over it. We walked in silence until she found a bench.

'There's something I need to ask you,' she said.

But first she had to light a cigarette.

It was then that I heard something. Was it a man rustling in the bushes behind us, or was it a stray cat?

Nella didn't seem to hear because she made no comment. Sucking in on her cigarette and exhaling through her nose, she said, 'I just don't understand, I thought we were on the same side. Whose idea was it to bring the troops?'

'It wasn't anyone's idea,' I said. 'It's just . . . it's just . . .' My teeth were chattering and I was trembling so much that I could barely breathe.

'Washington's on red alert,' I finally managed to say.

'Oh, it is, is it?' She didn't sound like she cared too much, so I continued.

'It's worse than you think! A lot worse! It's so bad that . . .'

'That what?'

'It's . . . it's . . .'

'It's what?'

'One minute to midnight,' I gasped.

'According to who?'

'The nuclear . . . the nuclear . . . the nuclear clock!'

'Are you *serious*?' Nella cried, tossing her cigarette to the ground. 'They told you *that*? The bastards. *Honestly*! Do they have no shame? You listen to me,' she said, as she rubbed her cigarette into the ground. 'If those guys think that damn clock of theirs is going to shut me up, they have something else coming!'

Sibel's summer house was a cube of steel and glass squeezed between two unpainted Ottoman mansions and as Nella pulled me down the garden path, I could see right through the house to the veranda where a maid was setting out food and drinks on a long table while Sibel rushed in and out with chairs. The unexpected visitors milled about uncertainly, their backs to the cypress trees through which I glimpsed patches of sky and sea.

And a shadowy figure, just beyond the garden wall.

Who was he? Was he trying to spy on us or was he trying to run away? I turned to see what Nella made of this strange, elusive shadow, but she was too busy looking for her soon-to-be ex-husband. Spotting him in a huddle at the end of the terrace, flanked by his fellow spies, she denounced him as a lowly coward. 'Look at you! For shame! You can't even talk to your own soon-to-be-ex-wife without surrounding yourself with heavies! Well, let me just tell you: I am not afraid. You do not intimidate me one bit. As for that nuclear clock of yours. You know where you can put that one. Don't you?'

'Now let's be reasonable. Isn't that what we're here for?' Rex was saying, the heat rising to his cheeks. Mr Wakefield called for calm and invited us all to sit around the table like the civilized people he knew us to be. After Sibel had poured *rakı* for the grown-ups, and Baby had knocked back two full glasses, Rex said his piece.

'So . . . well . . . let's begin by agreeing the ground rules. The point of us all coming out here this afternoon is that we are reasonable people.'

But Nella wasn't falling for that and soon Rex wasn't either. It wasn't long before his speech took a different turn and he was accusing her of returning to Istanbul to ruin his career. Why was she singing when she couldn't keep in tune? Her new friends were goons. To which Nella said, 'How interesting. Goons or not, they did help her make the rent. How else was she to survive now that he had cut her off?'

Here Delphine jumped in to say that despite her troubled personal history with Nella, she wasn't going to let another man get away with the same treachery she herself had suffered. Jabbing her finger at Rex, she said, 'Leave us in the lurch, fine! Do us out of our rightful inheritance. But by golly, you are *not* going to tell us how to keep a roof over our heads!'

'Keep this up,' Nella said, 'and you'll be sorry. You have no idea how much embarrassment I can cause you in this very city, with those gangsters as you call them. Everywhere you go, everyone you meet . . . Wherever I go, I promise you, *I shall be singing off-key*!'

Rex said something under his breath. My father, catching

it, rose to his feet, fists clenched. Hector held him back. Baby downed his glass of *rakı*, and poured himself another.

Sibel tried to restore order but Nella fended her off. 'Let go of me, why don't you. We're here to cut a deal. We want it all settled. Where their turf ends and where ours begins. What missiles we intend to send their way if they don't cooperate.'

Mr Wakefield cleared his throat. 'Please,' he said. 'Girls.'

'Girls? We are not girls!' Nella said.

'Ladies.'

'Not ladies either!'

'Then allow me to call you gentlewomen and call it a day so that we can turn our attention to more important matters. Like this crisis.'

'So what are you saying here?' Nella now demanded. 'We can't talk about the gross injustices visited by all the societies of the world, from the beginning of time, against the female sex because you guys . . . *you guys* . . . have manufactured another crisis?'

'Now Nella. Honestly!' Mr Wakefield said. Do you genuinely believe that to forge peace all we have to do is join hands and sing *Ring around the Rosie*? Do you think the missiles will melt away because the gentler sex has risen up, united, to stun us with the beauty of a single, irrefutable force?'

'Honestly,' repeated my mother. All heads turned to stare at her. She lowered her gaze and did not speak again.

Why not? What was she waiting for? How much lower did humankind have to stoop before she dropped her mask and said something?

What was she thinking? Why had she shut me out? Why, when I tapped her on the shoulder, did she just brush my hand away?

When I dug my elbow into her, she said it again. 'Oh, honestly.'

Honestly what? I wanted to know. But she wasn't about to tell me. With an abruptness that I'd never seen in her, she rose from the table and ordered me to follow her to the other end of the terrace. 'Now you listen to me. It is time for you to pull yourself together. And to calm down.'

'But I can't! I can't! We're running out of time.'

'Exactly,' she said. 'So stop wasting it.'

'What are you going to do, though?'

'You leave that to me.'

'Why won't you let me help you?'

'If you want to help me, you'll go straight inside, and sit down with Sinan, and do that sketch you should have started hours ago.'

She pushed me towards the door. Not very gently.

White Fang looked up from his book as the door swung shut behind me. 'Looking for your little satchel, I assume?'

Not seeing it, I asked, 'Where is it? Where did you put it?'

'Much as I would have liked to put it somewhere, I could not have done so,' White Fang said.

'Why not?'

'Because. It just so happens that I am not the one who stole it.'

In the commotion that followed – the house search, the veranda search, the street search, the examination of every bush alongside it and the slow, jagged procession back to the pier – White Fang refused to change his story. It was not his fault that I was delusional, he said. I could sob and moan all I liked, but the truth was the truth. 'And the truth, my dear Watson, is that this woeful creature had no satchel with her when she stepped off the ferry. And we can deduce from that, that she had no sketchbook with her, either.'

He had noticed, he said, because their absence was remarkable. He had never seen me without them. He'd assumed, of course, that I had left them at home for once. He'd hoped, that at long last I had seen the utter pointlessness of chronicling adult stupidity, especially on what could be the last sunny afternoon for all eternity. He'd only asked me indirectly anyway. In an age such as ours, how else could he keep his mind sharpened? He had thought it more amusing to drop hints.

And yes, like me, he had seen something lurking in the bushes. But unlike me, he had identified shadows. Not spies.

What I needed more than a sketchbook, White Fang announced, was a firmer grasp of reality.

'Oh, for God's sake,' Mr Wakefield said. 'Put her out of her misery. Tell me where you hid the poor girl's satchel.' When White Fang said nothing, he grabbed him by his collar and marched him off to the station master. They went inside his shack, and when they emerged, I could see my satchel in Mr Wakefield's hands.

*

It was the end of our long day trip to Büyükada. We were back on the ferry, returning to the city. According to my Mickey Mouse watch, it was 5.17. My sister and brother were asleep on the benches across the aisle and I'd been parked with them. The adults had gone off in search of food and drink they did not need. I didn't mind. I was grateful for the time alone, and each time my eyes fell on the sketch book spread across my lap, a wave of abject gratitude passed through me.

How exactly had I mislaid it? We had travelled together to all four corners of the Mediterranean, and not once had we parted company. But today . . . It must have been Dora's news. It must have distracted me. The red alert.

And now I was going to do what my mother had suggested and record that story so that next time – and there would be a next time – because the world was not about to end, because she was going to spring into action, any minute now . . . Another surge of panic clouded my line of thought, but then, it came back to me. Yes, that was it. That was what I had promised her. I would sit here and record the whole Summit, from start to finish, and the next time I lost all hope and faith, I could turn to these pages, and see how on Saturday, October 21st, I had lost hope and faith – and my sketch book – only to see them triumphantly restored.

I was not going to waste more than one panel for that ugly,

ugly scene on the veranda but I would find a way to squeeze them all in: Sibel with her hands on her head, the spies to her right and to her left, Nella, flanked by her defenders. Delphine at the far end, eyes as bright as a hungry bird's, and inside, next to the window, Dora playing with my brother and Sinan hiding behind his new book which was called *The Devils*.

A second panel for the moment when I first noticed the sketch book missing. A third for the hunt. I would make the spies look shifty, and the same went for the shadow in the bushes, which was not just a shadow no matter what White Fang said. In my sketch I would make this clear by giving him a hat.

I would put myself in the lower right-hand corner, caught inside a jagged lightning bolt, clutching the pieces of my heart. In the upper left hand corner, I would draw the nuclear clock.

The fourth panel would capture the happy moment of recovery. Somehow I would find a way of showing how the frantic hunt for my sketchbook had brought out our team spirit and how all the adults had somehow forgotten their differences and were friends again. My mother was right in wanting me to immortalize that moment. However, to make it clear that I didn't have high hopes for that fragile peace, I would save the lower left-hand corner for White Fang. I would show him sulking next to a fly in some ointment.

Next, a panel for our triumphant procession by horse and carriage to the centre of the island, and our walk up to the old monastery at the top of the island's highest hill. With my mother and me, bringing up the rear. I might need to make this a double panel to convey the monastery's unparalleled vistas. And the clouds gathering over the hills of the mainland. Still hours away.

The next panel would be for the things my mother said when we sat down on the bench to feast on that view: In one balloon I would put her hope about me learning from a fright that had, in the end, brought no loss or damage. In another I would put her promise that nothing bad would come from this missile thing, so long as we didn't let it distract us. In a third balloon I would put her assurance that the missing sketchbook had been a blessing in disguise because it had brought the tedious Summit to a speedy end, and not a moment too soon. I would arrange the speech balloons around the tops of the trees we had passed on our way downhill. Next to the shadow with the hat that we both saw lurking behind the bushes, and identified beyond a shadow of a doubt as Sergei, a speech balloon would show: 'Honestly. What is wrong with these people? Will this nonsense never cease?'

And then, in the final, glorious panel, the thing that had not happened yet. My mother putting an end to all this nonsense forever, and setting these silly people straight.

I could see the entire sequence in my mind. But could I fit all those panels on a single page, as my mother had suggested? While I sat on the bench in the ferry saloon, watching the rain pelt the sea outside, I longed to ask her but only when the time was right. When she was back inside the salon with me, her mission accomplished.

Meanwhile I sat across from my tormentor, White Fang, who still thought I was a baby for crying about my sketchbook. Next to him was Dora, whose eyes kept searching the spaces behind me. White Fang had just embarked on his seventh *gazoz* and his fifth toasted cheese sandwich which he chewed pensively, as if composing an insult.

It was 5.39. The waves outside were choppier, but the rain had stopped. I kept my head turned away, and my eyes fixed on the seagulls flying with our ferry, swooping low only to fall back. I pushed away something I didn't want to think about. About what my mother had said. That Dora wouldn't want to be my friend now that she was a real teenager.

The window next to me was smudged. Whenever the sun broke through the clouds, I could see the imprint of a hand. It blurred my view of the seagulls, so I moved closer to the window, and that was when I saw my mother, standing on the windswept deck. Behind her the sea glinted like wet slate, and across its expanse, I could see the domes and minarets of the Old City.

She was talking to the spies. All five of them. She was giving them a piece of her mind. They met her wrath with shoulders stooped and heads politely bowed. Only in their hands did I see their astonishment. The Turks held theirs clasped together but were unable to keep them still. The Americans patted their coats.

Never before had I seen her so sure of herself, not outside the house, certainly not facing five men in fedoras, and though I could not read her lips, I knew that she was saying to them what she'd already said to me, but with all the fire of the terrible beauty she had hidden inside her for so long. Once upon a time she had looked up to these men. She had trusted them to keep the world safe. Now she has seen, with her own eyes, how they operated. *And honestly.* The Hardy Boys could have done a better job.

I knew she was telling them that she was glad to have made their acquaintance and that she knew for sure that the Cold War was not a real war. It was a myth, but without gods and goddesses you could believe in. It was a string of suspicions and counter-suspicions, an endless inflation of second guesses, with each festering lie giving birth to yet another, until we arrived at today, the 21st of October 1962, when the stockpile of lies had reached proportions so epic that they thought nothing of purloining the sketch book of a child who happened to be her mother's eyes and ears. She told them that the least they could have done was help us get this work of beauty to our president before it was too late. And if it was too late already, if this crisis did eventually culminate with the annihilation of all the creatures on this earth except perhaps for cockroaches, well, they would have only themselves to blame.

The sketchbook. Just to say the word set my heart thumping. I reached for the buckle on my little leather satchel. I opened the warm leather flap and felt for the familiar roughness. Yes, it was still in there, its secrets intact. I stared out of the smudged window and saw my mother railing magnificently against these five men whose fat feet were planted on the deck. I saw behind them the city that had survived human error for more than two thousand years. My mother had her arms akimbo. She had put her proposal to them, and now, with bashful nods, they were agreeing to her request to send us to Washington and to arrange a meeting with our great president. Me and my mother and my sketchbook with all its secrets that would remain invisible until that fateful moment when we were standing in the Oval Office and I lit the first match.

Had she seen me through the smudge in the window? Was she beckoning for me to join her, so that we could seal the deal together? I jumped to my feet and rushed outside, my sketchbook still in my hand. Her eyes were on the door before I even reached it. She flicked me a quick smile, before returning to the spies, secure in the knowledge that it didn't matter if they'd put their paws on my sketchbook, because our secrets were still safe. Our invisible notes had gone undetected. Whoever had purloined my sketchbook earlier in the day had seen only the drawings of the ruins and museums we had visited, and the hotels and ships and train compartments where we had rested our tired heads, and the storms which we had turned into glorious parties that people would be talking about until the day they died.

The ferry was turning into Kadiköy, our last stop in Asia. Soon we would be across the Bosphorus and riding home across the Galata Bridge. As passengers streamed past me, I watched the spies regroup. William Wakefield brought out a packet of Marlboros. He offered it round, looking deeply into the eyes of the other four men as he held up his lighter to White Fang's father, and İsmet, and Rex, and finally the Admiral. Each man inhaled deeply and looked up at the sky. One at a time, they lowered their heads. I thought I could read in their faces their new admiration for the strong and confident figure that was my mother – with her arms locked in front of her and her great mane of black curls lifted by the wind. A red scarf I had never seen before billowed over her sleek black dress, which she had brought for grand occasions, and had not worn once, until today.

34

The reckoning

It is now the evening of Saturday, the 21st of October, 1962, and I am living in the present, like my mother suggested, ready to fling each spent day over my shoulder to make way for the wonders of the next one. My sketchbook is safe in the satchel where it belongs, and I'm reading in bed, but here comes my mother through the door.

'Your father wants to see you,' she says. As I climb out of bed, she averts her eyes. Am I in some kind of trouble?

When I enter the darkened living room, I see my father, ominously still in the pool of lamplight that makes his chair look like a throne.

'Sit down, darling,' my mother says.

My father watches as I sink into a chair. 'I heard something rather disturbing on the ferry just now.'

'Who from?' I ask.

'William. Rex. The Admiral. And of course Sibel's husband. Plus his sidekick. Is that enough?'

Struggling to keep my voice level, I ask what they told him.

'I think you know,' my father says.

He can, I think, see the gusts of dread blowing through me. Grimly, he waits for them to settle.

'So,' he says. 'Tell me exactly how you came to decide I was some sort of emissary from a shady-because-imaginary Washington cabal known for short as the No Camp.'

'The No Camp?' I squeak.

'Yes,' he says. 'The No Camp.' He folds his arms, clears his throat.

'Don't let me hold you up . . .' he says.

But where to begin? The horror, the horror. The ship, and its bowels. Dora and her warnings . . .

'It wasn't my idea,' I say. 'It was something . . .'

'Something Dora heard from her mother?'

'Actually, I think that maybe it was . . .'

'Who?

'I'm not sure.'

'Oh for God's sake.'

I gather up my courage. 'It could have been Mr Wakefield who told her.'

'Her.'

'Dora. They talk all the time, you know.'

My father leans forward. 'Do you have any idea, any idea at all, how much trouble you have caused?'

At last, my mother steps in. 'I'm not sure if you can blame . . .'

My father raises his hand. 'Gracie. Let me handle this.' He leans forward. 'Let's begin with this mission you dreamed up. What exactly was its purpose?'

'Peace,' I say. 'On earth,' I add.

'Aha. How admirable. And how exactly did you plan to achieve this lofty aim?'

'By melting people's hearts.'

'What the hell is that supposed to mean?'

'It means . . . it means . . .'

'Darling,' says my mother. 'Perhaps I can explain.' And she tries. And her intentions must be good, but I am upset to hear her tell my father that it was an idea she came up with, all the way back in America, originally with Mr Guttman, which is why he had given me the sketchbook. 'She was just so terrified, darling, it seemed like an innocent idea.'

'What did?'

'Oh, please don't make a mountain out of this.'

'Then don't make me pull out every awful detail. What is this idea that you cooked up with Mr Guttman more than two years ago without bothering to tell me?'

'It wasn't an idea,' I say. 'It's just that . . . when he gave me the sketchbook . . . and the satchel . . . he told me . . .'

'Told you what?'

Under my father's beady gaze, I can hardly grasp the wisps of desire and determination that made me decide to . . . do what?

'Perhaps we can begin,' my father says, 'with the object.'

'The object?'

'What you were hoping to achieve with this mission of yours.'

I steal a glance at my mother.

Can I tell him?

My mother seems to read my mind. She reaches for my hand.

'Just tell him, darling. Tell him the truth.'

'Are you sure?'

She nods.

I face my father. 'It's about beauty,' I say.

'About *beauty*?' he says. He turns to my mother. 'Is she serious?'

My mother casts her eyes downwards.

'So,' says my father, returning to me. 'Tell me what beauty has to do with all of this.'

'If you could just tell me what you're angry about,' I wail, 'maybe I could tell you!'

'Fine then, I will. Somehow, you managed to persuade everyone in this whole goddamn city that Mr Guttman is some kind of subversive, some kind of evil puppeteer.'

'No, I didn't! I just said . . .'

'You just said. You just said. Whatever you said . . . most particularly your postcard to poor Mr Guttman . . .' He pauses here to laugh hollowly 'I don't think I mentioned this, Gracie, but the day before we left for Egypt, Mimi sent poor Leo a postcard via the *diplomatic pouch* . . .'

'Oh, *no*!' says my mother. 'I didn't know *that*!' She pauses to glare at me. 'What . . . what did the postcard say?'

'As preposterous as this might sound, what she said was . . .'

'Only Mr Guttman can know what I said! It was private! I even sealed the envelope!'

My father sighs. The silence presses in. He clears his throat. 'Let me try again.' He leans forward, and I think he is going to whisper so the force of his voice hits me hard.

'Do you realise that, thanks to you, our poor friend Mr Guttman was dragged in by some goons for questioning, not once, not twice, but three times this year? Do you realise that thanks to your damn postcard, and no doubt with some help from Delphine and her minions, thanks to these pea-brained busy-bodies, my dear, dear friend, without whose kindness and encouragement we never would have made it here in the first place, is now under suspicion of *treason*?'

'For what?' I ask stupidly.

'For trying to set up secret links between the peace lovers of the Soviet Union, whoever the hell they are, and this goddamn No Camp, which I am pretty sure has never existed, if for no other reason than it was born in the overworked mind of a nine-year-old.'

'I'm ten now,' I say.

And he says, 'Exactly.' He stares at me until I think his eyeballs are going to pop. 'Do you realise that these people have been watching my every move, and I mean, every move, ever since?'

'That's not just my fault!' I cry.

'Oh, I'm sure it isn't. But tell me, Mimi. Is it true that you've been keeping watch on me, too, and recording the details?'

'Yes, but that was only on the ship, when I still didn't understand . . .'

'About what?'

'About . . . about the beauty part.'

'The beauty part.'

'I still didn't know . . . the truth.'

209

'About what?'

'Our mission.'

'Our *mission*.' My father turns to my mother. 'Tell me, Gracie. Am I losing my mind or is she?'

My mother shakes her head, noncommittally. Why isn't she helping me more?

My father turns back to me. 'So where were we? Oh, yes. I remember. We were on the ship. But at this point you were, apparently, still not clear about the nature of our true mission. So, now what?'

'She asked me to be her eyes and ears!'

In my panic I must have pointed to my mother for now my father turns back to her.

'She was so nervous, the poor thing,' my mother says. 'I just wanted to give her a game to play. To keep her occupied. To calm her down.'

My father knocks his hand against his forehead.

'You set our own daughter to spy on me?'

'Not really,' says my mother. 'Of course not. But darling, it was a harmless game. And anyway, who knows what the fruitcake . . .'

'Don't call him that.'

'You're the one who called him that and now you're standing up for him?'

'I don't have to like a man to stand up for him.' He turns back to me. 'So tell me. When you were tailing me, what exactly did you see?'

'Not much,' I say, and I let my guard down a little. 'I knew they weren't going to make an approach, not on the ship, because the word was out and everyone was watching, but we knew Nella . . .'

'Ah. So now the plot thickens . . .' He turns to my mother. 'So is that what this is really all about? You getting your own daughter to spy on Nella, and on me with Nella, just because of your own goddamn and utterly unjustified suspicions . . .'

'We just didn't want you to get mixed up in anything,' I interject.

'We? Who are we?'

Dora, I say. And William Wakefield, and the Admiral's wife because she was the one who'd warned me, and of course the spies they'd sent on board to watch over us.

'The spies who'd been sent on board to watch us?'

I explain.

My father turns to my mother. 'Can you believe this, Gracie?'

She shakes her head as if she's never heard any of this before, but then I make the mistake of assuring my father that no one could have read anything in my sketchbook on account of my having used invisible ink.

'And who, may I ask, supplied you with invisible ink?'

I look in the direction of my mother who avoids my gaze.

'Jesus Christ. Jesus Christ Almighty. Why do you always do this, Gracie?'

'It was only lemon juice,' she says.

'Lemon juice.'

'I thought it was harmless fun. I really did.'

She did?

'Please, darling, try to understand how young she is. Be reasonable. Poor Mimi was out of her mind with anxiety, and by the time we got on that ship, she was very literally looking for Reds Under Beds, so it seemed like a lovely and harmless way to get her thinking about . . .'

'About what?' my father asks.

'About . . . nicer things.'

'Like beauty.'

'Why not?'

'Why not? I'll tell you why not.' He pointed his jabbing finger at the window and the blackest night beyond. 'It is because of this cockamamie story you two cooked up . . . Yes, Gracie, it was the two of you. Not Mimi alone. I can see that now. It's because of this insane mission that you conjured up to amuse your daughter that we have landed in the middle of an infernal mess. It's because of this goddamn No Camp.'

'No it isn't,' I say. 'It's because of beauty.'

'Oh really?'

'Yes, it is. But the thing is,' I say. 'Sergei is still half one thing and half the other. Beauty hasn't melted him yet.'

'Beauty hasn't *melted* him?'

I try to explain It's no good. 'He still has time, though,' I assure my father. 'Maybe if you could talk to him yourself. Maybe while we're in Washington.'

'What's this about Washington?' my father asks. I remember, too late, that this part of our plan is as yet unconfirmed. 'I mean, you could talk to Sergei yourself, and tell him you're not really angry at him, and then he will come out of the bushes and help us.'

'Help us how?'

'Help us get the missiles back to the Soviet ports they came from.' Recklessly, I add that this is what my mother had instructed him to do.

My father's hands are on his head again. 'Gracie. Am I hearing this correctly?'

'Darling, please. Of course I never said such a thing.'

But she must know that I know she is lying! I – her eyes and ears!

After a silence, my father says, 'So, let's sum things up, shall we? Gracie, you did not tell Sergei to put the missiles back where they came from.'

'No, of course not.'

'But you did tell our daughter – who by your own account is fragile, prone to over-imagining things – you told her that you had sent him on this mission.'

'Do you honestly blame me? Would you rather she was looking at the horizon and looking for mushroom clouds? Somehow, we have to protect the children . . .'

212

35

Nuclear clocks

It is Tuesday, 24th October, the day Kennedy breaks the news to the world. My father hears about his speech from his Turkish colleagues, and though my mother thinks there's no need to know more than the gist of it, my father says, 'No. It's essential for Mimi to hear it straight. Let's start as we intend to proceed.'

Why is it that my legs give in, every time I'm scared? Even after a day in bed, it is dizzying to be upright, but I can just about walk if I keep one hand on a wall.

We have to fiddle with the buttons so long that I am worried we'll miss the fateful broadcast, but at last we can hear the voice of President Kennedy, rising and falling in a sea of static. He tells his *fellow citizens* of the *unmistakable evidence of missile site*s on that imprisoned island, affording the Soviets and the Communist Cubans *a nuclear strike capability* encompassing *the entire Western hemisphere*, accusing them of having transported *weapons of mass destruction in flagrant and deliberate defiance* of their own public promises, *to constitute maximum peril* in a manner that this King of Statesmen can only call *clandestine, reckless and provocative* . . .

The President doesn't mention my name, but I can tell that he's angry.

He doesn't mention Sergei either, and my father says it's probably because Kennedy doesn't know who the hell Sergei is, and even if he did, he wouldn't care.

What can we do then?

'There's really not much we can do, beyond sit and wait.'

Wait for what?

'God only knows.'

But God doesn't exist.

'That's right,' says my father grimly. 'That's the crux of the problem.'

Tuesday turns into Wednesday. The sun rises and sets. The next morning the phone rings, and Violet comes in to tell me that today it isn't Lightie with an outraged and disgusted Keenie listening in on an extension, but Kennedy and Khrushchev. They are both on their way now, to teach me a lesson, she says. I tell her I'm not fooled. I roll over in bed and close my eyes. From time to time a light pierces my drawn curtains, and I think: this is it, the Big One. I hide my head between my knees and wait, while yet another searchlight sweeps across my room.

My mother brings me linden tea, and real tea with cinnamon toast, as well as hot toddies without the whisky, and hot milk with cinnamon and nutmeg, along with a few *New Yorkers* with cartoons that might make me laugh if I care to look at them.

I don't. I can't. How can she expect me to fiddle while Rome burns?

Why is she still here? She should be out there, saving the world.

My legs are so weak now that I can hardly make it to the bathroom, not without leaning on my mother's arm. She says this might be for the best, all things considered. My father listens to the news without me, but keeps me up to date: Kennedy has set up a *Quarantine*, to stop ships reaching Cuba. Kennedy has tightened the Quarantine, and put the nation on the highest alert ever, DEFCON2, to be precise.

This, despite the fact that they don't know what the hell they are doing.

He asks me if I know what *brinkmanship* means.

I don't and he explains. 'So that's what these two madmen are up to.'

Which madmen?

'Kennedy and Khrushchev. Right now, neither of them wants to lose face.'

He explains what that means, too. Then he unravels that *other bogus term, credibility. 'In the last analysis, it's something* only liars worry about.'

I ask him what he thinks might happen next.

'Well the whole point of the Cold War is to make the consequences so awful that neither side dares to take the first step. So for the next few days, they'll huff and they'll puff, and then when the whole world is scared out of its wits, they'll make a back room deal.'

'With the No Camp?'

My father bows his head and sighs.

Alone in bed with my cocoas and my linden teas, my unread *New Yorkers* and wrinkled *Time* Magazines, I think about the Big One that might be there already, above the hills of Asia, and billowing towards us. I imagine my grandmother back seat driving my grandfather as they set out to the doctor for their suicide pills. I see them back in their kitchen, clutching their deathly vials and praying for us to be there, with them, when the sky flashes white.

Coasting into unwilled sleep, I trace the line of hospital ships encircling the long and sinuous shadow that is Cuba. I follow the doctors and the nurses to their gun nests, and when we reach the top, we cup our hands over our eyes. Which are fixed on the horizon.

We pass the news down the deck, for others to take up to the bridge. The captain picks up the phone. In the Oval Office, our President puts down the receiver. He brings his fist down onto his great desk. 'What the hell do they think they're doing?'

He is just thinking out loud. He doesn't know I can hear him. Turning his back on the shadows that conceal me, he ambles over to the window, and I follow. When I look out, I'm expecting to see the lawn where they do the egg roll for children every Easter. Instead I see the jagged edges of an abyss, and smoke rising from a world of ruins.

I forget that I'm hiding.

I turn around to look our President straight in the face.

He folds his arms. He clears his throat and glowers.

'You're Mimi, aren't you?'

I say, I am.

This news does not please him.

He ambles back to his desk. He brings his fist down hard.

'Do you have *any* idea how much trouble you've caused?

*

'Darling.' I hear my mother talking to my father. 'Darling, I hate to bring this up so late in the evening, but I was wondering if we could talk about this truth campaign of yours. I was wondering if it might be time . . . to go a little easier on her.'

'Why?'

'Well, she didn't sleep at all last night.'

'But she's asleep now.'

'Yes, but . . .'

'So what's she been saying?' my father asks.

'It's not what she's saying. It's how she's feeling. She says there's a sour pit in her chest, and when she lies down, her heart starts fluttering . . .'

'I'm sorry if I've frightened you.' My father says this to me later that night, when my mother brings me out to join him in his pool of lamplight.

'It's not you,' I say. 'It's the missiles.'

'That may be true, but I should have explained things better. What I should have emphasised, and this is important, is something I have explained to you already. They can't let this go all the way. They'll find some way to make a deal.'

My mother squeezes my arm.

She smiles at my father who gives her a hopeful look.

She shakes her head.

'Oh, for Christ's sake,' he says.

She smiles at the floor.

'Just tell me then,' says my father. 'Gracie, please. Tell me what to say. In fact, why don't you just tell her yourself.'

'Perhaps that's a better idea all round,' my mother says graciously. She turns to me with a smile. 'What your father wants you to know is that there is actually cause for hope.'

I turn to my father. 'Are the two leaders talking yet?'

'I'm afraid not,' he says. 'The war of words continues.'

'Even in the back room?'

'Who knows. *We* certainly don't because they won't tell us.'

'Maybe we should ask Sergei,' I say.

'I suppose we could, if we knew where he was.'

'Oh, I do.'

'So where is he, then?'

'In the bushes.'

My father lowers his head into his hands.

Later that night, after the shouting match, after my father accused my mother of poisoning my mind with her *capricious myths*, I leave my room to speak to him again. He looks up from his book and his pool of lamplight. 'So how are you doing?' he asks.

I shrug my shoulders.

'You don't have to pretend with me,' he says. 'If you're scared, it's better to admit it.'

I admit it.

'So there now. Do you feel better?'

'Maybe a little,' I say.

'Fear is nothing to be ashamed of,' he tells me. 'Fear is something you just have to face. And you can learn how, Mimi. Just like I did.'

I ask him how, and he tells me a little more than last time about the gunner's nest, and being up there in the middle of a great storm, in the middle of the Pacific, to shoot at five Japanese planes that swooped out of nowhere, through the clouds.

'I thought I was going to die. I thought we were all going to die. But I had been in the bowels of the ship all day, scraping the rush off the walls. I took in a deep breath of sea air, and at that moment I felt more alive than I had ever felt. I could see the planes as clearly as if they were in the palm of my hand.

'And then, as quickly as they had come, the Japanese planes dispersed. It was on my way down that I realised I had forgotten to pray. I never prayed again,' my father says . . .

'You pray all the time, though,' I say. My father looks perplexed, until I remind him of his favoured figures of speech: *I pray to God. God help me. Dear God, what have I done to deserve this child?*

'You're right,' he concedes. 'It only goes to show how deeply I was conditioned.'

He leans forward. 'But you don't have to worry about that. We've never ground fear and blind respect into you, like our parents did. You never had a whole phalanx of teachers and parents and priests warning you of the horrors that would visit you if you set your sights too high. If you so much as asked a question. But you – you are free of all that. You can ask questions. Demand answers. Most important, you can refuse to let anyone, and I mean anyone, including me, including your mother, tell you how to think. Promise me you'll remember that from now on, Mimi. If you forget everything else, remember to *question everything, always* . . .'

'But I do,' I say. 'I think that's my biggest problem.'

'Who told you *that*?'

I do not say who. Perhaps it's my glance in the direction of my mother or the bedroom that gives the game away.

'Dear God,' my father says, shaking his head.

'There you go again,' I say.

He doesn't laugh. Nodding in the direction of the bedroom, he says, 'She's not teaching you to believe in God behind my back, is she?'

No, of course not. 'She'd never dare do something as dangerous as that.'

He takes my hand and leads me back to my bedroom. 'My guess is you'll sleep like a log tonight, if you just give it a try.'

I say I will, if he promises to wake me up if he hears the world is ending.

He promises. 'But on one condition.'

'Next time,' he added, 'something frightens you, you must remember that you are awake and breathing, with eyes sharp enough to see what's really there and a mind sharp enough to tell the difference. There is no better asset than a fearless mind, Mimi. It melts the walls that lock us in.'

'Like beauty?' I ask.

'No,' he says. 'Like truth.' He says that and he sounds like he means it, so I believe him. For a whole day I believe him, and I treasure my mind for its fearlessness, and I accept nothing at face value. Instead I ask questions.

Like, 'Why did you lie to me?'

This is to my mother. She has no answers. She just brings me more linden tea and real tea with cinnamon toast and limp apologies. She meant no harm, she was just trying to help me, and yes, I can go on accusing her of loving Violet more than she loves me, but the truth is she loves all her children equally and just wants us to be happy.

That night I hear her whispering to my father. She's at her wit's end, she tells him. She's tried everything, but she can't find a way to win me back.

'Give her time,' I hear my father say. 'She'll feel better when she's out of bed. Why don't you tell her she has to start trying? Take her down to Bebek tomorrow, so that she can remember she has legs that work. Tell her that she has to, or else she can't come with us to the End of the World party.'

What End of the World party?

I am asking my father. And this time he keeps his side of the bargain, even though it is late at night, and I should be asleep by now, and tells me: 'For the first time ever, and probably the last, Hümeyra is giving her Friday night soirée on Saturday, in defiance of the terror now engulfing the world, as Kennedy and Khrushchev escalate their war of words.'

The truth of the matter, and he knows I'm strong enough to take it, is that Kennedy has given Khrushchev until midnight to back down. What he'll do after that is anyone's guess, but at least we can be sure of one thing.

And what is that?

'When midnight comes,' my father says. 'We'll be with our dearest friends in the world, and we'll be dancing.'

But why will we be dancing? Why can't we stay at home, just us, for a change? If it's the last night of our lives, isn't that where we should be: together as a family? Why are we sitting in this taxi, breathing in these fumes instead? Why do they care about their friends more than anyone? Why doesn't my father understand why I'd ask that? Why does he expect me to be a good sport when the world could end tomorrow?

Why have they left me out here, sobbing in the stairwell? Aren't they worried that someone bad will glance in from the street and grab me?

They heartlessly leave it to Dora to come and find me. But at least, when she has shepherded me up all five flights, she doesn't take me straight in. Instead, she pulls me into her apartment, to wash the tears off my face, and straighten out my hair and tie in a ribbon in it. She pours me a cool glass of water and takes me into her mother's bedroom, pulling two chairs to the window so that we can watch the goings-on next door. 'Just like old times,' she says. But the room is not the same. Not like old times at all. There are more candles in this bedroom than I've seen in my whole life, and every single one is burning. And that makes the room look spooky. And for the first time ever, Delphine's four-poster bed has clean white sheets. Tossed onto the new silken bedspread, emerald green but reflecting rainbows in every ripple, is a bouquet of red roses that Dora picks up so that I can read the card dangling from its ribbon, which is white, like the ribbon in my hair. It says:

'To İsmet. From his adoring Dora. For the world may end, but never our love . . .' She explains what her plan is, taking care to assure me that it is a design to be fulfilled only if nuclear death is nigh. 'Because by then it won't matter that I'm underage. If you follow my drift.'

I cannot follow her drift, not even for a second. All I can follow are her eyes which are fixed on Hümeyra's morning room window, searching for İsmet, only İsmet, while the usual characters swirl past. The Tenor and the Society Photographer. The Translator and the Madame Xenia. Baby flexing his hands. Bunny Evans, pot belly first. Sergei, pursued by his hostess with her armful of shawls. She drapes a yellow one around his shoulders. And then a blue one, around his head. She adds a peacock feather. But for once I do not ask why.

I want to leave this place. I want to leave it forever.

And as soon as I can, I do.

36

But now

But now it's 2012. The world I left behind is dead and gone, swept away and erased. Or rather, cleaned and refurbished.

We have retired from the great room that was once known as the best place in Istanbul for a party, and that Dora has, after four years of hard work, transformed into the Foundation Hümeyra. We have moved across the landing to what was once Delphine's apartment and is now Dora's airy, open plan living space, with its pristine sofas and polished floors, its small but precious carpets, its İznik tiles and burnished copper trays. I gaze through her shining windows and the perfect views they frame, but my heart is in the room this used to be. I ache for Delphine's sunken chairs, and her elderly divans, and the swathes of tarnished scarlet satin draped over them. I ache for the dusty shafts of sunlight, funnelling through the tattered, half-closed brocade drapes . . .

Dora still wears her hair the same way as she did when I first knew her. Lank and shoulder-length, with a fringe that grazes her eyelashes whenever she shakes her head. It is the same dark shade of brown as her probing and appraising eyes. The bones that made her look gaunt as a thirteen-year old have given her distinction in middle age. It is a severe sort of elegance: no make-up. No jewellery. But when she turns to the man on the sofa opposite, she still lights up.

This man is none other than Sergei. His hair still stands

upright, like a brush, but it is white now. The eyes are the same, quizzical, and shining bright.

He sets down his glass, which still looks cold. He looks hard at me, perhaps trying to read my thoughts. Sighing, he glances at his large golden watch: 'So, the countdown has begun,' he says. 'In less than one minute, our party will commence. Unless,' he adds, 'You would prefer to honour the spirit of our absent hostess by being late.'

He winks at Dora in a way that makes me wonder how they became so close. Once again I am reminded of the gap between her and me. Life was just beginning when we went our separate ways, but that was fifty years ago. Fifty years exactly.

An ugly desire overwhelms me. I want to stand up, shake Sergei's hand, kiss Dora on both cheeks, and walk away. How I long to walk away.

I have to remind myself that I am here because others can't be. I am here because I can climb five flights of stairs. I am here because my mother, who has been looking forward to this party since the moment it was mooted, has sent me in her place.

I remember how hard it was to leave the house without her this evening. I imagine how much harder it must have been for her. I recall her parting words. *Don't forget now, you're my eyes and ears, and your father's, and don't forget my speech!*

I remember what my mother said when I suggested that maybe I shouldn't go either. *No, honestly. Go. Go. Dora is expecting you. Dora would be devastated. She's promised me another opening, when I'm stronger. But why don't you take your father with you, at least. He's been so low lately. It would cheer him.*

And my father: *She doesn't mean that. She is just trying to be generous. And even if she means it, it's out of the question. I could never go back there without her. Never.*

His last words, as I head for the door: Don't forget my toast to absent friends!

His call from the balcony: Don't forget to mention each and every one of them!

And so I mustn't forget that I'm not here for myself. I'm here for my mother, and my father, and Dora too. After we have risen from her pristine sofas, and made our way across the landing's newly polished tiles and greeted our already assembled guests in the smokeless, noiseless great room of the Foundation Hümeyra, with his polished floors, and dusted artefacts – after we have admired the views, and the baby grand, and lingered long enough in front of the photograph of my mother singing at the End of the World Party, and commented on her beauty, and the raffishness of the revellers surrounding her, and mingled just long enough to add a few bursts of laughter to the hush, Dora taps the side of her glass, silencing our guests as swiftly as if she had turned a dial, and I bow my head.

Dora gives her speech of welcome with no notes. She speaks first of Hümeyra. Her life and her art. Her flamboyance and her courage. Her legendary soirées. She points towards the morning room and the window through which once she and I had watched them. She talks about the dark ships that slipped past these windows, and the Soviet Consulate that was housed below. She describes sitting with me on the floor of her mother's bedroom, listening to Radio Moscow, struggling to crack its secret codes and unravel its mysteries. When in fact, she says, *we* were the mystery. We were the scintillating people the Cold Warriors could never understand. The bright lights that made them jump off ships in pursuit of truth, beauty, and love.

She says that, and somehow I stay smiling.

Then it is Sergei's turn. His task is to describe the party we are commemorating today. As he launches into his honeyed reminiscence, describing the 'impossible, invisible' world we then inhabited, and the great abyss over which we teetered, about which Dora and I were so astoundingly well-informed, I examine the sparse, attentive crowd that has gathered in a polite semi-circle in the centre of this great room. Most look under thirty; they are all, Dora has told me, involved in the arts. They are the ones who will inherit this room. Once it has taken off its party clothes – once the shawls and the peacock feathers have been returned to storage, and the antique chaise longue and the baby grand to their present owners – this great room will become their haven, to use as they see fit. It was Hümeyra's dying wish, as Dora has just told them, as Sergei has just repeated, in more flowery words – it was her gift to all the bright souls kept young by beauty.

And now Sergei is describing this great room as he remembers it. He is describing the man he was, on the occasion of his first visit. With great, vague flourishes, he takes his bright-eyed listeners through the whole absurd saga. He leaves out the details and the hard facts. There is only the eternal arc: a man is transfixed, a man is undone by beauty and then remade by it. He ends with a poem, written, he says, for the occasion. He recites it with his eyes closed, first in Russian, then in Dora's English translation, and finally, resoundingly, in Turkish. It is like watching a man pray.

How I wish that at this moment I could close my eyes too, close them on the details and hard facts littering the space between us. I wonder what thread in me was severed that night. Why I left this great room so determined never to return.

No mention, tonight, of the golden glow that finally fading or of the price they paid. He misses out the drunken accidents, the decaying marriages, and destroyed careers. The masterpieces that might have lost their lustre, had they ever seen the light of day. The early deaths and the quack doctors that caused them. The later deaths, in hiding and in poverty.

I think of my mother, waiting in her pool of light. I think of my father in his.

I read out my father's toast with its long list of names, and after we have raised a glass to each and every one, I add my mother's name, and my father's, and we toast them too.

And afterwards, as this pale shadow of a party dissolves again into its natural hush, I watch Dora circulate amongst her bright young things, and I ask myself where she gets her strength from, and what drives her. And what possessed her to dress the room like this? What exactly was she hoping to achieve? From the glance she throws me, I think she can read my mind, and it turns out I'm right, because later, much later, when all but a handful of bright young things have said their farewells, when it is just Sergei at one end of the great room, in sombre conversation with his Turkish translator and assorted disciples, and just us two standing at the window, our backs to the city lights, Dora says, 'I thought you would appreciate it. I thought it might take you back.'

She points out the black hood over the bust of Beethoven – 'the same hood Hümeyra placed on the great man for the end of the world party, do you remember?' – and the paintings turned against the wall. She points at Hümeyra's tricycle, at the copper vase into which she poured the remains of drinks and emptied cigarettes whenever Vartui the maid wasn't looking. As she fingers the signature shawls, she asks me if I remember when Sergei tried to hide underneath them. 'This would have been just minutes before midnight, when there was that false alarm about a raid . . .'

'And of course the baby grand where Baby played all night long, and your mother sang. Can't you see them together now?' Dora asks me. And even though I have no memory of that night, I can imagine it, my mother standing with one hand on the piano, Baby bowing before returning to the stool. He is closing his eyes as he lifts his beautiful brown hands above the keys, then opening them wide, then wider still, as he lowers his hands into position.

'Do you realise that the End of the World party was your mother's one and only visit to this great room? I was just flabbergasted when I heard that,' says Dora. 'Not least because over the years that we were renovating the Foundation, when your mother and I talked about this great room, she could remember every last detail.'

'And there, just there,' she adds. She points out the far leg of the baby grand. 'That was where you stayed the entire night.'

'Not all night, surely!'

'You came out when one of us contrived to pull you out. Sergei did, if I recall. And your father, and your mother, and Nella and Sibel, and Vartui with her *böreks*, and I tried . . .'

'When you could pull yourself away from İsmet.'

'Well, I did have hopes in that department, I admit.'

I wait for her to recall the candle-lit bedroom she'd prepared for her deflowering. I wait to hear how the romance faded. Had he promised to wait for her? Had she come back from that gulag of a boarding school to discover that actually, he wasn't her type?

She talks about none of this. Instead she talks about the Foundation, which took so much longer than she originally envisaged because Hümeyra's legitimate heirs initially refused to deal with her informally adopted 'children', especially the son of the fabled trigamist.

She explains that she became involved in the project almost by chance, having taken a leave from her university job in the US to care for her mother, who by then was suffering from emphysema and other mysterious complaints never diagnosed by her quack doctor. Delphine couldn't manage the stairs but still she had refused to move. Dora had had to bring in private nurses and oxygen that cost thousands of dollars.

She tells me about Delphine's deathbed conversion to Protestantism in order to avoid the family plot and to make sure she was buried next to her friends. Fortunately the Anglican padre had refused her suggested epitaph: *Finally – my big scoop*.

'Baby's buried in that same cemetery. Did you know that Mimi?'

I didn't.

Dora says, 'That reminds me.'

She picks the iPod off its stand. 'This might interest you. It's his last known concert, in Moscow, circa 1963. There's no voice, which is a pity. I suppose you could say that, without Grace, he couldn't see the point.'

I recognize the first piece from the first few bars: *If I Die before the Night is Through*.

228

'This is your copy, by the way,' she says, handing me a CD. 'You must take it home to Grace. You must recreate every detail of the evening for her. Do I have your solemn oath?'

Once again, she tells me how tirelessly 'dear Grace' had stood by her and never so passionately than in the aftermath of this party we are commemorating today. In the troubled months before the Admiral's wife and other righteous well-wishers had stepped in and carted Dora off to the gulag boarding school, she and my mother went to church together every week. Do I at least remember that?

How strange. But never mind. The important thing is that my mother is the only person from the entire city of Istanbul who'd stayed in touch.

Which was why, when Dora returned to Istanbul four years ago, they fell right back into their old ways with secret visits to church for as long as my mother could manage them and outings to the new museums. Until my mother's eyes began to fail her, she continued to go with Dora to new cafes. And even when the world began to darken, my mother had retained that uncanny sixth sense. She was the only person in the entire city of Istanbul who noticed when Dora started to sink into despond.

'When was it exactly?' Dora asks herself. 'The autumn before last, I think. The lethal combination of the legacies of Delphine and Hümeyra had again driven me to the brink. Grace was the one, the only one, to pick up on my despair, and the manner of her consolation so ingenious, so astute. We were sitting in this very room, which hadn't yet been cleared. We started off sitting over there, on the stool of the baby grand. Then we moved to the ancient chaise longue, while I continued describing my ruptured and oh so jaded version of the old days. She listened in silence to my lament about grown men and women refusing to face facts, refusing to take the end of the world seriously. As we sipped our linden teas, I recalled my strange and, let's be frank, wholly inappropriate and, yes, *demented* infatuation for İsmet, and under Grace's solemn, all-accepting gaze I dared to ask out loud what the *hell* I'd thought I was doing, pretending to myself that the fate of the world lay in our teenage hands . . .'

Taking my hand now, Dora asks, 'And do you know what Grace said after I had poured out my soul? She told me that she had watched me most carefully throughout the End of the World Party, from the moment of her arrival in this great room to the moment of her departure. She gave me an assurance that – for me, at least – it had been a truly momentous evening. She went so far as to say I had savoured every moment, living each with the utmost intensity, and in the present tense, in harmony with all those giddy blyth spirits in my midst . . . Those were Grace's own words. On that evening half a century ago, in that roomful of spies with their silent but visibly palpitating terror of what might lie in wait, I alone had held my nerve, she said. I alone had gazed out the window and seen beyond the monuments of the Old City and the hills of Asia to the shimmering secrets that the horizon still nurtured. I alone had taken communion with the stars.

'And then . . .' Dora squeezes my hand. '. . . and then Grace told me why she thought my work on this Foundation had been so troubling for me. She said it was not Hümeyra's dust or Delphine's clutter that stood in my way, it was my own dust, my own clutter, my own urn anguish, honed and polished during my long and lonely years in that boarding school when I sought to understand why I had been banished from paradise. Of course she knew exactly what she was talking about because she too had lost so much on that same day. For Grace too, the party had marked the end of the world. At least, her world.'

'In what way?' I surprise myself by the sharpness in my own voice.

Dora smiles, and I think I see pity in her eyes. 'Well, she never sang again, did she?'

'Can that be true?' I rack my brain. Stranger than the thought of her never singing again is the thought that I can't remember if this fact is true.

'Think of what she had been through that week, Mimi. She

had you to deal with, and your father, and Sergei racing around in Dr Abrakadabra's truck. She was the disputed object of desire and yet she had done nothing wrong. At the same time the world was just possibly coming to an end, but that seemed to bring out the worst in people. So when she looked around this great room, at the people who seemed so keen to hear her voice, though they had no interest whatsoever in what she might have to say, she saw . . .' Dora chooses this moment to cast me a hooded, disapproving glance. 'She saw her dreams tarnished. She looked at those great characters, in this great room, and she saw that they, too, were paper thin. Then she looked at her family. One by one she looked at them, and they were the opposite of paper thin. They were three-dimensional. And something died in her . . .'

'Did she actually say that?'

Dora looks at me with a sadness that seems infinite.

'But enough! What's done is done. What matters is the time we have left.'

Again, she takes my hand, and I can feel her desperation as she takes me to the back room she has decorated from objects salvaged from Hümeyra's *atelier*. 'Did you ever visit the real thing?' Dora asks. 'It was just around the corner from here, and utterly enchanting. You would walk into what looked like a normal apartment building, and step out into a courtyard, and there it was, that little house, in the heart of the city but as quiet as a mountain top in winter. It had a coke-burning stove and a sofa that always felt damp to the touch, and along the walls there would always be a jumble of the Society Photographer's latest offerings which she used to such arresting advantage in so much of her work.'

Here, in the Foundation's modest mock-up of that vast and ramshackle *atelier*, Dora has pinned a careful arrangement of photographs to a cork board. She traces the shapes and shadows that can also be seen in the studies that decorate the opposite wall. Then Dora takes us back into the corridor to show us the work for which Hümeyra is now best remembered, *Sailing through Byzantium*, dedicated, in a charcoal scrawl, to 'Butler, my love'. It is long and thin like those panoramas of the city from the early twentieth century, one of which served as her inspiration. But Hümeyra's skyline is thick with revellers. They stand on the domes. They hang from the towers and the minarets. They clog the decks of the passing ships, striking poses caught first by the Society Photographer. Amongst them are emperors and drunken soldiers, golden mosaics and holy fires.

The sky is a collage of ripped and crumpled paper. A Byzantine eagle glows on the face of a moon. The sea is torn by dolphins and gongs, and when you look very closely, you can see long spiralling lines of poetry shaping the currents and the waves. 'It's all Yeats,' Dora says, 'even if the languages keep changing. Do you know?' she adds. 'I found this rolled up and stored beneath that damp sofa I was telling you about. I shall never quite understand it, I mean how cavalier they all were and how little they thought about the preservation of their work. I sometimes wonder if they thought about posterity at all!'

'Why would they?' I say. 'Even the morning after was too far ahead.'

'Too true,' says Dora. 'Too true.' She leads us back into the great room, where Baby Mallinson is still playing for Moscow, but without Grace to accompany him.

'So tell me, Mimi,' Dora says with a sweep of the hand. 'Have we captured something? Or have we not?'

'You have,' I lie.

Dora looks long and darkly out the window, as we listen in silence to the fading last notes of *Pera Nights* followed by rapturous applause from Moscow, circa 1963.

We listen in silence to the opening notes of Baby's next song.

'*Mayhem on the Mediterranean*,' I say.

'What a memory you have,' she says.

As we stand there at the great windows, listening to Baby play his storm in the middle the Mediterranean, I ask Dora what she misses most about those days.

Dora says it is the sense of enclosure – 'if that is the right word'.

'There we were, hiding in our secret haven, while the gods streaked the sky above with their lightning bolts, while Communists walked amongst us, radiating mystery and the unknowable promises of peace . . .'

When it's my turn to list what I miss, I say, the smoke and the rolled up carpets. I miss waking up in the middle of the night and hearing a low humming voice telling a story on the other side of my closed door, until, all at once, all at the same time, as if in response to a cue from a conductor's baton, countless people I can't see burst out laughing. I miss the hordes of men in tired suits on the damp, narrow pavements of İstıklal with Delphine wending her way through them in one of her Knock 'Em Dead dresses. I miss walking with Nella into Nuran Hanım's studio, and almost but not quite believing that we are almost floating over the currents of the Bosphorus. I miss the garden cafés where waiters pinched my cheeks after serving *gazoz* and *böreks*. I miss the stink of ship paint in third class cabins, and the trains whose dining cars vanished in the middle of the night. I miss getting lost on ships, and careening into the lounge to hear Baby playing *Mayhem on the Mediterranean*. I miss getting lost in cities I'd never known existed. I miss returning home to our balcony to watch the dark shadows of Soviet ships slip through the straits towards distant revolutions, while every glass in the house clattered. I miss believing in metaphors that always seemed to have an exact meaning. Most of all, I miss believing in my mother's stories.

'But Mimi,' says Dora. 'It wasn't that you stopped believing in your mother's stories. *You stopped listening.*'

37

Listening

I have run out of ways of avoiding Sergei when Dora takes a call, removes herself to the next room and leaves me alone with him. He sits down on the ancient chaise longue, inviting me to do the same. Once again he says how sorry he is that my 'sainted parents' aren't with us, 'tonight of all nights'. I say how sorry I am, too.

'Is it true?' he asks. 'Is it true that you, with your prestigious memory, cannot remember a single thing about the End of the World Party?'

'It's true,' I say.

He shakes his head, sagely, and I feel an angry flame shooting up inside me again. I ask him, point blank, what he thought he was doing back then. If he really thought himself so important. If he genuinely believed he could bring the world back from the brink of nuclear war. And he says . . .

Of course there had been moments, late at night, when his mind had soared, forging a great arc over the oceans; when he had dared to imagine that, even in Kennedy's sabre-rattling cabinet, there might be a man like him – not a fellow traveller, perhaps, but a spiritual brother, a divided soul, an only-skin-deep warrior, dreaming his way through the icy walls of war.

He could not deny that he had entertained such thoughts. In secret. And perhaps, on hearing the first rumours of a No Camp, his heart had missed three beats. It had missed many more with the discovery that the man believed to be the No

Camp's emissary had booked a passage on a Soviet ship. When Baby had brought these unexpected tidings, in the first dark days of 1962, Sergei had felt the tingling of a tiny hope which had not survived the confusions of that difficult winter passage on the *Felix Dzherzhinsky*. It was not what had propelled him overboard into the Bosphorus some nine months later.

Neither was it Beauty alone that had spirited him into the wild currents on that crisp October afternoon. It was equally the spectre of a world turned to Dust. It was Duty rendered paper-thin by silent, gnawing doubt. It was a Heart heavy with secrets. It was the Domino on which he teetered and an animal urge to escape it. But most of all, it was the mad hope that seized him when he saw us waving from our balcony. At last, he had thought. At last.

Only when he had arrived at our door had he finally seen the madness in his grand gesture. The chattering teeth, the squelching shoes, the brightly striped towel so heavy with the sea and the icy drag of his sopping black suit were sharp little memories that still assaulted him, and still he wished to strike his temples when he recalled that awkward interchange with dearest Grace in her living room when she had stood before him with her hands clasped and her beauteous eyes that were never to be his, and he had sat in what turned out to be her husband's reading chair, infusing it so deeply with sea water that it must have remained damp to the touch and a most unwelcome reminder of his fleeting visit for many weeks.

He had been in the bath – a bath that dearest Grace had kindly drawn for him – when he heard the tread of heavy footsteps. There followed a pause, and an ejaculation of affronted surprise. Papa Bear wished to know who'd been sitting in his chair! Papa Bear was rattling the locked door! While his beloved was saying, Darling, please. Calm down. I can explain, if only you would sit down but it would have to be on the balcony on account of the chair Sergei had ruined. Meanwhile he, Sergei, feeling his nakedness most keenly, had lingered in the bath water, first to grapple with the animal urge to flee, second, to rail against the gods for afflicting him with this impossible passion, and finally to ask himself if he'd have acted any differently if he had been the one to return home to hear that a man he knew only as a ship's librarian had arrived in a great puddle to burden the angel of the house with news of an impending Armageddon.

The missiles. Dear God, the missiles. How they had weighed on him. How often had he looked up at a darkening ceiling in those dim, dark early hours of the morning and thought: This is madness! This is the moment for all good men on earth to join hands and say: No more! Never again!

However, it was one thing to imagine, but it was another to stand in the home of a married woman to whom you had just bared your heart, and to see that woman anxiously placating the husband who would soon be storming in to demand satisfaction, while her children watched on darkly from the doorways. And then? And then! I had betrayed the motherland, and chosen a married woman as my vessel of hope. Those were my memories of that time. Stupid, idiotic Sergei! Of course she was going to tell her husband everything. And now he was going to have to confront the man who was now wearing the husband's most wrinkled and faded corduroy suit.

Sergei continued. He said he mustered his courage – what was left of it – and balking at the final ignominy of shuffling out to the balcony wearing the man's slippers, he sat down and put on the old tennis shoes dearest Grace had left for him. Then, of course, he chose the wrong chair, the telltale chair, so that the dry faded corduroy trousers had a large damp patch in the most embarrassing place. Rising to his full height, he struggled to compose the right words in order to convince this jealous husband that he meant no harm, and most crucially, nurtured no designs on his lovely wife. That he wished only to honour her spirit by doing the right thing, and that, as it happened, the secret he had divulged was, quite literally, earth-shaking. They had to forget their differences, if for no other reason than the enormity of the duty now facing them as citizens of the world. They had no choice but to rise to the occasion, whatever sorrows or angers their hearts might harbour.

He had gathered his words. He had looked around him, at the doorways. And in each, the dark enquiring eyes of a child.

'Is the world really going to end?' the eldest had asked.

'My dear little thing, I sincerely hope not. It is my hope that . . .'

From the balcony came a cry of male fury. Nodding towards it, the girl silently asked: 'Are you going out there?' Sergei replied with a noncommittal shrug of the shoulders that perhaps betrayed his inner turmoil. With sorrow, the girl said, 'Maybe you should wait a little.'

Wait a little. These words reverberate in Sergei's addled brain. And he thinks: Yes, he should wait. Wait and examine the madness of his heart, and his rash gesture. Wait and consider the doors that are still open, and the ones that have slammed closed. Better perhaps to wait next to the front door. Perhaps a walk would do some good. Perhaps a run . . .

There followed what he can describe only as the dark days of madness: He is alluding now to his nights of histrionics at Kulis, to his misadventure with Dr Abrakadabra's megaphone, and to his ill-advised and ultimately doomed attempt to conceal himself on a summer island out of season. In the end, he knew he had no choice but to turn himself in, first to his opposite numbers, so that they could bring pressure to bear on the man with the key to the fabled No Camp, and then, with the free world's knowledge and blessing, to his own people.

At first his people said, Sergei, have you taken leave of your senses? But then they too cherished hopes. They too could understand how this missile gambit would end. They too said, Yes, Sergei, you are right. Go forth into the decadent circles that might have been the death of you. Find the No Camp and save our souls!

His search was fruitless. It was darkest night, on the Saturday, the 27th of October, and it was far, far too late to save our souls because only today a U2 pilot had been shot down over Cuba and the US troops were gathering thick and fast along the coast of Florida, not to mention the base at Guantanamo, and Kennedy had given Khrushchev until midnight to back down or the ruthless US president would unleash his fury.

On Hümeyra's ancient chaise longue, he struggled to entertain thoughts of the present, only to be taunted by regrets and dashed hopes. He denied hell's flames only to see them reflected in the faces of his companions. They refused to believe. He found some comfort in their wilful ignorance. There were just a few hours left, and he wanted to think only of beauty, and of Grace, and of how things might have been, had they met when they were both young and unattached. The many humiliations he had endured that week in her name kept crowding his mind. There was anger too at her remoteness when time was of the essence, but anger led him back to the old places . . . what might have been, if only he had dared, if only she had listened, if only he had found a way through the ice.

Against all reason, his heart had leapt at her sudden entrance into this great room on the fateful evening in question. She had come! She had come to him, at last! And then this tiny hope broke into a thousand pieces when he saw her husband approaching, with the little girl beside him.

Smiling grimly, his rival walked across the room with his free arm extended, and again Sergei dropped his guard, as he heard the no longer jealous or even menacing man say that he should not have flown off the handle at the mention of a No Camp. That he hoped that Sergei would at least understand why he might feel exasperated, that he had been plagued by these baseless rumours about this so-called No Camp for more than a year, that each time he denied any knowledge, people seemed to believe him less. His former foe declared that finally he had gotten to the bottom of it. He knew the author of the entire dangerous fiction and he thought Sergei deserved to know too. In fact, he wanted to thank Sergei for having the generosity to believe that there could even be such a thing as a No Camp in a cabinet as bellicose as Kennedy's. Alas, and as usual, the truth was otherwise.

With these words, he sat the girl down. She lacked her mother's beauty. Her shoulders sagged. It was clear she did not wish to speak, and at first she could not find a single word to say, but her contrite father lingered, and talked on. He reminded Sergei that he was a scientist, a nuclear physicist, no less. Unlike so many of the blithe souls in their midst, he knew what lay ahead. He considered it a point of honour to stare squarely at the future, without having recourse to false comforts. Like Sergei, he answered to no god.

If only! Sergei thought mirthlessly. If only! The man kept talking. He had taken his daughter's hand again. Tell the truth, he said to her. The truth will set you free. Was he drunk? Sergei wondered. Well, they were all drunk by now. Except for the little girl, perhaps. He wished he could remember her name.

She didn't want to tell the truth about the No Camp, and he didn't wish to hear it.

'She didn't come up with this nonsense alone,' said her grimly satisfied father, when she was through. 'She had the help of her fellow junior sleuths.' He pointed across the room, first at Sinan, who was sulking behind another book, previously identified by Sergei as *The Devils*, and then at Dora, who was failing to hide her infatuation for the young secret policeman, who must have convinced himself that it did not matter since they only had a few hours left. These two would be sorry tomorrow. If there was a tomorrow.

'Exhibit A is over there,' the girl's father continued, 'if you want to see for yourself.' He gestured towards the baby grand, and where there should have been a sheet of music there was an open sketchbook that Sergei remembered from the ship. The girl had carried it with her everywhere in a small and battered leather satchel.

With a long face and a heavy heart and still sagging shoulders, she walked across the room to fetch it. 'My father says I should show it to you,' she announced, wearily, on her return. She placed it on the table before them. The father was gone by now. The girl looked up.

'Is this the end of the world?' she asked.

'I sincerely hope not,' Sergei replied.

She said, 'You don't know Khrushchev, do you?'

He sighed and shook his head. Then he smiled, to make up for the sigh: 'Let's see this sketchbook, shall we?'

The girl had scarcely opened it when Humeyra herself came over on her tricycle and claimed it back.

'Is it not sublime?' she asked, when she had restored it to its appointed place. Gathering a few reprobates around her, she rifled through its pages, and even from a distance Sergei could see the childish hand in the crude and cluttered designs. Hümeyra talked on, mostly in English, with detours into Turkish and French. She was telling the story that Sergei had just heard, but quite differently.

This time, it was about the great and secret powers of Art which, at the outset, had eluded this young child.

'But here,' Hümeyra raised her right arm in a flourish. 'Here is the moment when she finally understood!'

Hümeyra was pointing at a crude sketch of a low mountain being observed by the shadow of a little girl standing between two colossal pillars. Her posture was odd. She appeared to be leaning against the air, when in fact she was leaning against the golden mean. Hümeyra traced the faint line the artist had artfully left behind. Was that not precious? Was that not innocence made anew? 'And now look,' she said, 'look at this cloud. Remember this is Egypt, the land of clear blue skies. And now look at its shape. Its mushroom shape. But do not fear, my friends! Look at its edges, which are blurring! Look at the ice on those baked Egyptian hills. And there you see it! Art is truth and beauty. Art is melting the ice of the Cold War!'

Hümeyra's great peal of laughter cracked the air like a whip.

Even from his perch on the ancient chaise longue, Sergei could see that the blithe spirits, though charmed by the idea behind this sketch, were only pretending to be amazed by its execution, and the little girl could see this too. She only pretended to smile when Hümeyra embraced her. Sergei almost got up off his seat to tell her to stop. To leave the poor girl alone.

She was a slip of a thing, with a head that was too big for her body. He watched her skirting the edges of the party in a room with pictures turned inwards and a bust of Beethoven hidden inside a black hood. Now and again, Vartui emerged to feed her a *börek*. Sensing Sergei's eyes on her back – the blessed woman was rightly proud of her intuition – she crossed the room to feed him next. They were fresh from the oven, those *böreks*. He remembered how he cut them open to let the steam flow out in case they burned his mouth.

By now he had settled into his perch on the ancient chaise longue. He did not care that Hümeyra was turning him into a shawl model. There was even a shawl, fashioned into a turban, encircling his head. He could only guess what a spectacle he looked, so much so that new guests stopped to stare at him. They fell short of actually pointing at him, finding more polite ways to draw attention to the bizarre character. Sergei did not mind being thus pigeonholed, especially after his week of taunts and fisticuffs, bitter accusations and impossible demands, and rocks in such hard places and, most of all, his spiritual anguish. Filmy as they were, these shawls provided him with a thin comfort and shielded him from the eternal ice of unrequited love. And from the chill that seeped into his flesh as he realised the truth about the No Camp. He had been a fool. A shivering fool.

Was the girl cold, too? Had she, too, lost her cloak? He thought back on her confession. It had connected the dots but in so doing, it had erased the little girl. He could barely remember her flitting with her sister through the ship's narrow passages.

He wished he could have read her mind. He wished he could

have told her that there were, as yet, no marauding bands concealed in the bowels of their ship. He might have told her what he himself was only just learning, at that very moment, as he sat there in his ridiculous assortment of shawls. He watched the girl weaving her sad way through the crowds and desperately wanted to tell her: Forget the darkness outside, for you shall never know it. Cherish the beauty of the here and now, for it cannot last.

When the dancing began the girl took refuge behind the far leg of the baby grand. That's where she was in the print he procured the next day from the Society Photographer. In it, the girl is leaning in that same awkward way as she does in her own sketch, but there is no golden mean, only the air that cannot hold her. Her eyes show her absence. She is clutching that satchel, though it must be empty, because the sketchbook is propped, thick and dog-eared, on the stand.

There are other prints Sergei cherishes: the one taken much earlier, just minutes after there has been a cry from the door. The spies are coming! They are halfway up the stairs! Sergei found himself diving for cover without forethought, under a few more of Hümeyra's shawls. Baby draped himself on top and his new friend, the no-longer-jealous-husband, draped himself over his feet. Then the lights went off. The photographer used his flash. The print showed the panicked adjustments of shawls under cover of darkness. And Delphine who was emerging from behind the ancient chaise longue on all fours, in the dress she called her Saturday Night Special, clutching an orphaned but very fine high-heeled shoe.

There was a print of the spies, his opposite numbers, laughing, taken immediately after the lights went on again. There is a lightness in William Wakefield's demeanour as he peers over the top of his glasses. The Admiral is telling a joke which his wife, standing with arms folded, a few paces away, does not find amusing. They must have known by then that the crisis was moving towards a resolution. They glowed with a happy shared secret, a glow Sergei would see again later on.

In this print the Admiral's wife has joined him on the ancient chaise longue: he in full shawl regalia, but sitting square-shouldered, straight-backed while she wears an odd but undoubtedly handsome suit that she dismissed, following a compliment, as something of a museum piece, bought in Paris at her single moment of enrapture with haute couture.

They had talked about Paris after the war, and Berlin, and Vienna. They had talked about the refugees, and the cafes, and the characters. They had discovered one in common: a rascal with seven passports. She had shown him quiet mercy. Without offering specifics, the Admiral's wife had somehow managed to imply that the end of the crisis was nigh.

You can see all this in the print. You don't need to hear the words. It's the same with the print of Nella and Sibel leaning over the legendary punchbowl, with its fruits of the season floating in pure alcohol. The two sirens are dressed in black from head to toe. Their little pillbox hats have little veils; Sibel is already puffing smoke through hers and Nella is about to light up, but first she will compose the conspiratorial confidence already dancing on her lips. Behind them is Baby, resting a finger against his nose, while looking right through them.

In the mirror you can see the Society Photographer, snapping.

Here are Nella and Sibel again, bending most alluringly. Between their lovely legs you can see the girl being pulled from her retreat beneath the piano. The girl is a veritable portrait of reluctance. The next print is perhaps more arresting. Nella and Sibel are doing the twist, and until this moment the girl has been dancing too, but she is caught immobile. Perhaps the Society Photographer's flash has startled her. Sergei, though, sees something in her pose that he can recognise. He calls it the abyss.

In the next print we see Delphine in the alcove, lamenting the big scoop that never was, and next to her is Bunny Evans, frowning obediently while stealing a glance at his watch, while behind him a much smaller city glitters.

Next, a print of Hümeyra doing the tango by herself, while Grace's no longer jealous husband prances behind her. He has put on that silly goat herd skin, and a white Venetian mask, and he is suspended awkwardly in mid-air, eyes open wide, as if to fend off the floor towards which he will crash the moment the shutter closes. And here: Vartui, on the sofa in the alcove, with my brother and sister both asleep on her lap, their heads just touching. Below you can glimpse the chicken that she has refused to kill or cage, so that it too can enjoy its last few hours on earth. Here again: Vartui standing in the kitchen doorway. In this other print she is bent over the old phonograph, placing the needle onto a stack of 45s, and exuding sadness, even though her face is hidden. And dear Nuran Hanım, whom he misses so much, linking arms with her daughter, Semra.

Here now is Hümeyra lying as if dead on the floor. This must have been taken at one minute to midnight while Baby plays his song of the same title. Behind her a rolled up carpet and yet another lost shoe. In the next print we can see Hümeyra again, at one minute past midnight, still in the same place but seated majestically on a shawl that has the air of a magic carpet, head thrown back and raising a goblet high. Those present would never forget what she was saying at that moment:

'Life is but a pied à terre!'

There are also prints of the Tenor and the Translator and Madame Xenia the Accordion Lady and a contrite Dr Abrakadabra in a hallway's shadow, and even Hümeyra's legitimate son, arm in arm with the illegitimate son of the trigamist. This print catches them speaking and weeping together, for the first and last time.

Sergei cherishes all these images, but his favourite will always be one that now graces the Foundation's wall. It cannot have been taken long after the arrival of the spies, for Sergei is still under the shawls, as well as man-covered, and only a hand

and the very tip of a shoe protrudes. The frame is wide enough to include the baby grand in its entirety, and Sergei is sure I could, if I put my mind to it, identify most if not all of the revellers draped against its sides. Baby is playing, Grace singing. But what? Which tune?

They played everything that night, Baby's set-pieces and my mother's, and the glorious compositions he claimed, somewhat misleadingly, to have prepared for this occasion: *A corner of a foreign field. Nuclear clocks. In the old bohemian quarter. Sultry in October.* This last contained lyrics that made a mockery of Sergei's own recent antics; there were phrases that stabbed him in the heart. But Baby played them so well: with Grace's voice added, his well-varnished quips had taken on the glow of truth. Never more than when playing the tune for which he would be best known.

It must have been while savouring the last notes of *Hell or High Water* that Sergei asked himself, was this heaven? Was he perhaps dreaming? And Baby read his thoughts because he wheeled around to assure Sergei that, no, this was the Other Place. Most definitely.

It is only if you look closely that you can see the girl beneath the piano, in the forest of legs, leaning in that awkward way against the golden mean that cannot hold her.

Later on, her mother coaxed her out. She held her close as she sang *Stormy Weather*. She let all who listened know it was a song for her daughter, and the girl swung this way and that, embarrassed by this announcement. After it was over, she slipped away through the crowds that had gathered around the baby grand to crawl back into her hiding place. Later still, when in the midst of another of his silly goat dances, her father spotted her there, and called for her, but she hung back.

Her mother sang on, and although she did not look once in Sergei's direction, he could tell that dearest Grace was in some other way watching over him, and that in some other way, she was also watching over the goat-dancing husband and the sleeping children and the girl resting on the far leg of the baby grand. With his own eyes closed, he could almost hear the invasion of these distractions. He could hear her voice growing hollow, as Duty summoned.

Sergei said that he did not particularly like the print he now held in his hand. Grace was of course ravishing in her simple blue dress with its white collar and sash but he, poor Sergei, looked farcical, bowing while garbed in the shawls. She let him kiss her hand, though. She thanked him, quite formally, for 'doing the right thing, or at least trying.' She thanked him also for his kindness to her daughter. 'The poor little thing was afraid you were going to kill her.'

'Such a thought!'

'One day we'll all sit down together and laugh about it,' she said.

'If there ever is another day,' he said.

And she said, 'There will be.'

When Sergei woke up amongst the shawls the next morning, the great room was silent. The first thing that caught his eye was the sketchbook, still on the baby grand's music stand. The satchel he could not locate. He decided, in the end, that the girl must have taken it home, perhaps without the knowledge that it was empty, or perhaps she had left the sketchbook behind because she no longer had faith in it.

All this he saw through the pained veil of the worst hangover he'd ever known. Other thoughts followed: what he could have done differently, what he should never have done at all. He thought about the angel he would never possess, and the fallen idol, half submerged under the ancient chaise longue, but still clinging to his hand.

He pulled his hand free. Baby groaned in his sleep. Sergei went to sit on the bench of the baby grand and absently opened the sketchbook. On the first pages were landscapes that spoke to him despite their crudeness. He turned the pages. The style kept changing. The crude landscapes gave way to cubist crowd scenes and geometric landscapes, and here and there you saw the fudged edges of erased images, and in spaces left mostly blank there were the imprints of scratched words. There were portrait phases, and a longish Egyptian phase, and it was at the end of this sequence that he found the sketch that Hümeyra had so theatrically admired: the girl herself, standing between two colossal columns, looking out at the melting hills. He could not help but notice the lemony scratches that rippled out from the horizon in all directions.

This was not art. It had been cruel of Hümeyra to have suggested it, however generous her motives. When he looked at these compositions, what he sensed most powerfully was the abyss between the girl's vision and her technical ability, the gulf between her mother's beauties and her father's harsh truths. What she wanted to capture was so very far beyond her grasp, but in every line and scratch, he could feel her trying, trying, trying, and he ached for her, because someone should have told her that it was enough to try. He wondered if she would forgive herself. Perhaps that is why, after he had taken the sketchbook off the baby grand, where anyone could thumb through it and perhaps fail to see its soul and laugh, and had found a safe place for it in a corner of Hümeyra's coat-filled bedroom, he forgave himself, if only a little.

Here Sergei pauses. He sinks back into the ancient chaise longue, as if consumed by his own words. 'And you?' he asks. 'Can you forgive me, too, if only just a little?'

'You have a way with words,' I say. I do not mean it generously, but Sergei smiles. He goes on to tell me how glad he is, that I have warmed to his turns of phrase. He is, in fact, a published poet. He is also, as of the previous year, if only in a manner of speaking, a monk. It has brought him peace.

There was, however, no respite for Sergei in the years after the missile crisis. After the relief that came with civilisation being restored, there was the Soviets' humiliation in the eyes of the world. In time, however, Khrushchev and his lost face were replaced and forgotten. Sergei made a home for himself, and framed the prints whose reproductions we have just been viewing. He placed them around his study in Odessa, and each time his eyes fell on the little girl amongst the forest of legs, he feared that she might still be there, leaning against a golden mean that wasn't there. He was glad, on first renewing his acquaintance with my parents, to hear how far I'd travelled since that day. But now he fears for what I might have left behind there.

He says he is sorry to hear I have yet to track down the sketchbook. Dora probably alluded to the elation she and Sergei shared when they found it buried beneath the detritus of decades, not in Hümeyra's apartment, but in the battered suitcase containing Baby's remaining personal effects. To think that this precious, ruined man had taken it with him all the way to Moscow, and then back again, and held on to it, and never said a thing. Of course, it had been a treasure trove for him, or rather for his lyrics which tragically hadn't survived. Only the music. But never mind. The sketchbook was rediscovered and returned. And yes, Sergei is certain. It is now enjoying the shelter of my father's study. He says he is sure because he had himself carried it to the house. I must ask Dora, he says, who accompanied him when he went to pay his respects to dear Grace and my splendid father who had welcomed him with open arms, and had forgiven him so generously.

What a very fine man I have for a father! A gentleman of the first order. Isn't it the greatest of wonders that a person can, in an entire chapter of his life, fail to see a single redeeming feature in a man – because that man is his rival– only to return, many chapters later, to find a soul in flower! Had Sergei been in my father's shoes, had he been the one to open the door to find his old and decrepit rival, he would have brandished his fist. Most certainly he would have sent the interloper packing. Instead, my father had opened his arms. He had led Sergei to a chair, saying, 'Watch out now. It's still damp!' Oh how they had laughed, all three of them, just as dearest Grace had predicted so long ago.

That night, she was as Sergei remembered.
She made no mention of that darkness fast descending.
She spoke of happy things. And only happy things.

And how it grieved him. Even after all those years, it was the shadows he longed for, and these she had denied him. But slowly he was learning. And one day, perhaps I would, too.

'We must embrace the angel's silence,' he says, 'if we are to see through her eyes.'

38

Seeing

After we have begun our long goodbyes, and Dora has found the courage to share with me her deepest concern, held back all night, and I have found the courage to listen, and apologise, and vow to change my ways, and she and I have embraced, and Sergei and I have done the same, and everyone has promised everyone to meet again soon – perhaps even tomorrow – it takes my taxi an unusually long time to reach the sea, but we get there eventually, and the traffic flows well through Dolmabahçe and even Beşiktaş. It is in Ortaköy that we end up at a standstill for over an hour.

Outside the gargantuan night club that has replaced the coal depot I remember, I tell myself that the prognosis may not be as gloomy as Dora says it is.

I am stung again by Dora's last words: *How can we hope that this new operation will work, when all the others didn't? What will become of your dear mother, if she can no longer see Beauty?*

We shall see, I think, as the taxi leaves the shore to climb the Aşiyan. After I have paid the driver and have waited for my receipt, after I have made my way down the dark path to my parents' house, these words stay with me: we shall see. We shall see.

I do not recognise the ground beneath my feet. I have to watch out for the dips and depressions. As I pick my way through the shadows, I try to avoid distractions and keep a blank mind, but then I see some mark or flaw in the dark pavement, and Dora's words hit me again.

The bird clock is chiming as I walk into the apartment. Three in the morning, but my mother is still up. She calls me into the living room.

She is still in the armchair where I left her so many hours ago. Peering at me from her pool of light, she says, 'Oh good. Dora's given you a copy of her book. I was hoping she'd do that. I think you'll like it. Well, at least most of it.'

She peers across the room. 'Your hands are shaking,' she says, and it's a relief to know she can see my hands at all.

'It was pretty overwhelming, being back there after all these years,' I say, in case she notices my red eyes as well.

'I'm sorry to hear that,' my mother says. 'Though I do understand. She's such a delightful person, that Dora, but she can say the most extraordinary things.'

'I had no idea you two were so close.'

'Oh, well you know how much I always liked here . . . and since she moved her permanently . . .'

'How long ago was that?'

'Oh, let me see . . . four years? Five? It was when you were in all that trouble . . .'

'With *Enlightenment*?'

'Yes, it was around that time. We were worried, naturally. And generally quite upset. All that politics. Until Dora stepped in. She was really very helpful.'

'So you see quite a lot of her.'

'Oh, yes. We do have wonderful talks.'

'And did you really correspond with her during all those years?'

'Is that what she said?'

'Yes, she did.'

'And what did you say?'

'That you'd written to me about three times in my entire adulthood.'

'Well, then, I must have written her about the same number.'

251

'Did you really go to church with her every Sunday in those months before they sent her away?'

'Oh Dora! What a vivid imagination she has! To think she's a historian. What will she come up with next?' she says, and for a moment I am convinced.

'So,' she says. 'How was the party?'

I tell her that it was lovely, even if it was but a pale shadow of the original. I tell her that it was good to have a chance to talk to Dora.

'So tell me what you talked about until three in the morning,' my mother says.

I take a breath and I almost tell her. I almost tell her what I have been told. About the cataracts my mother hid from me and the haemorrhage in her left eye. The string of accidents, small and not so small. The bruises, burns and falls. The vertigo that has kept her housebound. I, too, would have noticed all of that had I not waited so long – so very, very long – to come back. I want to ask her why she hid it from me but the words stick in my throat.

Instead I list the other things Dora and I talked about: The Foundation. Her mother. The ship.

'Oh, not the ship again,' says my mother.

'Sergei gave one of the speeches,' I say, moving on again.

Without missing a beat, she says, 'How was he?'

'In very good nick.'

'Well, I'm glad you had a chance to talk to him. Did he tell you about our forth-coming journey?'

I say: 'What's he offered? A trip to Odessa? A tour of the Sevastopol shipyards?'

'That, too. But he's a wealthy man these days, you know. He has a yacht. No, what he's proposed is a trip to Cuba.'

'To retrace the route he would have followed himself had he not jumped off that ship?'

'Well, that's one way of putting it.'

'Are you serious? Do you really want to cross the Atlantic with that . . . .that fruitcake?'

'Even after all these years, I still hate that word.'

'He's a lovely man. I didn't mean it.'

'Of course you didn't. And neither did I,' she says. 'You know, I've always wanted to see Havana. It was so very generous of him to invite us along. If it ever happened, it would be wonderful, don't you think?' Perhaps to change the subject, she says, 'By the way, I have that painting back.'

That painting is the water colour she created from the photograph of me at Queen Hatshepsut's temple when I draw my famous sketch. She gestures at the picture hanging above my head. I turn around and look at it, and nod, even though it's a water colour of some other temple, not Queen Hatshepsut's. 'I've always wanted you to have it,' she says. 'I know how much that day meant to you.'

I thank her, for remembering.

'Well, I'm sorry I missed the party,' she says, 'but I'm glad you and Dora had a chance to meet again. She really does have a very generous heart. In that respect, she's like her father, I suppose . . .'

'So we know who her father is now?'

'Oh dear, didn't I tell you? Yes, well . . . it turns out to be none other than Sergei.'

'You must be joking.'

'I'm afraid not. He seems to have been in Istanbul at the auspicious moment.'

'And he's acknowledged it?'

'Oh, yes.' She says this somewhat grimly.

'You were there, I take it. When Dora found out.'

'Yes, and that was one Dora Soirée you can count yourself lucky to have missed.'

'I wonder why she didn't tell me.'

'Oh, she will, I'm sure. She genuinely wants to bring you back. If not to live here, then at least to spend more time . . .'

Which reminds me of the CD I had meant to bring home with me.

'Don't worry,' she says. 'He's already given us our copy.'

She sends me to the study to look on my father's desk. Next to his laptop are the proofs of my father's latest book, *Light in the Dark Ages*. Beneath them I find the last known recording of Baby Mallinson, in Moscow, circa 1963.

Returning to the living room, I tell my mother that Dora played that recording for me after the party.

'We were listening to it, too, just a few hours ago, your father and I. Would you mind putting it on again?'

I do, and we listen. With the first note from Baby's piano, my mother closes her eyes. Here they come again, the first bars of *Stormy Weather*, but then the first reworking, and the next and the next, each one more insistent, and then the explosion, and the party, and then the silence and the slow return. Very soon I am not listening but sailing through the Mediterranean in midwinter and gazing at my mother, who is gazing at the horizon and beyond.

I wonder if she really did tell Dora how much she wanted to shed us, all of us, and fly away by herself. If on the night of the End of the World party, something inside her died. If this was the night when she said farewell to her grand illusion, and accepted her lot. Does she think I abandoned her? Did she ever sing again? To anyone? Was it really ten years before she took up painting?

I wonder if she ever forgave me for going on and on and on about marauding bands of Communists while failing to protect my sister from her molester. Is that why there are no pictures of me on her desk? I wonder if she blames me for all the trouble I caused her, and my father, and poor Mr Guttman, and the spies I fooled, by making up stories and annotating my sketches with suspicions in invisible ink. I wonder if she knows I was doing it for her. If she knows that when I look out across the Bosphorus, over the hills of Asia, I can still see the faint outline of a mushroom cloud rising out of Khrushchev's bald head.

I wonder if she knows how often I think of all these things.

The music ends. My mother opens her eyes and smiles.

'Now wasn't that beautiful?' she says.

Acknowledgements

When the world as I knew it really did come to an end last year, I came to depend on the kindness and generosity of friends, family and strangers. It is thanks to them that I was able to bring this book into the world. Lynn Michell of Linen Press came into my life on the worst day of all, so we started at the deep end. Our almost daily conversations about edits and revisions, mothers, daughters, and fathers, brought light into a very long winter.

So, too, did my father, John Freely; my sister, Eileen; my children: Matthew, Emma, Helen, and Pandora; my step-children, Kimber and Rachel; my present and future children-in-law, Özge, Matt, and Camilla, my brother-in-law, Tony; and my grand-daughter, Mina. They are heroic and I am proud to know them.

I would also like to thank Celia Pyper, Nicci Gerrard, Sally Muir, Shanti Fry, Jan Attah, Judith Longstreth, Lucy Longstreth, Elizabeth Shepherd, Bryn Jones, Anita Bennett, Joan Porter MacIver, Jennifer Potter, Ayça Wheating, David Morley, Peter Blegvad, Will Eaves, Sarah Moss Catherine Bates, Anna Lea, Loredana Polezzi, Silvija Jestrovic, Dragan Todorovic, George Ttoouli, Naomi Alsop, Bethan Ellis, Gill Frith, Jeremy Treglown, Daniel Hahn, Kate Griffin, Antonia Lloyd-Jones, Jo Glanville, Müge Sökmen, Ba ak Ertur, Nakiye Boran, Hale Akay, Emin Saatçi, Ben Pyper, Sean French, Lee Hennessy, Helen and Mal

Lewis, Karen Prees, Theo Papadopoulos, Emma Carmel, Rebecca Waters, Joseph Olshan, Anne O'Brien, Angela Cockayne, Bob Fearns, Geoffrey Wheatcroft, Nicole Pope, Lanning Aldrich, Carol Sanford, Andrew and Caroline Finkel, and Alison and Simon Gittens in more ways than I can count. I am grateful to my colleagues and students at the University of Warwick and to my many dear friends at the Translators Association and PEN.

I am in awe of the eagle eyes of Louise Santa Ana, Becky Pickard and Lola Boorman at Linen Press for catching all those rogue commas and runaway sentences. And when I say that I am eternally indebted to my friend and agent, Derek Johns, I mean that literally!

I thank Dolores Freely, my beloved mother, for her beauties and mysteries.

I thank Frank Longstreth, my beloved husband, for giving us everything he had. May he rest in peace.